Paulin

UNWILLINGLY TO EARTH

A TOM DOHERTY ASSOCIATES BOOK
NEW YORK

NOTE: If you purchased this book without a cover you should be aware that this book is stolen property. It was reported as "unsold and destroyed" to the publisher, and neither the author nor the publisher has received any payment for this "stripped book."

This is a work of fiction. All the characters and events portrayed in this book are fictitious, and any resemblance to real people or events is purely coincidental.

UNWILLINGLY TO EARTH

Copyright © 1992 by Pauline Ashwell

All rights reserved, including the right to reproduce this book, or portions thereof, in any form.

Cover art by Boris Vallejo

A Tor Book
Published by Tom Doherty Associates, Inc.
175 Fifth Avenue
New York, N.Y. 10010

Tor ® is a registered trademark of Tom Doherty Associates, Inc.

ISBN: 0-812-51929-9

First edition: August 1992

Printed in the United States of America

0 9 8 7 6 5 4 3 2 1

Part One:
UNWILLINGLY TO SCHOOL

THIS MAY LOOK LIKE A MOVIGRAM OF BROWNIAN Movement but no such luck; it is Russett Interplanetary College of Humanities Opening Day, four thousand three hundred twenty-seven other freshers milling around and me in the middle with a little ticket on my chest says Lee, L. because my given name is something not to mention; they say these kids came from four hundred twenty-four planets just to study at Russett but personally of all points in the known continuum this is the one I would rather be any place But.

Freshers come all sizes, all colors but a fair number are girls so there is one thing we will be finding in common anyway.

This may come as a surprise, that I am a girl, I mean. My tutor at Prelim School says my speech is feminine as spoken but written down looks like the kind of male character who spits sideways.

I reply that I talk like my Dad, he is a character all right, male too, but does not spit, if you spent your formative years with a filter in your kisser neither would you.

He says my flair for seeing the functional significance of the minutiae of behavior is obviously what got me chosen for the Cultural Engineering Course.

Huh.

I know what got me into that all right I am not so dumb as I look.

You think I flatter myself? Brother, by what goes on I look dumb indeed. Maybe this is because of my hair, curly and pale colored—all right, blonde. My eyes are blue as they come which is by no means sky color whatever the books say, my skin is pink in some places white others when washed and a visitor we had once said I had a rosebud mouth.

I am seven then, I do not hold it against her right away there are no roses where I grew up; when I landed here on Earth I hunt one up to see was it a compliment.

Brother.

I find later they come other colors but this one is frostbite mauve, and the shape!

I wish to state here my mouth has two lips like anyone else.

Where I grew up is Excenus 23, how I got hauled off it is due to a string of Catastrophes but the name of the biggest is D. J. M'Clare.

Excenus sun is what they call a swarmer, ninety-seven small planets in close orbits plus odd chunks too many to count. Twenty-three is the biggest, gravitation one point oh seven Earth, diameter a fraction less. If you ever heard of the place it was because they mine Areopagite there, Ninety-four percent production for sale in the known volume of space comes from mines on Twenty-three; but for that, no reason to live there at all.

Unwillingly to Earth

My dad started as a miner and made his pile, then he took up Farming and spent the lot. He has it all back again now.

Areopagite forms only in drydust conditions meaning Humidity at ground level never above two and one half percent Rainfall None, hence from this farming on Excenus 23 is something special, but miners are like other people they have to eat too.

When Dad started there was him and Uncle Charlie and their first year they fed 954 men, nowadays the planetary population is Three thousand three hundred twenty and there are seven other farmers, most of them started working for Dad and graduated to farms of their own. Nobody on Excenus 23 eats concentrates now.

Uncle Charlie is Hon. as in secretary meaning no real relation. He is an engineer, when Dad met him down on his luck but able and willing to build diggers, harvesters, weathermakers for ten thousand acres, out of any junk to hand. Had to be done like that because Excenus Haulage Company, the big company did all the shipping in and out of the planet, sold food concentrates. No competition welcome therefore no shipments of Seeds, agricultural machinery, all that, would have been allowed through.

It takes Charlie two years to do his job, meanwhile Dad bones up on the agricultural side. Nowadays there are a lot of books on drydust farming, they cover soilmaking, microbiology, economical use of weather, seed selection, plenty more; at that time there were fewer and Dad read them all.

If he had sent for the usual texts E.H.C. might have caught on and had a little accident in transit, so Dad gets them in as *books* I mean antique style, chopped in pieces and hinged together down the side. They are labeled Curio Facsimiles and disguised with antique picture covers mostly showing the damnedest females you ever saw, dressed in bits and pieces mostly damaged; some of them dead. People collect these things for some reason. Dad has one or two put on top with texts to match the outside, rest are textbooks on Agriculture like I said.

Charlie offers to make reader-reels from them but Dad turns him down. He still has all those books packed in a row, when I was little he used to tell me how he learned all his farming studying that way, without using Reading Machines, it just showed you could still do it if you had to. Dad never had any education and it bothers him; I used to think that was why he kept on telling me this.

Well there are plenty of troubles not least with E.H.C. but Dad is not the type to give up; reason he started farming in the first place was he caught on E.H.C. were making it Impossible for people to do just that; Dad does not like people to try and stop him even if it was not what he wanted to do in the first place.

I am born soon after the farm is really set. My mother walked out when I was three. She was fresh out of college with an agricultural degree when Dad met her, maybe the trouble was he caught on she knew less about drydust farming than he did, maybe other things—Excenus 23 is no place for a woman they say.

It is O.K. by me but I was born in the place.

Dad and Charlie raised me between them like the crops, which is to say carefully.

There are plenty more people now in Green Valley where the farms are, fifty or so and they change all the time. People who come out farm for a bit make their pile then go. We even get women from time to time. People's wives from Town come out to board sometimes, Dad lets them because he thinks they will Mother me.

Well mostly I manage to steer them off and no hard feelings, it is My home after all they got to be reasonable about it if they want to stay. Seems they do as a rule. Town is kind of tough to live in. Several stayed a year or more. So it is not true to say I grew up in a Wholly Masculine Environment, I knew up to seven women for quite a while.

Green Valley is outside the mining area and about six hundred miles from Town. This has to be. Town gets most of its water combing the air and so do the weathermakers for the farms; anyway mining and farming do not mix so good. The Valley is twenty miles each way hedged by hill ridges up to seventy feet high. Outside is stone flats, dust bowl and tangled mats of *Gordianus* scrub. Forty miles around about it I know pretty well but the rest of the planet is about the same, except for Town.

This is where I was born, I was all set to stay there before Dad had his Accident; first Catastrophe on the way to this place.

I am up one day in a helivan watching the harvest on a thousand-acre strip at the edge of the farm, there is a moderate wind blowing from over the hill, so we are keeping the weather-lid over each row until just before the harvester gets there so as to keep the dust out of the grain. I am directing this.

Here at the edge the weather-lid is just above the crop, it runs from the weather-maker in the middle of the farm in a big cone like a very flat tent, fifty feet high in the middle and four miles across. You cannot see it of course unless the wind blows dust across, or there is rain inside; the lid is just a layer of air Polarized to keep dust one side, water vapor the other; just now you can plainly see where puffs of dust go skittering across.

The harvester gets to the end of a row on the far side from the road. I signal Biff Plater at Control and he draws the weather-lid in twenty yards. The harvester lifts its scanner at the end of the strip, wheels, and comes through the next swath, with the big cutter pushing six inches above ground, stalks sliding back into the thrasher, bagged corn following on the trailer behind.

Then I see Dad come along the road riding the biggest kor on the farm. Kors are *Pseudocamelopus hirsutinaris*, part of the indigenous fauna we started taming to ride on about a year ago. Dad does not really enjoy it, he cannot get used to having no brakes but he will not give up. I see right away he is having trouble, the kor slipped its bridle and navigating on its own, long neck straight out and Dad slipping to and fro in the saddle; his mouth filter is bumped out and waving behind.

The harvester is half up the field. I do not want the kor to be scared. I yell to Biff, Turn it off quick! but the controls are on the other side of the shack from the weather ones.

Then the kor sees the scanner rearing on its stalk, it is not frightened at all thinks this is the Great great grandfather of the species and charges straight across to say Hello.

I am yelling to Biff and got my eyes shut, then he is yelling right back, I have to open them and look down.

The kor has gone straight into the cutter the second before it stopped. Dad has been thrown and the harvester stopped with one tread a foot from his head and the corner gone over his arm.

I bring the heli down yelling for help on all frequencies.

Dad is breathing but flat out; fractured skull, ulna and radius like a jigsaw puzzle, multiple injuries to the chest; the kor is in three pieces mixed up with the machine.

We call the hospital in Town and they direct First Aid over two-way visiphone while the ambulance comes. It takes seventy minutes and I am swearing to myself we will hire a permanent doctor if we have to shanghai him, after this.

The ambulance arrives and the doctor says we have done as well as can be expected, fortunately Dad is tough but it will be a two-month hospital job at the least.

They crate him up in splint plastic and load him into the ambulance. Buffalo Cole has packed me a bag. I get in too.

I am out again first thing, passengers Not Allowed.

I get out the long-distance heli and go straight to Town, I am waiting in the hospital when they arrive. I wait till they have Dad unpacked before I start to inquire.

These hospitals! It is all they will do to let me look at him; when I do he is lying in a kind of tank, his chest is the wrong shape, there is a mass of tubes round his head running to a pump, this for Resorption of blood clots in the brain; more too the other end for External aeration of the Blood, he is not going to use his Lungs for a bit.

I think this does not look real, Dad in all this plumbing; then I hear my breathing goes odd, next thing you know the doctors steer me outside.

They say it will be a week before the blood clots go and Dad wakes up but they will report by visiphone every day.

I say No need they can tell me when I visit each day.

They are deaf or something, they repeat they will call Green Valley each day at thirteen o'clock.

I say Is this when they would prefer me to call in?

At last they have got it, they say Surely I will not fly six hundred miles every day.

I say No I shall be stopping right here in Town.

Then they want to know what friends I am stopping with, I say At a hotel.

Consternation all round No place for young girls to stop in this town, they make it out the toughest hell-hole in the known volume.

I say Nuts, there are hotels for Transients and their wives too.

They flap wildly in all directions and offer me a bed in the Nurses' hostel which is Men Only ordinarily, but they will make an Exception.

I say Thanks very much, No.

In the end they tell me to go to the Royal Hotel it is the most respectable of the local dumps, Do not on any account make a mistake and go to the Royal Arms which is a pub in the toughest quarter of the town; they tell me how to go.

I put my luggage in my pocket; for some reason I have clutched it throughout; and I go.

Way I feel I do not go to the Hotel straight off, I walk around a bit. I have been into Town of course shopping with Dad, maybe twice a year, but I do not seem to know it so well as I thought.

Then I find I have got to the Royal Arms or just near it anyway.

It is now late evening, the sky is black except for stars, planets, and meteors crashing through every minute or two. The town is lit up but there are few in the streets, quiet folk are home in another quarter the rest still fueling up indoors. Way I feel some toughery would suit me fine to take my mind off, because Taming kors was my idea in the first place. Maybe I will get a chance to try out that Judo trick I learned from Buffalo Cole.

So I slip through the noise-valve doors one after another and go into the Pub.

Brother.

The Noise trap is efficient all right, outdoors no more than a mutter so there is a real wallop inside. Every idea in my head is knocked clean out of it, even the thought that I might go away. Among other things are three jukeboxes in three corners going full blast and I cannot hear them at all.

Part of the decibels come from just conversation, part is encouragement to a three-way fight in the middle of the floor. I am still gaping when two of the parties gang up on the third and toss him all the way to the door. I dodge just in time, he rebounds off the inner valve and Falls right at my feet.

Everyone turns and sees me, and the jukeboxes all become audible at once.

I go down on my knees to see if the Character I have just missed meeting is still breathing or not. His pulse is going all right but his face is a poor color wherever blood lets me see. I yell for water but Competing with the jukeboxes get nowhere. I am taking breath to try again when someone turns them off at the main, Silence comes down like cotton-wool.

I ask for water in a whisper, someone brings it and tries to take me away.

I find I am clinging to the guy yelling He is hurt, he is hurt! There is blood balling in little drops on my Evercleans and smeared over my hands, I am trying to wipe it off with a disposable, Not suited to this of course it crushes and goes away to dust and then the cotton-wool feeling in my ears spreads elsewhere.

Then I am lying on my back with water running down my chin and a sensation of Hush all round.

I try to sit up and something stops me. Someone murmurs soft Nothings that fail to make sense.

I keep quiet till I have it sorted and then I figure I have fainted clean away.

Me, Lizzie Lee.

I sit up and find I am on a couch in a sort of backroom and there are Faces all round. Half of them seem knocked out of shape or with knobs on, bashed recently or previous.

The faces all jostle and I hear they are telling those behind She is sitting up! and the glad news getting passed along.

Someone pushes through the faces carrying a tray with

food for Six, I deduce they think I fainted from Hunger or something.

I would put them right on this, but I realize the feeling in my middle is because I last ate ten hours ago.

I weigh in and they appear pleased by this.

So I feel an Explanation is owed and I tell them my Dad is in hospital with an accident, you would not think they could get so upset about a perfect stranger, Sure this will not last but it is a genuine feeling just now for all that.

There is more buzzing and a kind of Rustle and I find they are taking up a collection.

I am horrified, I cry No, no, they are very kind but I truly cannot accept.

And they think this is Proper pride or something, they start to mutter again and someone says Well then, no need to worry, Knotty will give me a job as long as I need it, won't he? Knotty is in the crowd somewhere, seems he is keeper of this Pub. He seems to agree and I figure he'd better.

I do not see why they are so sure I am Indigent until I happen to glance down. I am still in my work Evercleans I was wearing when Dad got hurt; also it breaks on me suddenly that this is the worst quarter of the Town, no girl would come here if she could afford to be elsewhere, even then not into the Royal Arms unless full of sweet innocence or something.

And I cannot Speak.

When a bunch of strangers are mooning over your problems because you are a Poor young thing you cannot tell them you walked in looking for a fight.

Truly, I could swear out loud.

In two shakes of a vibrator they have it fixed, Knotty will give me a job as long as I need one and I can have a room above the pub and at least fifty husky miners have sworn a personal guarantee no one within Miles will lift a finger in any way I could not wish.

Unwillingly to Earth

So what can I do?

I thank them and I walk out into the bar, when I get there I find the laws of human nature are not wholly Suspended, there is a fight going on.

My bodyguard behind me gives a concerted roar and the fight stops and they look sheepish at me.

It is so clear they expect me to look shocked and sorrowful that I cannot help it, this is just what I do.

I ask the cause of the fight and they shuffle and the bigger one says he is very sorry and would like to apologize Miss.

It turns out he has come in since I arrived and wishes to get drunk with Minimum delay, the assembled party tell him Damsel in distress back of the bar and he says to Hell with that, she is probably faking it anyway; he sees this was error and regrets it very much.

And I have to make a production over forgiveness, he will never believe me unless I do.

So I am Stuck.

You think all this will wear off in a day or two? Brother, so do I. At first, that is. But it does not. I have reformed the place overnight.

I begin to think getting drunk each night and working it off by fighting are not really their personal choice, all they need is a stimulus to snap them out of it; such as the influence of a Good woman maybe and looks like I am elected.

I get so busy listening to assorted troubles and soothing fights before they come to the boil, apart from any job Knotty can give me such as putting glasses in the washer and dishing the drinks, I hardly have time to think about Dad except at the hospital each day.

He is dead out for seven days just like they said, while the blood clots get loose from his brain; also they set his ribs and arm and tack up things inside. My miner friends all cheer me up, they say This is a good hospital and tell me all the times they have been put together again themselves. I say Oh and Ah so often I am quite tired, it seems to please them anyway.

Then Dad comes awake.

He does not do it while I am there of course, but I am allowed to sit with him two hours the day after; they have shifted him out of the tank into a proper bed and taken the Plumbing away. Towards the end while I am there he comes round and says Hello Liz, how have you been?

And I want to cry but I am damned if I will. I say I am fine. And he is already asleep again.

I ring home like I do every day. Charlie is out so I leave a message, then I go back to the pub. I feel truly I could sing all the way. I do not notice until Knotty says so that I am singing anyway. Knotty is in a sour mood but when I tell him about Dad he fetches out half a smile and says will I be leaving then?

I say No Dad has another one month and twenty-one days of Hospital to go.

At this his face falls under three gravities and he says All very well for me. I say why? can he not afford to pay me?

He says what troubles him is the pub. Since I came liquor drinking is down two fifths, if anybody starts to get drunk the rest stop him in case something occurs to Sully my pure girlish mind, it becomes clear that to Knotty this sobriety is not pleasing at all.

Well it is far from being my wish either, at least I think that at first then I think again Do I really want my pals back to the old routine drunk every night Dead drunk Friday to Monday? This do-gooding is insidious stuff.

I go on thinking about it when I have time, this is not often because the boys are so pleased to hear Dad is better they allow each other to get quite Lit, I have to head off one row after another.

Unwillingly to Earth

I begin to think anyway this situation cannot last long, the pressure is building up visibly something is going to Blow they need outlets for aggression and getting none just now. Also I must do something for Knotty. I could tell him Dad will pay back his losses but Knotty's head is solid bone; if I once got into it that I am not a Dear little down-and-out, he would let it out again at the Diagrammatic wrong time.

Things have got to end but they have got to end tidy with no hard feelings, I shall need help for this.

I get out that night as soon as Knotty is in bed and get to a public visiphone. I dial home, never mind that it is one in the morning I want Uncle Charlie.

What I get is Buffalo Cole looking sleepy, he lets out a Yip he learned from an old stereo and asks where I am and where I have been so long and so loud I cannot tell him for quite a while.

Then he tells me Charlie is here in Town.

He has assumed I am staying at the Hospital. They phoned today as usual, he asked for me and found I was somewhere on my own; he busted into town straight off like a kor calf in a cornfield and been hunting for me all over tearing out hair in bunches.

He is staying with a friend on the far side of town. I ring.

Brother.

Now he has found me he has no wish to talk to me I am to stay in the visiphone booth and not move till called for well I suppose I can wiggle my ears if I like?

Charlie arrives in a heli four minutes later and mad enough to burn helium, he gives me the kind of Character my pals sketch for one another when I am not supposed to be by.

He is not interested in Excuses, he will get me out of whatever mess I am in for my father's sake; I will come to a bad end some day but I can have the grace to keep it until the old man is on his feet again.

I have learned something these last few days; I do not yell back. I say I have been very foolish and need advice.

Do not think this Fools him but he is taken aback slightly. I get something said before he recovers and in the end I tell the whole thing hardly interrupted at all.

At the end he gives me a peculiar look like when one of the Chicken hatcharias gave birth to a parrot and says nothing for a while.

I say Look Charlie my idea is this; he says Liz your ideas are the start of this trouble in the first place, you have been getting Ideas ever since I knew you and every one worse than the one before, just let me think about this.

Then he says Well if you leave without explanations I suppose we will have these desperate characters hunting for you all over Town and if the truth gets out there will be a rumpus because of that, I guess you better go back there for tonight anyway, how are you going to get back in?

I say I have a key, does he think I Crawled out of a window? From his look I rather gather he does, Men are children at heart.

All the same I go back quietly and sleep like a tombstone.

In the morning I see Charlie at the hospital and he says he has an idea but seems he prefers to sit on it and see how it will hatch, I do not tell him what I think of this.

Then Dad wakes and says a few words and things look brighter and afterwards Charlie swears he has a real idea how I can get Out of this without any hurt feelings, it just needs a bit more Work on it.

* * *

Unwillingly to Earth

I go back to the Arms thinking my troubles are half over, Brother what error, this is where they *begin*.

That evening I am chinning to some types who cut up yesterday, I tell them how Shocked I am how surprised how sad because they have Backslid, they are always sure I feel like this. If I do not say it they get upset because they suppose my feelings too Deep for words; I can do this sort of thing No hands now.

Just the same it takes concentration, when the stranger comes in I hardly notice him at all.

He is a tall chap in the usual Evercleans with filter mask over his shoulder, all that is strange is that I have not seen him before, men stick to their own pubs as a rule.

He slides into a corner and swaps words with the regulars and I forget him altogether.

The clock strikes twelve, two hours to midnight closing, enter a tall dark stranger.

Short hair and big shoulders and the face that launched the campaign for Great Outdoors Shampoo, maybe twenty-two years old, he takes a quick look round and I guess he does not think much of the place.

Well he should have seen it a week ago, now there is only one single jukebox going and people are just chatting over drinks, not a Fight in the place.

He comes up to the bar and taps someone on the shoulder to make way; try touching anyone a fortnight back and Stand well clear! This time the fellow stops his fist before it goes six inches and then Moves over an inch or two and I am face to face with the stranger over the gap.

He looks at me and registers more Surprise than I thought his face could hold, I say What are you drinking Sir?

He swallows hard and says Beer please; something is displeasing him like mad but I cannot see how it is Me.

I give him his beer and he gives me an unloving look

and moves away, he horns in on one of the gatherings and starts to Chat.

I am busy but I keep an eye on him and it seems to me the chat is getting too emphatic for health, I beckon over a miner called Dogface and ask What goes on?

He says That character been annoying you Liz? I say No is he annoying anyone else? Dogface says he asks too damn many questions, someone will paste him any minute now.

I sign for another miner called Swede, these two are the steadiest around; I say Ride herd on this character and keep him out of trouble.

They say How? I say Get into conversation and stop him talking to anyone who is too prone to get Mad.

They look doubtful so I tell them to talk to him, he is asking questions well tell him Answers, tell him about life on Excenus, you can see he is a fresh-out Terrie, tell him about mining; that will be Instructive for him.

Next time I look Dogface and Swede are one on each side of him talking away, the other types have all drifted off.

The stranger stays for an hour and they stick by him all the while, when he leaves no one has laid a finger on him, I have done a Good deed this day. Dogface and Swede say they never knew they had so much to talk about, just the same the stranger did not look Grateful to me.

Next day I go to the hospital as usual wondering if Charlie has hatched his Idea.

Halfway there I feel Eyes on the back of my neck. I look round and there he is again, the tall dark stranger I mean.

He strides up and says he wants to Speak to me.

His tone is such that I think of Buffalo's judo trick but he looks the type to brush it off with a careless Reflex, I could wish there were more people around.

I say What about?

He says I know damned well what about, this is Poaching and he will not stand for it, he will Complain to something I do not catch.

I say he must be thinking of somebody else.

He Sizzles between his teeth and says I need not think I can get out of it by playing innocent because he will be able to trace me perfectly well. I obviously come from that establishment for muddy-minded morons Pananthropic Institute of Social Research; everybody knows Excenus is Russett's fieldwork place and no other school would crash it, let alone horning in on a Practical that way.

Furthermore the dodge I am using was corny in the Ark or earlier.

I am much perplexed but more angry and ask What he is proposing to do?

He says Don't worry I will find out later, I guess he does not know either; but before I can say so he goes striding away.

I walk on getting madder as I go, this Mystery on top of everything else is enough to drive one round the Fourth dimension, and he will catch on to his mistake and I shall *never* hear it explained; however when I arrive I forget him because Dad is awake and fit for talking to.

Several times I wonder Shall I tell him the whole thing? but he is still sick, this is no time to tell him I am serving in a Bar in the toughest part of the town.

We talk quietly about the farm and plans for next year and things we did when I was little, all of a sudden I want to cry.

Then Charlie comes. One visitor at a time I have to go, Charlie needs some instructions about the farm.

I think I will go out and walk around, I do not like waiting in the hospital much, they think Visitors get in the way; I am halfway down the outside steps when there is a shadow over me and a voice says Excuse me, Miss Lee?

I turn and stare.

Brother what is this, are they shooting a stereo on Excenus? this is the handsomest man I ever came across. He makes the one this morning look like a credit for twenty all from one mold, I am certain I never saw him before.

He says We met last night though that was hardly an introduction, he is glad of a chance to make my acquaintance now.

I think No this cannot be, Yes it is, this is the gink I hardly noticed last night; same face same voice same hands and I never looked at him twice, how in Space is it done—?

Brother! He called me *Miss Lee*!

I say There must be some mistake and turn towards the Hospital again.

He says the hospital clerk told him my name and he saw me come out of the Royal Arms this morning.

Sing Hey for the life of a Hunted Fawn, now I am good and Mad, just crazy. He says he thinks a talk would be Mutually Profitable, what I think is quite Different and I say it out loud. He has a way of doing things with his eyebrows to look amused, men have been Killed for less.

He says What would the clientele of the Royal Arms think of that?

I say What the hell is that to him?

He says he will be delighted to explain if I will give him the opportunity but this is hardly a suitable place to talk.

There are *no* places suitable and I tell him so.

He says he has a helicar there, if I would care to drive it anywhere I like he will give me the key.

I begin to see what will happen if this specimen opens his face to Knotty and Co.; I must know what his game is; I say OK.

We are just getting into the heli when the air is sun-

Unwillingly to Earth 21

dered, *LIZ!* here is Uncle Charlie and my reputation in pieces again.

He charges across and my companion says Mr. Blair? which is Charlie's name though I hardly remember, and he hands over a card with a name and some words on it.

Charlie reads it and looks Baffled but not mad any longer.

I sneak a look, it says *D. J. M'Clare* and a string of initials, *Russett Interplanetary College of Humanities, Earth*, it has *Department of Cultural Engineering* in little letters lower down.

Charlie says Liz what in Space are you up to now?

M'Clare says he has to make Miss Lee a rather complicated apology, this being no place to do which he has suggested a ride, it will be much better if Mr. Blair will come along too.

I do not know how it is done but ten seconds later Charlie is inviting him for a drink to the house where he is staying and I am tagging along behind.

The house is close to the hospital and well-to-do all right the air is Humidified right through. I choose lemonade to drink, I never cared for alcohol much and I am *more* tired of the smell; when Charlie has done bustling with drinks M'Clare begins.

He says he understands Miss Lee had an encounter this morning with his pupil Douglas Laydon.

I say Great whirling nebulae not the lunatic who called me a poacher? He says Very likely, Laydon came here to do a Practical test and finding I had anticipated him was somewhat upset.

He explains that students in Cultural Engineering have a fieldwork test after two years, this one had to make a survey of the principal factors leading to violence and try out short-term methods of abating same in a selected portion of the Community on Excenus 23 namely the Royal Arms pub.

M'Clare says Excenus 23 is a very suitable spot for this kind of field work, the Social problems stay constant but the population turns over so fast they are not likely to catch on.

Charlie nods to show he gets this. I get it too and start to be angry, not just Mad but real angry inside; I say You mean that dumbbell came out here to push people around just for the exercise?

He says fieldwork is an essential part of the course for a Cultural Engineering degree. I say Hell and hokum nobody has any right to interfere with people just for practice; he says Not everybody posesses your natural technique, Miss Lee.

I says Look that is different, *I* was not trying to find out what makes people tick and then fiddle with the works and think I did something clever.

Charlie says Shut Up Liz.

This man does not believe me, well I did not start this on Purpose but now I remember all the times I listened to someone tell me his troubles and thought What a good girl I am to listen to this poor sucker, how wise how clever how well I understand; I do not like thinking of this.

Then I find Charlie has started to tell M'Clare the whole thing.

I will say for Charlie he tells it pretty fair. He does understand why I cannot just let my pals find out I have fooled them, whatever he may have said; but why does he want to tell it to this character will not see it at all?

Then he says Well, Professor if I understand what Cultural Engineering stands for this is a problem right in your line, I would very much welcome advice.

M'Clare says nothing and Charlie says It is a very minor matter of course: M'Clare says There he does not agree.

He says if these tough types caught on that their dear little down-and-out was really Rich it would not stop at personal unpleasantness, the whole relation between the mining and farming communities might well be Upset.

I would like to sneer but cannot because it is perfectly true. Dad is pretty rich and has a big effect on local affairs; if the miners think his daughter been slumming around making Fools of them no knowing *what* comes after.

M'Clare says However it should be simple enough to fix things so no one can catch on.

Charlie says it is not so simple, Liz has to be got away where no one will chase after her; fortunately very few people in Town are in a position to recognize her but Where can she go now?

I say Look that is easy, give me a job on the farm.

Charlie says Suppose they take a fancy to visit you, you think Buffalo Cole is going to remember you are the Hired Help came there last Tuesday? That is the one place you can be certain sure someone will give you away.

Besides just at present they know your name but have not connected it with *Farmer* Lee. No, Liz, we have to get you a job as companion or something to someone here in Town, a respectable woman the miners will keep right away from.

I say Charlie there are maybe three respectable women in Town, if you park me on one all my pals will come round to make sure I have not hired into a Brothel by mistake. How will your lady friend care for that? Charlie says What worries him is where to find a woman anyone could believe would voluntarily saddle herself with a Hellcat like me.

M'Clare makes a little cough and Charlie asks What does he think?

M'Clare says our solutions are too prosaic and too partial, this is a classic example of a fauntleroy situation and should be worked out as such.

I ask What the hell is a fauntleroy situation? He says this means a situation in which one younger and apparently weaker person exerts influence over a group of adults by appealing to their protective instincts.

Appeal, hell! he says Unconsciously, no doubt. He says the situation can only be properly resolved if the subject appears to be in no further need of protection against the trouble, whatever it may be; in this case financial.

Charlie says You mean we should tell them Liz has come into money and moved to a hotel?

M'Clare says Again that would be only a partial solution, he thinks it would be better if Little Orphan Liz and her sick father were rescued by a Rich Uncle arriving next Wednesday from Magnus 9.

Charlie says Why is Liz short of money if she has a Rich Uncle ready to assist? M'Clare says he is also a long-lost uncle only recently made his pile and just managed to trace the one remaining Relative he has looked for ever since.

I say Why is this better than, he died and left me the Cash? He says Money for nothing morally unsatisfactory and a Bad ending, this way you give something in return; also your lonely uncle can take you and your father straight off to Earth and leave nothing for anyone to ask questions about.

I do not believe anyone will swallow this hunk of cereal, too convenient all round.

According to M'Clare that does not matter, it is the right *kind* of improbable event for this situation. My pals will think it quite Right and proper for their little ray of sunshine to be snatched up into unearned affluence and cheer the declining years of her rich relative and bring him together with his estranged brother-in-law; *right* ending to the situation: Statistical probability irrelevant to the workings of Destiny.

Charlie says Where will we find an uncle? He himself is too well known, to hire an Actor means going off the planet. M'Clare says as it happens he has to leave the planet this afternoon and will be returning next Wednesday himself.

Charlie says You mean *you'd* do it? That's really wonderful, what do you say Liz? What I *want* to say is I will not have this Cultural Corkscrew add himself to my family, but the lemonade tangles in my epiglottis; people have died that way but Do they care?

M'Clare says of course he must get Mr. Lee's permission for this masquerade, *I* just thought of that one now I am left with nothing to say except—Hellanhokum I ought to be back at the bar.

I do not trust M'Clare one Angstrom I could see he was thinking of something else the whole time, probably What interesting opportunities for Observation if the whole thing is given away. If Dad is really over his concussion he will put a stopper on the whole thing.

Does he hell!

Charlie takes M'Clare along, never mind Visiting hours are over, they spill the whole thing to Dad before the Professor catches his ship.

Well I will say they made a job of it. When I go along in the morning absolutely no bites in the furniture, Dad is still weakened of course.

He says Liz, girl, you are as crazy as a kor-calf, you got as much sense as a shorted servo, the moment I take my eye off you you stir up more trouble than a barrel of hooch on a dry planet. It is a long time since I was surprised at anything you do, here he goes off into ancient history not relevant to this affair.

This business, he says, has put the triple tungsten-plated tin top on it, even you must know what could have happened to you going into a place like that, Liz girl how could you do such a thing?

I say Dad I know it was crazy but you have it all wrong, miners may be tough but these types were real good to me.

He says Liz your capacity to fall on your feet is what scares me the worst of all, one of these days the probabilities will catch up with you all in one go. Look at this Professor M'Clare probably the one man in the Universe would know how to get you out of this with no one catching on, and he turns up here and now.

Well I was all set to get out myself, with Charlie helping, but it seems to soothe Dad to think about M'Clare so I let him. That smoothie put himself over all right.

It develops where he has gone is Magnus 9 in the next system to let an examinee loose on some suckers there; he has left a list of instructions with Charlie and Dad says I am to order myself according to these and not dare to Breathe unless so directed.

They are all about what I am to do and say, Charlie stands over me while I learn them by heart, he does not seem to trust me but Hellanall does he think I *want* to fluff in the middle of a script like this?

Tuesday evening is when the scene starts, my pals ask What is on my mind, they hope my old man is not worse is he?

I say I have had a message from a ship just coming within communicator distance and is landing tomorrow. I am to meet someone whose name got scrambled, at the Space Gate at five thirty in the morning; I cannot think who this can be it worries me a little Dad has so many troubles already.

At this my pals look grim and say If it is debts I can count on them and if it is anything else I can still count on them, I feel ashamed again.

Five-thirty is a horrible time to start. I am yawning and chilled through, the night breeze is still up and dust creeping in among the long pylon shadows in little puffed whirlwinds, the three ships on the field got their hatches down and look broken and untidy.

First a little black dot in the sky then bigger and bigger covering more and more stars, it does not seem to come nearer but only to spread, then suddenly a great bulging thing with light modeling its underside and right overhead, I want to duck.

It swings across a little to the nearest pylons. They jerk and the arms come up with a clang, reaching after the ship. There is a flash and bang as they make contact just under the gallery where it bulges, then a long slow glide as they fold and she comes down into place like a grasshopper folding its legs.

I find my breathing hitched up, I take a deep lungful of cold morning dust and start coughing.

My pals rally round and pat me on the back.

I thought there were only three present but there seem to be more. They stop me seeing the passengers get off until half are into the Gate, M'Clare is not in sight hell he did not see me perhaps he has ditched us all.

The speaker system makes with a crack like splitting rocks and says Will Miss Lee believed to be somewhere around the Gate come to the manager's office at once please?

I take another deep breath, more carefully.

My pals of whom I now have Seven on the premises seem to think it is sinister; they wish to come too. In the end they elect Swede and Dogface as bodyguards and the rest wait outside.

I cannot remember one single word I ought to say.

In the office is a man in uniform and another one not, I guess I look blank but not as blank as I feel the human face could hardly, how has he done it this time?

It was several seconds before I recognized him at all.

He looks older and kind of worn you would guess he had a hardish life and certainly not cultured at all.

I say I was called for, my name is Lee.

He says slowly Yes he thinks he would have known me, I am very like my mother, and he calls me Elizabeth.

Every word is clean out of my head, fortunately my pals take over and wish to know How come?

M'Clare looks at them with a frown and says neither of them is James Lee, surely?

I say No they are friends of mine, does he mean he is my mother's brother because I thought he was dead?

This is not the right place for that the script is gone to the Coalsack already.

M'Clare says Yes he really is John M'Clare, he brings out papers to prove it. My friends give them the once over several times and seem to be satisfied, then they want to know sternly Why had he not helped us before?

M'Clare brings out letters from a tracing firm that cover two years and a bit, I will say he is a worker he has vamped all this stuff in three days with other things to do, I suppose Cultural Engineering calls for forgery once in a while.

My pals seem satisfied.

I say Why was he looking for us seeing he and Dad never got along? This is the script as originally laid down.

M'Clare alters the next bit ad lib and I don't take it in but it goes over with my pals all right, they tell him all about Dad's accident which they think happened prospecting, and about me and the Bar; just then in comes M'Clare's acquaintance well to do in business locally meaning Uncle Charlie, apologizing for being late; M'Clare told him just how late to be.

My pals shuffle and say Well Miss Lee you will not want us now.

I say What is this Miss Lee stuff, you have been calling me Lizzie for weeks. I had to tell them my name or they will call me Bubbles or something.

Unwillingly to Earth

M'Clare says he has a great deal to discuss with his niece and Dad, not to mention Charlie, but he wants to hear all about my doings and I will want to tell my friends; maybe if he calls round to the Royal Arms in the evening they will be there?

They shuffle but seem gratified, they go.

Charlie sits down and the manager goes and Charlie says *Whew!* I sit down and do not say anything at all.

Well Knotty will be pleased to get rid of me that is one life brightened anyway.

I do not want another day like that one, six hours doing Nothing in a hotel. I see Dad about five minutes, he used up the rest of the visiting time with M'Clare or Charlie in and me *out*, then Charlie flies back home to get something or other and I want to go too, I want to go home! I will never come to this town again, I can't anyway until my pals have all left the planet. I wish all this lying were over.

Evening M'Clare and I go out to the Royal Arms.

Knotty has had a letter from me all about it, and of course everyone knows, minute we get inside the door I see everybody is Worked up and ready to fight at the drop of a hint, fauntleroy situation or not if they think my Rich Uncle is trying to snoot them all the trouble missed during the last fortnight will Occur at one go.

Then M'Clare spots Dogface and Swede at the back of the crowd and says Hello, five minutes later it is Drinks all round and everything Jo-block smooth, I could not have done it better myself.

Then he is making a speech.

It is all about Kindness to dumb creatures meaning Me, I do not listen but watch faces, judging by them he is going good. I hear the last words, something about Now he has found his niece and her father he does not want to lose sight of them and his brother-in-law has agreed that the whole family goes back to Earth with him in two days' time.

It occurs to me suddenly How am I going to get off the ship? They have found some sick cuss wants to get to Earth and will play my Dad ten minutes to get a free passage, but my pals are bound to turn up to see me off How am I to slip away?

Then I stop thinking because Dogface says slowly So this is goodbye, hey, Liz?

And someone else says Well it was nice while it lasted.

And I cry. I put my head down on the table among the drinks and cry like Hell, because I am deceitful and they are kind to me and I wish I could tell the Truth for a change.

Someone pats me on the back and shoves a disposable into my hand, I think it is one of my pals until I smell it, nobody bought this on Excenus 23! I am so surprised I wad it up and it goes to dust, so I have to stop crying right away.

I even manage to say Goodbye and I will never forget them, they say They will never forget me.

We say about ten thousand Goodbyes and go.

Next day the hospital say Dad overtired, they have sedated him, seems he was half the night talking to M'Clare and Charlie what the hell were they thinking of to let him? My uncle will call for me. I expect Charlie; what I get is M'Clare.

We are to go shopping buying some clothes for me to wear on Earth, it seems to me this is carrying Realism too far but I do not want any more time in the hotel with nothing to do.

Fortunately the tailoring clerk does not know me, we have a machine out at the farm. He takes a matrix and slaps up about ten suits and dresses; they will be no use

Unwillingly to Earth

here at all, no place for condensers or canteen I cannot even give them away.

However I am not bothered so much about that. M'Clare is all the time trying to get me to talk, he says for instance Have I ever thought about going to College? I say Sure, I count my blessings now and then.

We are somehow on the subject of Education and what teaching have I had so far? I say Usual machines and reels. I want to get off this so I start talking about Excenus 23, he cannot compete there. I tell him about our manners, customs, morals, finance, farming, geography, geology, mining of Areopagite, I am instructive right back to the hotel, I hope now he feels he has had Enough of it.

In the evening they let me see Dad.

They say You really ought not to be allowed in he has had his Quota of visitors already today, I say Who? but need I ask, it was that nice Mr. M'Clare.

The nurse says I am allowed to see Dad because he refuses to go to sleep until he has told me something, but I must be careful not to Argue it will retard his recovery if he gets excited again.

Dad is dead white and breathing noisy but full of spirit, the nurse says You may have five minutes and Dad says No one is rationing his time for him, when he is ready he will ring. The nurse is a sturdy six-footer and Dad is five foot four, they glare it out Dad wins in the end.

Well I intend to keep it down to five minutes myself I say Hello Dad what cooks?

He says Lizzie girl what do you think of this M'Clare?

I would love to tell him but I say He is very clever.

Dad says Sure he is clever, Professor at a big college on Earth gets students from all planets in the known volume, I been talking to him and he says you have a Flair.

I say Huh?

Dad says I have a flair for this cultural engineering business, Professor M'Clare told him so.

I say I promised already I will keep it under control in the future.

Dad starts to go red and I say Look, two minutes gone already, what did you want to tell me? say it straight, and he says Going to send you to College, girl.

I say What!

Dad says Liz, Excenus is no place for a young girl all her life. Time you see some other worlds and I cannot leave the farm and got no one to have an eye to you. Now M'Clare says he will get you into this College and that is just what I need.

I say But—!

Dad says They got schools on Earth for kids like you, been on an outback planet or Education restricted in other ways, they are called Prelim Schools; well you got the Rudiments already; M'Clare says, after three months Prelim you should be fit to get into Russett College of Humanities, he will act as your official guardian while on Earth, Do not argue with me Liz!

The nurse comes back and says I must go in thirty seconds not more, Dad is gray in the face and looks fit to come to pieces, I say All right Dad of course you know best.

He says Kiss me Lizzie, and Goodbye.

Then the nurse chases me Out.

This is M'Clare's doing, playing on Dad when he is mixed in the head, he knows damned well this thing is impossible if he were only in his right mind. I go Tearing back to the hotel to look for M'Clare.

I find he is Out.

I sit there seething one hour twenty-seven minutes until he comes in. I say I have to speak to him *right now*.

I do not know if he is looking bored or amused but it is an expression should be wiped off with a rag, he says, Certainly, can it wait till we reach his room?

Unwillingly to Earth

We get there and I say Look what is this nonsense you have talked Dad into about taking me to Earth or something? Because it is straight out crazy and if Dad were right in the head he would know.

M'Clare sits down and says "Really, Lysistrata, what a spoiled young woman you are."

Who the hell told him, that name is the one thing I really do hold against Dad.

M'Clare goes on that he did not understand at first why my father refused to have me told until it was all fixed, but he evidently knew the best way to avoid a lot of fuss.

I say I am not going to leave Excenus 23.

M'Clare says I cannot possibly avoid leaving Excenus 23, I have got to go on the ship tomorrow haven't I?

I say they can send me back by lifeship, he says it is far too late to arrange that now.

I say Then I will come back from the first stop on the way.

He says he is Officially my guardian from the moment we leave the planet and he cannot allow me to travel alone, reason for all this rush is so he can see me to College himself, What is the matter with me don't I want to see the World anyway?

Sure, some time, but I don't have to go to College for that.

M'Clare says that is my mistake, Earth has such a rush of sightseers from the Out Planets entrance not permitted any more except on business. Only way I can get there is as a student except I might marry an Earthman some day. I say Hell I would rather go to College than that.

Just the same when I have had enough of it I am coming straight back home.

M'Clare says I will do no such thing.

Great whirling nebulae he cannot keep me on Earth if I want to go! He says On the contrary he has no power to do anything else, my father appointed him my guardian on condition I was to do a four-year course at Russett. Of course if I am determined to return to Excenus Home and Dad rather than make the effort to adjust myself to an Environment where I have not got everyone securely under my thumb there is an easy way out, I have to take a Prelim test in three months and if I fail to make it no power on Earth could get me into Russett, and he would *have* to send me back home.

We have to start early in the morning so Good Night.

I go to my room, if there was anything I could bite holes in that is what I would do.

I will pass that exam if it takes twenty-eight hours a day, No this is to be on Earth well all the time that they have; I will get into M'Clare's class and make him Sorry he interfered with me.

What does he take me for? Dad too, he would have sent me to school long ago except that we both knew I would never make the grade.

I am next thing to illiterate, that's why.

Oh, I can read in a way, I can pick up one word after another as they come up in the machine, but I cannot use it *right*; Dad is the same.

Dad used to think it was because he learned to use it too late, then when I was old enough to learn he found I was the same, some kink in the genes I suppose. Both of us, we cannot read with the machine any faster than an old-style book.

I did not know this was wrong until I was eleven. Dad hid the booklet came with the machine, then one day I found it, part of it says like this:

> It has sometimes been suggested that the reading rate should be used as a measure of general intelligence. This is fallacious. The rate at which information can be absorbed, and therefore the rate at which words move across the viewer, is broadly cor-

related with some aspects of intelligence, but not with all. Mathematicians of genius tend to read slower than average, and so do some creative artists. All that can safely be said is that people of normal intelligence have reading rates somewhere above five thousand and that it is exceptional for anyone to pass the ten thousand mark; the few who do are usually people of genius in a narrowly specialized field.

My reading rate is so low the dial does not show, I worked out with a stopwatch it is eight hundred or thereabouts.

I go and ask Dad; it is the first time he ever lets me see him feeling bad, it is all he can do to talk about it at all, he keeps telling me it is Not so bad really he got on all right and he cannot read properly any more than me; he shows me those old books of his all over again.

After this we do not talk about it and I do not want to talk about it now. Not to anyone at all.

That is the longest night I remember in my life, nineteen years of it.

In the morning we go to the Gate. My pals are there seeing me off. I do not cry because I have just found out something makes me so mad I am just waiting to get in the ship and tell M'Clare what I think of him.

Then we go into the ship.

I cannot say anything now we have to strap in for takeoff. The feeling is like being in a Swing stopped at the top of its beat. I cannot help waiting for it to come down, but after a bit I grasp we are up to stay and get unhitched.

In the corridor is a crewman, he says Hello miss not sick? I say Ought I to be?

He asks am I an old traveler? when I say First time up he makes clicking noises to say I am clever or lucky or both.

We are getting acquainted when I feel eyes on my backbone and there is M'Clare.

M'Clare says Hello, Lizzie, not sick?

I say I do not have to pretend he is my uncle any more and I prefer to be called Miss Lee, I will not have a Person like him calling me Lizzie or in fact anything else, as of now we are not Speaking any more.

He raises an eyebrow and says Dear him. I start to go but he hooks a hand round my arm and says What is all this about?

I say I have been talking to that poor sucker come out of hospital and pretending to be my Dad. He is a heartcase thinks he will be cured when he gets to Earth able to get around like anyone else, I *know* if he could be cured on Earth he could be cured on Excenus 23 just as well, he will simply have to go on lying in bed and not even anyone he knows around, it is the dirtiest trick I ever knew.

Well he is not smiling now anyway.

He asks have I told the man he will not be cured, I say What does he take me for?

He says "I could answer that, but I won't. You are quite right in thinking that it would do very little good to take a man with a diseased heart to Earth, but as it happens he will not be going there at all.

"Close to Earth," M'Clare goes on, "there is a body called the Moon with approximately one-sixth the Gravitational pull. There is a big sanatorium on it for men like this one, the rare cases not curable by operation or drugs; they will grow him a new heart and graft it in. Meantime if he cannot live quite a normal life he will at least be able to get out of bed, and probably do some sort of job. This has been explained to him and he seems to think it good enough."

Sweet spirits of sawdust I have heard of that sanatorium before, why does the deck not open and swallow me up?

I say I am sorry. M'Clare says "What for?"

I say I am sorry I spoke without making sure of the facts.

I do not beg his pardon because I would not have it on a plate.

M'Clare says my father gave him a letter to deliver to me when the ship was under way, he shoves it in my hand and goes away.

It is written with Dad's styler, he fell on it during the accident and the L went wobbly, what it says is this.

Dear Liz,

About this College, I know when you said I know best you did not mean it, just the same I reckon I do. You got to look at it another way. At my old school when they found I could not use Readers they reckoned I was no good for learning, but they were wrong. There is more to being educated than just books or you could sit and read them at home.

You and I are handicapped same way so we have to use our heads to get over it. All that is in books came out of somebody's head, well you and I just got to use our own instead of other people's. Of course there is facts but a lot of books use the same facts over and over, I found that when I started to study.

There is another thing for you, they told me at school I would never be any good for studying but I reckon I did all right.

It is high time you saw some other worlds than this one but I would not send you to College if I did not think you could get through. M'Clare says you have this Flair. We will look forward to seeing you four years from now, don't forget to write.

Your loving father
J. X. Lee.

P.S. I got a list of books you will want for Prelim School and Charlie had Information Store copy them, they are in your cabin. J. X. Lee.

Poor old Dad.

Well I suppose I better give it a try, and what's more I better get on with it.

The reels are in my cabin, a whole box of them it will take me a year to get through, the sooner the quicker I suppose.

I jam one in sit down in the Machine put on the blinkers and turn the switch.

There is the usual warmup, the words slide on slow at first then quicker then the thing goes *click* and settles down, the lines glide across just fast enough to keep pace with my eyes. I have picked myself something on Terrestrial Biology and Evolution, I realize suddenly I will be among it in a couple of weeks, lions and elephants and kangaroos, well I cannot stop to think now I have to beat that Exam.

Most of those weeks I study like a drain.

They have cut day-length in the ship to twenty-four hours already. I have difficulty sleeping at first but I adjust in the end. Between reading I mooch around and talk to the crew, I am careful *not* to be the Little Ray of Sunshine but we get on all right. I go and see the man with the sick heart a few times, he wants to know all about the Moon so I read up and relay as well as I can.

It sounds dull to me but compared to lying in bed I can see it would be a high-voltage Thrill.

He thanks me every day during the whole voyage. I keep telling him we only did it because we wanted someone to impersonate Dad. I think there ought to be ways for people like him to get enough money to go to the Moon, how can you earn it lying in bed? he agrees but does not seem to get ideas very much, I think I will write about it to Dad.

We stop at the Moon to put him down but no time to look round, M'Clare had to be back at Russett day before yesterday. I suppose he lost time picking me up, well I did not ask him to.

Dropping to Earth I am allowed maybe half a second in the control room to look at the screen, I say What is all that white stuff? they say It is raining down there.

More than half of what I see is water and more coming down!

When the Earthbound ask what strikes me most on Earth I say All that water and nothing to pay; they do not know what it means getting water out of near-dry air, condensing breath out-of-doors, humidity suit to save sweat on a long haul. First time on Earth I go for a walk I feel thirsty and nearly panic, on Excenus 23 that would mean Canteen given out rush fast for the nearest house.

They told me it was raining; all the same when we walk out of the ship I think at first they are washing the field from up above. I stand there with my mouth open in surprise; fortunately M'Clare is not looking and I come to quite soon.

Seems all this water has drawbacks too, round here they have to carry rainproofing instead of canteens.

I spend three days seeing sights and never turn on a book.

Prelim school.

Worst is, I do not have a Reader of my own now, only Reading Rooms and I have to keep it private that I read more than two hours a day or someone will catch on and I will be Out before I have a chance to try if what Dad says will work out.

There is more to teaching than books; for one thing Class Debates; these are new to me of course but so they are to the others and these I can take. Man to man with my tutor at least I can make him laugh, he says The rugged unpunctuated simplicity of my style of writing is not suited to academic topics even when leavened with polysyllables end of quote, but it is all these *books* are getting me down.

In the end I find a system, I read the longest reel on each topic and then the one the author doesn't like, that way I get Both sides to the question.

Three months and the Exam; afterwards I keep remembering all the things I should have put down until I take a twenty-four-hour pill and go to bed till the marking is over.

I wake up and comes a little blue ticket to say I am Through, please report to Russett College in three days for term to begin.

Well, what am I grinning about?

All this means is four *years* more of the same and M'Clare added on.

I go for a walk in the Rain to cool off but I keep grinning just the same.

It comes to me as a notion I may not get through Russett term without telling M'Clare all about himself, so I get round and see as much of Earth as I can; more variety than at home.

So then three days are up and here I am in Russett entrance hall with more people than I ever saw in my life at one time.

There are these Speaker mechs which are such a feature of Terrestrial life, all round the room. One starts up in the usual muted roar like a miner at a funeral, it says All students for Cultural Engineering Year One gather round please.

This means me.

Cultural Engineering is not a big department, only fifty of us coagulated round this mech but like I said they come all kinds, there is one I see projecting above the throng so brunet he is nearly purple, not just the hair but all over. What is the matter with him? he looks like the longest streak of sorrow I ever did see.

Well there are other ways to get pushed into this place than through Basic urges thalamic or otherwise, just look at me.

The mech starts again and we are all hanging on what drops from its diaphragm, it says we are to file along corridor G to Room 31 alpha and there take the desk allotted by the monitor and No other.

This we do, even by Terrie standard it is a long hike for indoors.

I wonder what is a Monitor, one of these mechs without which the Earthbound cannot tell which way is tomorrow? Then we are stopped and sounds of Argument float back from ahead.

That settles it, Terries do not argue with mechs and I am conditioned already, it is a way to get no place at all; there is someone Human dealing with the line.

We go forward in little jerks till I can hear, it is one of those Terrie voices that always sound like they are done on purpose to me.

We come round the corner to a door and I can see that this Monitor is indeed Human or at least so classified.

It is only me that this could happen to.

Each person says a name and the Monitor repeats it to the kind of box he carries and this lights up with figures on it. I wonder why the box needs a human along and then I remember, one hundred twenty-four different planets and accents to match, I guess this is one point where Man can be a real help to Machine.

I am glad I saw him before he saw me; I tell him Lee, L. and he looks at me in a bored way and then does a double take and drops the thing.

I pick it up and say Lee, L. in cultivated tones and it

lights up just the same; Q8 which means the desk where I have to sit.

The desks are in pairs. When I track Q8 to its lair Q7 is empty, I sit and wonder what the gremlins will send me by way of a partner.

I do not wait long. Here she comes, tall and dark and looks like she had brains right down her spinal column, she will have one of those done-on-purpose voices in which I will hear much good advice when the ice breaks in a month or so. Brother this is no place for me.

She looks straight past my shoulder and does not utter while she is sitting down.

I cannot see her badge which is on the other side. She has what looks to me like a Genuine imitation kor-hide pouch and is taking styler and block out of it, then she looks at me sideways and suddenly lights up all over with a grin like Uncle Charlie's, saying as follows, "Why, you must be Lizzie Lee."

I do not switch Reactions fast enough, I hear my voice say coldly that my name is Lee, certainly.

She looks like she stubbed her toe. I realize suddenly she is just a kid, maybe a year younger than I am, and feeling shy. I say quick that I make people call me Lizzie because my real name is too awful to mention.

She lights up again and says So is hers, we ought to found a Society for the Prevention of Parents or something.

Her brooch says B Laydon, she says her first name will not even abbreviate so people here got to call her just B.

I am just round to wondering where she heard my name when she says That stuffed singlet in the doorway is of course her big brother Douglas and she has been wanting to meet me ever since.

Here Big Brother Douglas puts the box under his arm and fades gently away, the big doors behind the rostrum

Unwillingly to Earth 43

slide open as the clock turns to fourteen hours and Drums and Trumpets here comes Mr. M'Clare.

B Laydon whispers I think Professor M'Clare is wonderful, don't you?

Brother.

I know M'Clare is going to deliver the Opening Address of the Year to Cultural Engineering students, it is my guess all such comes out of the same can so I take time off for some thought.

Mostly I am trying to decide what to do. Prelim School was tough enough, so this will be Tough^2, is it worth it going through that just to show M'Clare I can do it?

Sure it is but *can* I?

I go on thinking on these lines, such as what Dad will say if I want to give up; I just about decided all I can do is wait and see when suddenly it is Time up, clock shows 15:00 hours exactly just as the last word is spoken and Exit M'Clare.

Some timing I will say.

I look round and all the faces suggest I should maybe have Listened after all.

B Laydon is rapt like a parcel or something, then she catches me looking and wriggles slightly.

She says We have been allotted rooms together, sharing a study, do I mind?

I assume this is because we come together in the alphabet and say Why should I?

She says Well. On the form it said Put down anyone you would like to room with, and she wrote Lizzie Lee.

I ask Did she do this because mine was the only name she knew or does she always do the opposite of what Big Brother Douglas tells her, she answers Both.

O.K. by me anyway.

Our rooms are halfway up the center tower, when we find them first thing I see is a little ticket in the delivery slot says Miss Lee call on Professor M'Clare at fifteen thirty please.

Guardian or no I have seen him not more than twice since landing, which means not more than twice too often; still I go along ready to be polite.

He lets me sit opposite and looks thoughtful in a way I do not care for.

He says "Well, Miss Lee, you passed your qualifying exam."

I say Yes, because this is true.

He says it was a very economical performance exceeding the minimum level by two marks exactly.

Hells bells I did not know that, marks are not published, but I swallow hard and try to look as though I meant it that way.

M'Clare says the Admission Board are reluctant to take students who come so close to the borderline but they decided after some hesitation to admit me, as my Prelim Tutor considered that once I settled down as a student and made up my mind to do a little work I should get up to standard easily enough.

He says However from now on it is up to me, I will be examined on this term's work in twelve weeks' time and am expected to get at least ten percent above Pass level which cannot be done by neglecting most of the work set, from now on there are no summarizing texts to rely on.

He presents these facts for my consideration, Good afternoon.

I swagger out feeling lower than sea level.

It is no use feeling sore, I took a lot of trouble to hide the fact that I worked hard for that Exam, but I do feel sore just the same.

The thing I want to do most is to get one hundred percent marks in everything just to show him, I got a feeling this is just exactly how he *meant* me to react, because the

Unwillingly to Earth 45

more I think about it the more sure I am that very few things happen by accident around M'Clare.

Take rooming, for instance.

I find very quickly most people in Cultural Engineering have not got the partners they put in for, this makes me wonder why B got what she wanted, namely me.

Naturally the first thing I think of is that she has been elected Good Influence, this makes me pretty cagey of course but after a day or two I see I must think again.

B always says she does not *look* for trouble. This may be true, she is very absent-minded and at first I suppose she just gets into Scrapes through having her mind on something else, but later I find out she has Principles which are at the back of it.

First time I hear about this is four nights after Opening, there is a knock at my bedroom window at maybe three hours. I am not properly awake and do not think to question how somebody can be there, seeing it is five hundred feet up the tower; I open the window and B falls inside.

I am just about ready to conclude I must be dreaming when B unstraps a small antigrav pack, mountaineering type, and says Somebody offered her the beastly thing as a secondhand bargain, she has been trying it out and it doesn't work.

Of course an antigrav cannot fail altogether. If the space-warp section *could* break down they would not be used for building the way they are. What has gone wrong is the phase-tuning arrangement and the thing can be either right on or right off but nothing in between.

B says she stepped off the top of the tower maybe an hour ago and got stuck straightaway. She stepped a little too hard and got out of reach of the tower parapet. She only picked that night for it because there was no wind, so she had no chance of being blown back again. She just had to turn the antigrav off, a snatch at a time, and drop little by little until the slope of the tower caught up with her. Then she went on turning it snap on and snap off and kind of slithering down the stonework until she got to the right floor, and then she had to claw halfway round the building.

B says she was just going to tap at the window above mine and then she saw that frightful Neo-Pueblo statue Old Groucho is so proud of, then she came one further down and found me but I certainly take plenty of waking.

Well I am wide awake now and I speak to her severely.

I say it is her career, her neck, neither of them mine, but she knows as well as I do Jumping off the tower is the one thing in this University utterly Forbidden and no Ifs.

B says That's just because some idiots tried to jump in a high wind and got blown into the stonework.

I say Be that as it may if she had waked up Old Groucho—Professor Emeritus of Interpenetration Physics and ninety-three last week—she would have been expelled straightaway, I add further She knows best if it would have been worth it.

B says she is a practicing Pragmatist.

This turns out to mean she belongs to a bunch who say Rules are made mostly for conditions that exist only a little bit of the time, e.g. this one about the tower, B is quite right that is not dangerous except in a high wind—not if you have an antigrav I mean.

B says Pragmatists lead a Full Life because they have to make up their own minds when rules really apply and act accordingly, she says you do not lead a Full Life if you obey a lot of regulations when they are not necessary and it is a Principle of Pragmatism not to do this.

B says further it is because Terries go on and on obeying Regulations unnecessarily that Outsiders think they are Sissy.

I say Huh?

Unwillingly to Earth 47

B says it is not her fault she never had any proper adventures.

I remark if her idea of an adventure is to get hauled in front of the Dean why did she not go ahead and wake up Old Groucho instead of me?

B says the adventure part is just taking the risk, everybody ought to take some risks now and then and Breaking rules is the only one available just now.

This causes me to gawp quite a bit, because Earth seems to me maybe fifteen times as dangerous as any planet I ever heard of so far.

There are risks on all planets, but mostly life is organized to avoid them. Like back home, the big risk is to get caught without water; there is only about one chance in a thousand for that to happen, but everybody wears humidity suits just the same.

On Earth you got a sample of about all the risks there are, mountains and deserts and floods and the sea and wild animals and poisons. Now it occurs to me Terries could get rid of most of them if they really cared to try, but their idea of a nice Vacation is to take as many as possible just for fun.

Well later on it occurs to me I would never have understood this about Terries but for talking to B, and I look round and find a lot of the Terries got paired with Outsiders for roommates and maybe this is why.

I say to B some of what I think about risks and it cheers her up for a moment, but she goes on getting into trouble on Pragmatic Principles just the same.

Me, I am in trouble too but not on principle.

The work at first turned out not so bad as I expected, which is not to say it was good.

Each week we have a different Director of Studies and we study a different Topic, with lectures and stereos and visits to museums and of course Books.

Further we have what are called Class Debates, kind of

an argument with only one person speaking at a time and the Director to referee.

Terries say this last is Kid Stuff, but the Outsiders met it mostly in Prelim School if then so they really study hard so as to do it good. Next thing you know the Terries are outclassed and trying hard to catch up, so a strenuous time is had by all, I begin to see there is a real thing between the two groups though no one likes to mention it out loud.

Class Debates I do not mind, I been used to arguing with Dad all my life, what gets me is Essays. We do one each week to sum up, and all my sums come wrong.

Reason for this is we get about fifteen books to read every week and are not allowed more than three hours a day with a Reading Machine, this is plenty for most people but I only get through about a quarter of the stuff.

If you only know a quarter of the relevant facts you get things cockeyed and I can find no way round this.

My first essay comes back marked Some original ideas but more reference to actual examples needed, Style wants polishing up.

The second has Original!! but what about FACTS, style needs toning down.

More of the same.

After four weeks I am about ready to declare; then I find B gets assorted beefs written on her essays too and takes it for granted everybody does, she says Teachers always tell you what you do wrong not what you do right, this is Education.

I stick it some more.

I will say it is interesting all right. We are studying Influences on Cultural Trends, of which there are plenty some obvious some Not.

Most of the class are looking forward to becoming Influences themselves, we have not been taught how to do this yet but everyone figures that comes next. It seems to me though that whatever you call it it comes down to

Pushing people around when they are not looking, and this is something I do not approve of more than halfway.

There is just one person in the class besides me does not seem to feel certain all is for the best. This is the dark fellow I noticed on Opening Day, six foot six and built like a pencil. His name is Likofo Komom'baraze and he is a genuine African; they are rare at Russett because Africans look down on Applied studies preferring everything Pure. Most of them study Mathematics and Literature and so on at their own Universities or the Sorbonne or somewhere, seems he is the first ever to take Cultural Engineering and not so sure he likes it.

This is a bond between us and we become friendly in a kind of way. I find he is not so unhappy as he looks but Africans are proverbially Melancholy according to B.

I say to Komo one time that I am worried about the Exams, he looks astonished and says But, Lizzie, you are so clever! turns out he thinks this because the things I say in Class Debates do not come out of any book he knows of, but it is encouraging just the same.

I *need* encouragement.

Seventh week of term the Director of Studies is M'Clare.

Maybe it makes not so much difference, but that week I do everything wrong. To start with I manage to put in twice the legitimate time Reading for several days, I get through seven books and addle myself thoroughly. In Debates I cannot so much as open my mouth, I am thinking about that Essay all the time, I sit up nights writing it and then tear it up. In the end I guess I just join together bits that I remember out of the books and hand that in.

B thinks my behavior Odd but she has caught on now that I do not regard M'Clare as the most wonderful thing that ever happened.

The last debate of the week comes after Essays have been handed in, I try to pay attention but I am too tired.

I notice Komo is trying to say something and stuttering quite a bit, but I do not take in what it is about.

Next day I run into Komo after breakfast and he says Lizzie why were you so silent all this week?

What we studied this time was various pieces of Terrie history where someone deliberately set out to shape things according to his own ideas, I begin to see why Komo is somewhat peeved with me.

Komo says "Everybody concentrated on the practicability of the *modus operandi* employed, without considering the ethical aspects of the matter. I think it is at least debatable whether any individual has the right to try and determine the course of a society, most of the members of which are ignorant of his intentions. I hoped that the discussion would clear my mind, but nobody mentioned this side of it except me."

I know why Komo is worried about this, his old man who is a Tartar by all accounts has the idea he wants to re-establish a tribal society in Africa like they had a thousand years ago; this is why he sent Komo to study at Russett and Komo is only half sold on the idea.

I say "Listen, Komo, this is only the first term and so far as I can see M'Clare is only warming up, we have not got to the real stuff yet. I think we shall be able to judge it better when we know more about it, also maybe some of the stuff later in the course might be real helpful if you have to argue with your Dad."

Komo slowly brightens and says "Yes, you are a wise girl, Lizzie Lee."

Here we meet B and some others and conversation broadens, a minute later someone comes along with a little ticket saying Miss Lee see Professor M'Clare at 11:30 hours please.

Wise girl, huh?

Komo is still brooding on Ethics and the conversation has got on to Free Will, I listen a bit and then say "Listen,

Unwillingly to Earth 51

folks, where did you hatch? you do what you can and what you can't you don't, what is not set by your genes is limited by your environment let alone we were not the first to think of Manipulating people around, where does the Freedom come in?"

They gape and B says Oh but Lizzie, don't you remember what M'Clare said on Opening Day?

This remark I am tired of, it seems M'Clare put the whole Course into that one hour so Why we go on studying I do not know.

I say No I wasn't listening and I am tired of hearing that sentence, did nobody write the Lecture down?

B gasps and says there is a recording in the Library.

It was quite a speech, I will say.

There is a good deal about Free Will, M'Clare says Anyone who feels they have the right to *fiddle* with other people's lives has no business at Russett. But there is no such thing as absolute freedom, it is a contradiction in terms. Even when you do what you want, your wants are determined by your mental makeup and previous experience. If you do nothing and want nothing, that is not Freedom of will but Freedom *from* will, no will at all.

But, he says, all the time we are making choices, some known and some not; the more you look the more you see this. Quote, "It has probably not occurred to you that there is an alternative to sitting here until the hour strikes, and yet the forces that prevent you from walking out are probably not insurmountable. I say 'Probably' because a cultural inhibition can be as absolute as a physical impossibility. Whatever we do means submitting to one set of forces and resisting others. Those of you who are listening are obeying the forces of courtesy, interest or the hope that I may say something useful in examinations, and resisting the forces that tend to draw your minds on to other things. The more we consider our doings the more choices we see, and the more we see the better hope we have of understanding human affairs."

Here there are examples of how people often do not make the Choice they would really prefer, they are Got at for being sissy or something. Or social institutions get in the way even when everyone knows what should be done, Hard Cases make Bad Law and Bad Law makes Hard Cases too. M'Clare says You are always free to resist your Environment, but to do so limits all your choices afterwards, this comes to Make environments so they do not *have* to be resisted.

There is lots more but this bit has something to do with me, though you may not think so yet.

If I have any choices now, well I can throw my hand in or try to Do something, all I can think of is telling M'Clare how I cannot use a Reading Machine.

I am not so sure this is a choice, when he said Inhibitions can be absolute, Brother no fooling that is perfectly true.

Right now I can choose to sit here and do nothing or go and get some work done, there is a Balance of forces over that but then I go along to a Reading Room.

I have a long list of books I ought to have read, I just take the first, dial for it and fit it in the machine.

I think, Now I can choose to concentrate or I can let my mind go off on this mess I got into and What Dad is going to say, no one in their senses would choose that last one. I set my chronoscope for twenty past eleven and Put the blinkers on.

I switch the machine on, it lights and starts to go.

Then it goes crazy.

What should have warned me, there is no *click*. There is the usual warm up, slow then faster, but instead of a little jump and then ordinary speed it gets faster and faster and before I realize it I am Caught.

Unwillingly to Earth

It is like being stuck in concrete except this is inside me, in my head and growing, it spreads and pushes, it is too big for my skull it is going to *burst*.

and then I have let out a most almighty Yell and torn out of the thing, I find later I left a bit of hair in the blinkers but I am Out of it.

There is no one around, I run as though that machine had legs to come after me, I run right out in the campus and nearly crash with a tree, then I put my back to it and start Breathing again.

Whatever I have done till now, judging by the feel of my ribs Breathing was no part of it.

After a bit I sit down. I still have my back to the tree, I leave thinking till later and just Sit.

Then I jump up and yell again.

I have left that Crazy machine to itself, someone may sit in it this minute and get driven clean out of their head.

I run back not quite so fast as I came and burst in, someone just sitting down I yell out loud and Yank him out of it.

It is a Third Year I do not know, from another class, he is much astonished.

I explain.

I guess I make it dramatic, he looks quite scared, meanwhile a small crowd has gathered round the door.

Along comes Doc Beschrievene expert at this kind of Machine to see Why breach of rule of Silence in this block.

He trots straight in and starts inspecting the chair, then he says Exactly what happened, Miss Lee?

I say Mygod I have to see Mr. M'Clare!

I have been scratching my wrist for minutes, now I find the alarm of my chronoscope is trying to make itself felt, once again I am breaking records away from there.

I arrive one minute late but M'Clare has a visitor already so I can even get my breath, I also catch up on my

Apprehensions about this interview; seems to me the choice is Getting slung out as a slacker or Getting slung out as a moron and I truly do not know which one I care for less.

Then the visitor goes and I stumble in.

M'Clare has a kind of unusual look, his eyes have gone flat and a little way back behind the lids, I do not get it at first then I suddenly see he is very tired.

However his voice is just as usual, not angry but maybe a little tired too, he says "Well, Miss Lee, they say Actions speak louder than words and you certainly have given a demonstration. You've made it quite clear that you *could* do the work but you aren't going to, and while it would be interesting to see if you could gauge the requirements of the examiners so exactly this time I don't think it would justify the time taken to mark your papers. What do you want to do? Go back to Excenus straight away or take a vacation first?"

I simply do not have anything to say, I feel I have been wrapped and sealed and stuck in the delivery hatch, he goes on "It's a pity, I think. I thought when I first saw you that there was a brain under that golden mop and it was a pity to let it go to waste. If only there were something that mattered more to you than the idea of being made to do what you don't want to do—"

It is queer to watch someone getting a call on a built-in phone, some do a sort of twitch some shut their eyes, M'Clare just lets the Focus of his slide out through the wall and I might not be there any more, I wish I was not but I have to say something before I go away.

M'Clare has been using a throat mike but now he says out loud, "Yes, come over right away."

Now he is not tired any more.

He says "What happened to the Reading Machine, Miss Lee?"

Unwillingly to Earth 55

I say "It went crazy." Then I see this is kid's talk but I have no time to put learned words to it, I say "Look. You know how it starts? There is a sort of warm up and then a little click and it settles down to the right speed? Well it did not happen. What I think, the Governor must have been off or something, but that is not all—it got quicker and quicker but it did something else—look I have not the right expressions for it, but it felt like something opened my skull and pasting things on the Convolutions inside."

He has a look of wild something, maybe Surmise maybe just exasperation, then Doc Beschrievene comes in.

He says "Miss Lee, if it was a joke, may we call it off? Readers are in short supply."

I say if I wanted to make a joke I would make it a funny one.

M'Clare says "Ask Miss Lee to tell you what happens when you start the Reader."

Beschrievene says "I have started it! I connected it up and it worked quite normally."

Now the thing has gone into hiding, it will jump out on somebody else like it did on me. I have no time to say this: M'Clare says "Tell Dr. Beschrievene about the Reader."

I say "It started to go too fast and then—"

He says Start at the beginning and tell what I told before.

I say "When you sit in a Reader there is normally an initial period during which the movement of the words becomes more rapid, then there is a short transitional period of confusion and then the thing clicks audibly and the movement of the words proceeds at a set rate. This time—"

Here Doc gives a yell just like me and jumps to his feet.

M'Clare says What was I reading in the Machine?

I do not see what that has to do with it but I tell him,

then he wants to know what I remember of it and where it stopped.

I would not have thought I remembered but I do, I know just where it had got to, he takes me backwards bit by bit—

Then I begin to catch on.

M'Clare says "What is your usual reading rate, Liz?"

I swallow hard. I say "Too low to register on the dial, I don't know."

He says "Is your father handicapped too?"

I lift my head again, I am going to say That is not his business, then I say Yes instead.

He says "And he feels badly about it? Yes, he would. And you never told anybody. Of course not!" I do not know if it is scorn or anger or what. Beschrievene is talking to himself in a language I do not know.

M'Clare says Come along to the Reading room.

The chair has its back off, M'Clare plugs in a little meter lying on the floor and says "Sit down, Liz."

There is nothing I want less than to sit in that chair, but I do.

M'Clare says "Whether or not you have a repetition of your previous experience is entirely up to you. Switch on."

I am annoyed at his tone, I think I will give that switch a good bang. I feel I have done it, too.

But the light does not go on.

M'Clare says patiently "Turn on, please, Miss Lee."

I say "You do it."

Beschrievene says "Wait! There is no need to demonstrate, after all. We know what happened."

Then M'Clare's fingers brush over mine and turn the switch.

I jump all over, the thing warms up and then click! there is the little jump and the words moving steadily through.

And you know, I am disappointed.

Unwillingly to Earth

Beschrievene says He will be the son of a bigamist, I jump out of the chair and demand to know What goes?

M'Clare is looking at a dial in the meter, he turns and looks at me with exactly the same expression and says "Would you like to repeat the experience you described?"

Beschrievene says "No!"

I say "Yes. I would."

M'Clare bends and does something inside the Machine, then he says again "Sit down, Lizzie Lee."

There it is again, words slide across slow and then quicker and quicker and there is something pressing on my brain; then there is a Bang and it all goes off and Beschrievene is talking angry and foreign to M'Clare.

I climb out and say Will they kindly explain.

M'Clare tells me to come and look, it is the Reading-rate dial of the machine it now says Seven thousand five hundred and three.

Beschrievene says How much do I know about the machine? seems to me the safest answer is Nothing at all.

He says "There is an attachment which regulates the speed of movement of the words according to the reaction of the user. It sets itself automatically and registers on this dial here. But there is also another part of the machine far more important, although there is no dial for it unless you fit a test-meter as we have done; this is called the Concentration Unit or Crammer."

I did know that, it is what makes people able to read faster than with an old-style book.

He says, "This unit is compulsive. When the machines were first made it was thought they might be misused to insert hypnotic commands into the minds of readers. It would be very difficult, but perhaps not impossible. Therefore in the design was incorporated a safety device."

He pats one individual piece of spaghetti for me to admire.

He says "This device automatically shuts off the Crammer when it encounters certain cortical wave-patterns which correspond to strong resistance, such as is called forth by hypnotically imposed orders; not merely the resistance of a wandering mind."

I say But—

He looks as though I suddenly started sprouting and says "M'Clare this is most strange, this very young girl to be so strong, and from childhood too! Looks are nothing, of course—"

M'Clare says "Exactly so. Do you understand, Lizzie? One of your outstanding characteristics is a dislike of being what you call pushed around, in fact I believe if somebody tried to *force* you to carry out your dearest wish you would resist with all your might. You are set not so much on Free Will as on Free Won't. The Crammer appeared to your subconscious as something that interfered with your personal freedom, so you resisted it. That isn't uncommon, at first, but not many people resist hard enough to turn the thing off."

I say "But it worked!"

Beschrievene says that the safety device only turns off the Crammer, the rest of the machine goes on working but only at the rate for unassisted reading about one tenth normal rate.

M'Clare says "You, my girl, have been trying to keep up with a course designed for people who could absorb information seven or eight times as fast. No wonder your knowledge seemed a bit sketchy."

He sounds angry.

Well hells bells I am angry myself, if only I had told somebody it could all have been put right at the start, or if only the man who first tried to teach Dad the Reader had Known what was wrong with the way he used it, Dad would have had ordinary schooling and maybe not gone into prospecting but something else, and—

Unwillingly to Earth

Then whoever got born it would not have been me, so Where does that get you?

Beschrievene is saying "What I do not understand, why did she suddenly *stop* resisting the machine?"

M'Clare says "Well, Liz?"

It is a little time before I see the answer to that, then I say "We cannot resist everything, we can only choose the forces to which we will submit."

They look blank. M'Clare says Is it a Quotation?

I say "Your speech on Opening Day. I did not listen then. I heard it just now."

This I never thought to see, his classical puss goes red all over and he does not know what to say.

Beschrievene wants to know more of what was said so I recite. At the end he says "Words! Your students frighten me, M'Clare. So much power in words, at the right time, and you are training them to use such tools so young! To use them perhaps on a whole planet!"

M'Clare says "Would you rather leave it to chance? Or to people with good intentions and no training at all? Or to professional axe-grinders and amateurs on the make?"

I say How do I stop doing it?

Beschrievene rubs his chin and says I will have to start slowly, the machine produced so much effect because it was going fast, normally children learn to read at five when their reading rate is low even with the Crammer. He says he will take out the safety but put in something to limit speed and I can have a short session tomorrow.

I say Exams in four weeks three days why not today?

He laughs and says Of course I will be excused the exam—

M'Clare says Certainly I will take the exam, there is no reason why I should not pull up to pass standard; work is not heavy this term.

Beschrievene looks under his eyebrows but says Very well.

After lunch I sit down in the doctored machine.

Five minutes later I throw up.

Beschrievene fusses and gives me anti-nauseant and makes me lie down half an hour then I start again.

I last twenty minutes and come out head aching fit to grind a hole. I say For all sakes run it full speed, it is this push and drag together turns me up, this morning the Machine only scared me.

He does not want to do this, I have to go all out to persuade him; I am getting set to weep tears when he says Very well, he is no longer surprised my Will was strong enough to turn off the Machine.

This time it comes full on.

The words slide across my eyes slow, then quicker, then suddenly they are running like water pouring through my eyes to my brain, something has hold of me keeping my mind open so they can get in, if I struggle if I stop one microsecond from absolute concentration they will jam and something will *break*.

I could not pull any of my mind away to think with but there is a little corner of it free, watching my body, it makes my breath go on digs my nails into my hands stops the muscles of my legs when they try to jerk me out of the chair, sets others to push me back again.

I can hear my breath panting and the bang of my heart, then I do not hear it any longer, I am not separate any longer from the knowledge coming into my mind from the machine

and then it stops.

It is like Waking with a light on the face, I gasp and leap in the seat and the blinkers pull my hair, I yell What did you do that for?

M'Clare is standing in front of me, he says Eighty-seven minutes is quite sufficient come out of that at once.

Unwillingly to Earth

I try to stand and my knees won't unhinge, to hear M'Clare you would think it was his legs I got cramp in, I suppose I went to sleep in the middle of his Remarks anyway I wake tomorrow in bed.

In the morning I tell it all to B, because she is a friend of mine and it is instructive anyway.

B says Lizzie it must have been awful but it is rather wonderful too, I do not see this I say Well it is nice it is over.

Which it is *not*.

Four weeks look a long time from the front end but not when it is over and I have to take the Exam.

I have made up my mind on one thing, if I do not pass I am not asking anyone to make allowances I am just going straight off home, I am too tired to think much about it but that is what I will do.

Exam, I look at all the busy interested faces and the stylers clicking along and at the end I am certain for sure I have Failed by quite a way.

I do not join the post-mortem groups, I get to my room and lock the door and think for a bit.

I think That finishes it, no more strain and grind and Terrie voices and Please Tune In Daily For Routine Announcements and smells you get in some of this Overoccupied air, no more high-minded kids who don't know dead sure from however, no more essays and No More M'Clare, I wish they would hurry up and get the marks over so I can get organized to count my blessings properly.

However sixty four-hour papers take time to read even with a Crammer and M'Clare does them all himself, we shall get the marks day after tomorrow if then.

There is a buzz from the speaker in the Study and B is not there, I have to go.

Of all the people who should be too busy to call just

now it is Mr. M'Clare He says I have not notified him of my Vacation plans yet.

I say Huh?

He says as my Guardian he ought to know where I am to be found and he wants to be sure I have got return schedules fixed from wherever I am going so as to make certain I get back in time for next term.

I say Hell what makes you think I am coming back next term anyway?

He says Certainly I am coming back next term, if I am referring to the Exam he has just had a look at my paper it is adequate though not Outstanding no doubt I will do better with time. Will I let his secretary have details of my plans, and he turns it off on me.

I sit down on the floor, no chair to hand.

Well for one thing the bit about the Vacations was not even meant to deceive, he did it just to let me know I got Through.

So I have not finished here after all.

The more I think about studying Cultural Engineering the more doubtful I get, it *is* pushing people around however you like to put it more fancy than that.

The more I think about Terries the more I wonder they survived so long, some are all right such as B but even she would not be so safe in most places I know.

The more I think—

Well Who am I fooling after all?

The plain fact is I am not leaving Russett and all the rest of it and I am so pleased about it, just now I do not care if the whole damn College calls me Lysistrata.

Part Two:
RATS IN THE MOON

S O THIS IS A RAT.
It reminds me of a man back home on Excenus 23 tried to sell my Father a mine once.

The mine turned out a good one I believe, which maybe shows you should not Judge by Appearances, but anyway Dad had all the money he knew what to do with already.

It is just about par for today that earlier this afternoon I spent nearly an hour watching for Rats, and now this one comes sliding out of a tunnel when I have to catch up with Clarence and do not have time to look.

Oh, well, I can spare ten seconds I suppose . . . It sits up and is looking down its teeth as much as to say It spent half an afternoon waiting to see a Person and all it gets is Lizzie Lee. (Actually it is on the wrong side of a sheet of one-way glass which to Rats seems the end of the World I suppose). I decide it is short on personal charm especially the tail, but considered as Ultimate Horror gnawing the Heart of the Universe my reaction is No.

The Rat turns suddenly and flicks back into its tunnel and I go on my way trying to practice the rules for Lunar Locomotion at Maximum Speed with Minimum Effort . . . (Certainly I am on the Moon, these days they do not allow Rats anywhere else.)

How I got there is kind of complicated and goes like this:

I have finished one semester as a student of Cultural Engineering at Russett College, Earth, and to my surprise I had to go on a Vacation.

Naturally I am aware that for students Vacations form part of the Total Experience. I just never expected to last so long, because of my Educational Handicap. Terries say they did not spend 500 years getting their Pop. down to reasonable figures just so as to be swamped by 1,000,000,000 tourists, every footloose person in the Inhabited Volume wants to visit the Mother of Mankind, so they do not let anyone land unless they have Legitimate Business on the planet. Studying is Legitimate provided you work at it which you have to prove by passing Exams; there was one at the end of the first semester and I expected to be thrown out as soon as I failed.

However four and a half weeks before that M'Clare found out about my Educational Handicap and got it put right, and by studying every minute I actually passed the Exam with a few marks to spare.

Next morning his Secretary calls by Communicator to ask about my Vacation Plans; M'Clare as my temporary Guardian needs to know where to find me, perhaps she might suggest—There is a heap of documents on my desk relating to Holiday Trips for Outsiders, I pick up the first one and inform her I shall be going on a Tour of the Monumental Achievements of Pre-Industrial Man.

She says Really? and I state that I owe it to my Education to go, the oldest work of Man on my home planet being aged fifty-seven and that is a hole in the ground.

She replies that I will find the Tour very Impressive. M'Clare has gone to a Conference but left a message for me. I am to enjoy myself stay out of trouble and not forget my Holiday Task.

Hell.

That must mean the Vacation Project Priority Catford handed out four weeks ago. I would just as soon have gone on forgetting it.

Next semester we are due for a series of Seminars on Fictional Concepts in Relation to Contemporary Society and in preparation for this each member of the class has a Topic to read up and write an Essay on. The first ten or even fifteen are on subjects I have at least heard of but mine was number 47 and entitled *The Concept of Absolute Evil in Fiction of the Age of Impotence*.

Well it could have been worse I suppose, my friend and roommate B Laydon has drawn *The Theory of Emotional Equivalence as Exemplified in "Cubic of Solomon."* Okay for her she claims to *enjoy* Three-dimensional poetry but that gadget you have to read it with gives me a headache in 10 seconds flat.

I did not complain because I assumed I would be gone before it was time to hand in the Essay, so now I am stuck with it. Also with this Tour, it is a circular one and the Office tells me I can join it in Peru if I catch the Transequatorial Ferry in two hours' time.

So I set the Robolaundry to Pack and stuff clothes in with one hand while I hunt for the Reading List for the Project with the other. I finally get it set in the Library slot in time for book spools to start spilling out just as the Laundry starts to deliver also, and what with 2 dozen friends dropping in to say See you next semester I am still shoveling spools and encapsulated Garments into a traveling bag when my cab arrives. I have just got it programmed when I hear the noise the Library gadget makes when it has finished a List, followed by the sound of a spool dropping into the tray.

Oh what the hell I already have books by Andersen Buchan Chesterton Donaldson Ellison Fortune Garner Howard Innes Jacobi Koontz Lewis Merritt Norton Orwell Price Rice Sapper Tolkien Vance Wheatley Yates Zelazny and a few others not to mention several volumes of *Appalling Science Fiction* and *Magazine of Fear and Wonder*, one more cannot really matter. I lock the window and Go.

I am much impressed by Cuzco and Machu Picchu which were built by hand of stones cut square with stone tools, also by Newgrange Stonehenge Lascaux Pompeii Rome Knossos Delphi, I am not sure at what point Impression first becomes tinged with Depression but as we go on to Petra, Baalbek, Nineveh, Gizeh it deepens and halfway round a temple called Karnak I realize I am finished, done; if I have to look at one more Sight Site Saite or whatever I shall justabout pop a convolution.

What I need now is a Rest somewhere with no History at all.

Then I see the Moon rising over this very Historical river the Nile and realize that is just what I require. Oh sure Man first stepped there 800 years ago but all the Buildings are still in use, no Ruins, no monuments except a plaque saying *Neil Armstrong Stepped Here*; also I have a friend there, Clarence Dalrymple, waiting for a new Heart and meanwhile has a job looking after Rats.

Why this is relevant; having read the marked sections in ⅔ of those books I still do not feel I have the hang of this Evil business. The books are full of words like Unnatural, Abominable, Monstrous for which the Authors seem to use a Dictionary I don't know, but whenever they

Unwillingly to Earth

want a real concrete symbol of Evil, half the time what they use is a Rat.

It seems Rats are very Evil being Fundamentally Inimical to Man.

So okay, maybe it won't help to look at one but it can't hurt. I arrange to travel by the Lift the following day.

Landing on the Moon from Earth has not much formality, you stick your passport in a slot and walk up a dim tunnel using Lunar Locomotion as taught on the Lift (the last 6 hours of the journey are done under deceleration at ⅙ G so everybody has been able to practice) while various machines check you are not carrying concealed weapons or diseases and your face does not match any of the Million Most Unwanted, then you get your Passport back at the top and can catch a Slider to your Hotel.

Would you believe it the first thing I see as we emerge from the Space Gate is a parade of giant red letters saying HISTORY IS BEING MADE HERE!

Then they reform to read FIVE PLANETS CONFERENCE and I relax. There was some talk about this on the Lift; it is just Cincinnatus Lamartine Discus Karel and Ved being Got Round A Table at last; no doubt the sorting out of quarrels been running ever since the planets were settled is History but not the sort to cause Monuments.

Plaques, maybe.

I had to cross 11 Time Zones to get the Lift and had no sleep on board, so having checked in at my Hotel the Royal Cynthia I go straight to my room stick my clothes in the Robolaundry and throw myself at the bed, such is the effect of Moon G that I am asleep before I hit.

When I wake up I have missed half the morning so after dialing breakfast and flicking the first outfit to hand out of its capsule I start out to get in touch with Clarence. The whole Pop. of the Moon would not fill one small city back on Earth so there is only one Directory and when I key in

Clarence's name I get a number right away; but when I transfer that to the Communicator I see not Clarence but a woman with remarks embroidered on her tunic reading SUPERVISOR AMBULANT EFS.

She is Not very pleased to see me and wants to know Why I am attempting to communicate with Clarence, I explain and she softens somewhat and says Oh yes Dalrymple has mentioned me.

However he will be in Supportive Therapy all morning. I exclaim Good Lord has he got Worse then? but she says No, his condition is stable but it will be seven months before the new Heart being grown from his tissues is mature enough to graft, meanwhile the old one needs all the help it can get. Seeing me should not do Dalrymple any harm however if I obey the Rules, she will have him call me this afternoon.

I say I would just as soon come and see him in person then; she looks surprised and says Am I in Labsville already? I knew this was a town 200 km from Lunarburg but had not realized what this means in Moon terms, viz. going there is a Major Undertaking. There is a tunnel running between the two but the traffic is One Way, meaning One Way at a time. A single train goes from Lunarburg to Labsville taking 2 hours for it and then after a 20 minutes turnaround it runs Back again. If I want to visit with Clarence for more than 20 minutes I must be prepared to spend 8 hours on it.

Well okay that is still what I came for; it is already too late to start out today so I say Tell Clarence I will come out tomorrow by the train leaves here at 09:00 gets in 11:00 unless I hear to the contrary; and she promises to do so.

So now I am free to work on my Project, dammit.

According to the Brochure this Hotel has a Commodious Reading Room so I set out in search of it. Evidently this is the oldest part of Lunarburg, tunneled before they

Unwillingly to Earth

learned how to make a Disruptor cut square; all the passages are tubular and the Reading Room has been cut by driving three tunnels parallel and overlapping and then scraping the Ridges off the floor. The ones on the ceiling are still there and the bulges at the side have been screened off except for three alcoves with Reading machines in them, two occupied one not.

However I do not observe this straightaway because the rest of the room is occupied by about a dozen people engaged in Competitive Conversation, and not a single one looks any younger than 70 years old; if the Lunar Handbook is right and living on the Moon takes 10 years off Apparent Age they must all be well over 80 and they are all looking at me as much as to say *What* is this twentygenarian doing in Our hotel?

Before I can sink any distance into the floor I am rescued by a small fluffy lady in pink who flutters over with Remarks wafting ahead of her: "Oh, my dear, I really must apologize, you must be Miss Lee of course, I really meant to be there when you arrived but the General, so difficult to make up a four since poor Mrs Ogbanishah left us. I did peep into Reception but they told me you had already gone to bed. If there is anything I can do to help you at any time do please let me know."

I say Nothing, thanks, I would just like to use that Reading Machine.

She says Oh but the Colonel will be here any minute now.

I say I am not looking for a Colonel, I just want to read.

She says Oh but *really* the Colonel will be here any minute.

Bysitters now take a hand and I finally grasp that The Colonel always reads the *Lunar Times* from 11:30 to 12:15 on this Machine.

Well When will one of the Machines be free? after a lot of discussion it is borne in on me that these Machines are booked to the Permanent Residents one after another right through the day, the reason one is Vacant right now is that the lady using it met an old friend in the obituary column and has gone to write a letter to the Relict.

I thank them for the information and Go.

I will just have to hire a portable Machine somewhere.

The Pink lady who is apparently the Manageress has fluttered out after me so I ask her Where and she lends me an Autoguide set for the nearest shop. I find the place all right but return in a state of Shock; they told me Living on the Moon was Expensive but this is ridiculous.

She is still in Reception and asks how I got on. I am still searching for words that will not be Unsuitable when she says Many Transients are surprised to see the effect of Freight charges on the prices here.

The hell with that. Freight costs a lot more to Excenus 23, but I am feeling Insulted; the man in the shop refused to hire me a Reading Machine although the sign in the window distinctly promised he would. I offered to Deposit the full price but he seemed determined all Transients were in a Conspiracy to cheat him, in the end I had to buy the damn thing.

It is secondhand and cost 3 times as much as the better one I left at the Lift Terminal on Earth. The Manageress puts on enough distress for politeness and says A nice girl like me would never believe the dirty tricks some Transients get up to, it is so easy to hand in a damaged gadget when the Hirer is too busy to check it, claim the Deposit and go on board before the owner finds out what is wrong. Once on board the Captain usually will not permit Passengers to be taken off, it upsets the Manifest, so it is very difficult to make them pay.

I say But according to the *Lunar Handbook* there is a new Law or Court or something that allows a man to be arrested by Bailiffs on a civil complaint, up to 10 minutes before Liftoff. She looks totally puzzled for a moment and

Unwillingly to Earth

then says "Oh! You mean the Piepowder Court! But, Miss Lee, that is only for Transients; it's no use to *us*."

She insists that the Court with the funny name does not act on complaints from anybody with a Residence permit for more than 2 weeks; this seems more than odd as How many people find things to Sue about when they are only here for a day or two? surely not enough to make a special Court worth while.

However I finally understand that the Complaints usually relate to events on the long voyages before arriving at the Moon, lots of business is done on the big Interstellar liners and some of it goes sour, also there are Conmen among the travelers. If a sucker is cautious enough to register his purchase of Waterfront lots on Martian canals, or whatever, soon after touchdown he may discover that he has been Had before the Haver's ship leaves the Moon, in which case the Respondent can be taken off by Bailiffs even if the ship is just about to go. It still sounds odd but the Manageress gives me to understand it is mostly a Gimmick to make Transients feel the Moon really takes care of them, there is a drive on to encourage Tourists.

I retire to my room and get to work. In the afternoon Clarence calls and will be Pleased to see me tomorrow, he looks much fitter than when I saw him last, this thing about Low G taking the strain off a Bad Heart really does work. I finish the last of the books and go to bed early.

I spend the train journey next day planning my Essay.

When I started this Project my first impression was that the only connection between Absolute Evil and Social Conditions was that the Authors of these books had a living to make; I mean when they thought of a Plot which called for some Picturesquely wicked proceeding and there was no reason in the Universe why any sane person would Proceed in that particular way, then the Motive can be *Absolute Evil*.

Like when a Good Guy has been a nuisance to a Bad Guy and the Bad Guy gets hold of him, you would expect the Bad Guy just to Shoot the other one and that would be That. But an *Absolutely Evil* Guy will dream up a nasty form of Execution and even then he does not get on with it but keeps the Good Guy waiting in order to Gloat.

So of course that gives the Good Guy time to be Rescued or to get away. Gloating is very Evil; it is Inefficient, too.

One trouble is I do not know much about conditions in the Age of Impotence, in fact I never heard of it till this Essay. B Laydon lent me a Work called Pocket History of World Literature from the Earliest Times, it has so many spools I guess it nearly would fill a Pocket at that; this says the Age of Impotence is a name for the middle years of the Twentieth Century, so called because the great Message of so many writers was simply that they Could Not Cope (it was also a time when the sexual sort of Impotence was fashionably blamed for everything from Murder to Materialism but apparently that is *not* the Point).

This book says Guilt was a very popular emotion in Literature of the period and the books I have read confirm it, seems you were supposed to feel guilty about Injustice and Deprivation suffered by anybody anywhere whether you had anything to do with it or not. Never mind whether this attitude was Socially Useful; the Authors seem to have felt people including Bad Guys had a Human Right for Good Guys to feel guilty over clobbering them no matter what Wrongs they had done. However those who went in for *Absolute Evil* could be counted as *in*Human. Sometimes this is just an excuse for them to be extinguished in a complicated and Sadistic manner but sometimes it is More than that; Evil could be dealt with decisively and heroically without any need to feel Guilty afterwards and I can see where Authors and Readers both might find that a Relief.

Unwillingly to Earth

I begin to feel I have Got something and get busy finding suitable Quotations. Then the Reading Machine tugs gently at the straps behind my head after which it slides back and raps me between the eyes; the Train which has been standing for some time in the airlock just before Labsville has now made the final push into the Station and people start to get out all round.

I shove the machine hurriedly into its case and grab my pouch of book reels and step out onto the sidewalk just in time to see Clarence's back walking slowly towards the other end of the train.

I remember not to yell in case it startles his Heart; then I take off after him fall over my feet stop to remember where I am and finally manage to get in front of Clarence just as he reaches the last door of the train.

What the Devil is wrong?

For a moment he does not seem to recognize me; then he says heavily "Oh. There you are, Liz."

He reaches out, takes my Reading Machine and pouch and slings them over his shoulder, then turns and leads the way into a sort of Foyer.

Clarence does not look like a man with a bad Heart, he is big and broad with Muscles to match. He is wearing ordinary clothes, not Hospital ones, except that he has an armband with big black letters E_F and little letters beside them which I cannot read because of the creases. The puffiness has gone from his face but it is set like Cement in a No Expression and if yesterday he was really glad to know I was on the Moon, this morning he is Not.

It is right on the tip of my tongue to ask What Gives, but I am doing my best to Keep it there and not let it off; once on the ship from Excenus M'Clare told me "Never bother a sick man with silly questions and remember any question is silly unless you know what to do with the answer." If I ask Clarence whether this visit is Mistimed he will either not hear me or say "What an Idea!" and start Exerting himself. If he wants me to know what is on his Mind he will tell me. So the only question is Should I stay here or get Tactfully back on the train and go away?

Only it would not be Tactful if he suddenly remembers and finds me missing, that could start a Moonwide womanhunt; besides he is carrying my Reading Machine . . . At this point I learn what is written on his Armband, there is a poster on the wall with the same black letters but now I can read the little ones which say "xertion orbidden". Under them it says in red

> MEANS
> EXERTION FORBIDDEN

Then in black:

> Do not on any account ask wearers of this armband for physical assistance. They must not under any circumstances be hurried or harassed. If any wearer of this armband seems to be ill or in difficulties go to the nearest Incom box and ring 1111.
> *(Illegible Squiggle)*
> DIRECTOR
> HUMAN HEART FOUNDATION

Presently the Elevator arrives. According to the Indicator there are VII Levels and the Station is on Level IV: we go right up to I and I follow Clarence off. He leads me a little way down the corridor—Labsville architecture is cut Boxy rather than Drainpipe—and into a little space with doors on three sides, and Switches himself on.

I mean suddenly he seems his normal self. He looks me in the eye and begins to speak.

This is a mild shock because always before he spoke

Standard which is a sort of colorless flavorless Essence of Communication with no Racial Social or Planetary overtones, most people use it on Excenus 23 because we have people from 50+ planets each with its own unintelligible Localese; what Clarence speaks now is Something Else.

"Liz m'dear, according to the Supervisor you want the Grand Tour and let's face it, I'd be a washout. I don't get the sense of a quarter of what goes on round here. But so happens a bunch from this Five Planets jamboree are swanning over here today and three of the junior Eggheads have been laid on to show 'em around. I had a word with the Great Panjandrum and he'll be happy for you to tag along. Then I'll meet you for lunch and we can go on to have a squint at the Rats; they aren't on the Five Planets itinerary; not enough class. Okay?"

Okay! the only problem being Not to show how relieved I am.

The Five Planets party are on the far side of one of the doors, in a large space which comes the nearest to plushy of anywhere I have yet been on the Moon; it has a carpet instead of plastic coating and there are Murals on the wall, depicting mythical Moon fauna I think. Several people in lab coveralls are handing round coffee and cookies but I am not thirsty and don't know anyone so I pass the time studying the pictures. Presently I decide to look at those on the other side.

Halfway across I run into some Legs.

There is a Body on top, also long and knobby and so are the arms, but it is the Legs make themelves conspicuous; I try to sidestep and we have a bit of this-way-that-way, every time I try to Dodge in a particular direction so does he. I do not know whether this is accidental or a Joke but presently I give up and go back the way I came.

There is a sound behind me which might be a Voice but at that moment the Eggheads we are all waiting for come in and ask us to divide into 3 groups and each go out by a different door.

I do not want to put myself forward so I wait to tag along behind whichever group turns out to be the smallest. Something makes me turn round and I see Lanky with the Legs talking to one of the men who handed coffee and they are both Looking at me. This reminds me uncomfortably that whenever I went to see a Sight on Earth I had some sort of Permit and here I have none. I wait to see which party Lanky will join but he just goes on glaring at me as though wondering by What Right—? in the end I glare back and he turns suddenly and dives after the tail end of one group, and I tag after another.

The Tour is fine if you like Laboratories; I should say most of this group can take them or leave them alone. There are polite Ohs and Ahs when some Technological Marvel does its stuff, otherwise they are mostly enjoying a good gossip. I wonder why they are here instead of Conferring in Lunarburg but presently conclude that the Top People are having a quiet day together for Horsetrading Hornswoggling and other Political Pursuits and have pushed the Second Strings and Encumbrances off here out of the way.

There is one man in the group however seems to feel he is here to Work, a short solid man with a corrugated face looks like it has been pleated while soft and the folds have then set hard. He is one of several who have Labeled themselves and the label reads SENATOR G. GASSETT-LOW, CINCINNATUS.

The way he Works is to ask the cost of everything in an accusing voice. I think half the time the Egghead does not know but manages to keep a straight face while Making it up; finally the Senator forgets where he is and asks how much the Cincinnatan Taxpayer—here the Egghead nips in smartly with Nothing At All; Experiments on this level are funded entirely from Earth.

Unwillingly to Earth

The Senator makes a recovery and asks How about other Levels, then: the Egghead replies that Labsville has a few projects of special interest to certain planets and funded partly by them, but so far as he knows Cincinnatus only contributes to the Antibody Reserve Production Fund like the rest of the Outer Worlds, the Production unit is on Level VII.

A voice in my ear murmurs, "Poor old George! If only he knew!"

I am being spoken to by a Strange Man.

Not all that strange, he is one of the Five Planets party and I heard him being addressed as Tolly in tones indicating that if he is on the Second String he must be near the Top of it.

My Mother did not tell me Never to Speak to Strange Men because she left when I was 3; every other adult woman on Excenus 23 must have told me that one time or another but Dad's injunctions were more about Judgment and Common Sense. Common Sense tells me I cannot get into difficulties in the middle of a crowd and Judgment tells me this man is far too comfortably set in his own niche in the Universe to be dangerous to girls young enough to be his daughter . . .

Grand-daughter maybe, he has that Well Preserved look. He is not handsome but full of Presence and Charm. I have had enough of being instructed and feel ready to be Charmed for a change so I murmur back "If he only knew what?"

He flashes a smile at me, a good one even if he has Practiced it.

"The Senator equates Public Expenditure with Public Waste; that's the one Political principle he really is quite sure about, and how he loves to apply it!! So it's bad luck that the only project here on which his planet has spent money should be an absolutely impregnable Sacred Cow—don't you think?''

He twinkles his eyes and waits for me to spot that there is More to Come; it is like being back at Russett in a Seminar but I may as well play up.

I say "Sacred Cow? You mean the Antibody Reserve?" I fake a bit of shock to keep him happy but come to think of it maybe I could supply the Real Thing.

I mean the Reserve Antibody Production Fund is one of the very few examples of all planets working together for the Common Good: it saved thousands of lives during epidemics on Miranda and Lemonchik and Yudhisthira, millions if you count people on other planets who might have got the diseases if they had not been Stopped. It was in my very first History book.

Tolly smiles again to show he Understands.

"Don't take me wrong, m'luv, it was a great idea when it started. Trouble is, it's out of date. The point is to have stocks of vaccine ready to be rushed where they are needed, right? But what actually happens if an epidemic breaks out on one of the Outer Worlds, these days?"

I think back to the last time somebody landed on Excenus 23 with a cold in the head, back when I was 8, and say "The planetary Hospital makes cultures and grows a vaccine of its own."

"Right! With modern automated plants they can get vaccines tailored to the precise strain involved, in ten days or so, whereas to get it from the nearest Regional Depot might take several weeks . . . A good many of the scientists here feel that the Sacred Cow has grown into a White Elephant. They'd like to be able to use the space and manpower for something else."

I say "Why don't they? Labsville is run by the Scientists, isn't it?"

Tolly shakes his head.

"No, m'dear. When you get down to bedrock, no. The

scientists get the use of the facilities, but they don't own the place. It was set up originally by three or four big charitable foundations and they still have control. Why d'you think heart cases are employed to carry out simple routine jobs when it would be so much simpler to use automation? Because about two thirds of Labsville belongs to the Human Heart Foundation. It wasn't excavated originally for scientific purposes but to house and treat anybody with an incurably bad heart who could get himself here, and supply him with a new one, free. A handful of really rich men who didn't want to burden their families with too many billions set it up. Then the medical staffs found that keeping men around for a year or two with nothing useful to do created problems in itself. So they offered space and facilities and grants to any scientist who'd design his work so as to provide jobs for EFs. Tricky—a lot of brilliant men have walked out in disgust over the difficulties. Lot of others have made their reputations here, though. More EFs the scientist employs, more space and money he gets from the Foundation.

"However, they don't own Reserve Antibody, of course. The snag there is the Lunar Gov. They don't want it cut down."

I say "Why not?" and Tolly smiles again.

"Tourism, m'dear. It's the biggest sightseeing attraction on Luna. Practically an Ancient Monument."

The whole party has been walking for some time down several of the long steep slopes they have here instead of stairs, and right now we are entering the Department of Reserve Antibody Production, so when I wince I guess Tolly takes it for a start of Amazement or maybe Awe.

It is a huge long wide space that looks very low because of its Proportions, actually the ceiling is five meters up which is high for Labsville but the effect is that we have all crawled into a vast horizontal Slot.

The Culture Units are enormous glass sausages, they

rest on cradles which can be Swung Tilted or even Shaken and inside are more glass Compartments Channels Racks Plates and so on than I can distinguish. The cradles pivot on thick glass columns with liquids flowing inside, these reach the Ceiling and appear to hold it up but being transparent they give me a feeling of Insecurity.

Tolly has gone off to charm somebody else. The Egghead is busy explaining why it is Not dangerous to breed pathogens *en masse* in a totally enclosed Armorplated environment. This is not what worries me, I am prepared to believe the Authorities know what they are doing; what I do *not* enjoy is the Impression that the ceiling is slowly coming down as in one or two of the books I recently read, so I make unobtrusively for a way out.

There are several very wide gaps in the side wall making this place more cr less continuous with the corridor beyond; I am in mid-stride and nearing Escape when there is a shout behind me of "Junior!" Would you believe it Lanky appears suddenly before me on a Collision course.

We each put down a toe and manage to Steer sideways and this time he goes the opposite way and Rebounds off the side of the gap. I stop politely to see if he has broken anything but when he untangles his legs they seem to be Working so I go on my way.

It is time to join Clarence for lunch.

The Cafeteria is another great big slot. I think perhaps I prefer my Architecture tubular but at least this has pillars of solid rock. Clarence still has Things on his Mind but is putting a lot of effort into being an Entertaining Host so I fix my thoughts on being Entertained and by common consent we get through the meal quickly and prepare to go.

On the way out Clarence is nailed by a Senior-looking Egghead and I withdraw out of Earshot, at least I thought

I had until I heard the Egghead exclaim "Why in Luna should she object, under the circumstances?"

Turns out two of the Five Planets party want to see Rats and the Egghead wishes to attach them to Clarence and me.

No of course I can't object. We arrange to meet them in the Rodent Habitats section in ten minutes' time; now I shall never learn what is eating Clarence I suppose.

The Rats inhabit long oblong blocks separated by corridors. Clarence switches on a red light inside one of them and shows up an absolute hurrah's nest of tunnels going Up down and along at every angle but all sooner or later turning inwards and out of sight. He explains that all the Scientific observations are made by Sensors inside the block connected to Computers and Screens, the glass panels are just for sightseers like me.

Also like the two members of the Five Planets party now approaching under the escort of the Senior Egghead. Oh Hell and Handbaskets they are the Senator from Cincinnatus and Lanky Junior.

The Egghead introduce Senator Gossy Lowell and his Nephew and departs.

The Senator is Not pleased at being misnamed and puts that right in a gravelly growl, adding that since his Nephew insists on seeing Rats we might as well get on with it.

Okay by me but unfortunately the Rats do not cooperate.

The first block is full of wild-type *Rattus norvegicus* according to Clarence, who has started to recite their History when the Senator who has been inspecting a notice affixed to the Environment interrupts.

"That's all written out here. We can read it for ourselves."

I state loud and clear that I am using *my* eyes to look for Rats and would like Mr. Dalrymple to Continue, please.

The Senator gobbles, Junior utters a faint snort, Clarence goes on talking and I continue to watch for Rats which would be Sucks to the Senator except that there aren't any.

Rats, I mean. After 20 minutes we decide there must be something Special going on in the middle of this block and move on to the next.

The next block is inhabited by a Mutant strain with white hair and pink eyes which must look especially Evil I think, but unfortunately after another 20 minutes I am still unable to Confirm this.

It is all just a Statistical Accident otherwise known as Bad Luck but the Senator decides it is a Conspiracy. Junior starts to say something but is snapped to silence by his Uncle who demands that Clarence take them to rejoin the rest of their party. Clarence starts to insist on my Right to see a Rat if it takes all Night and he is Not going to leave me here alone; so I look at my watch and announce it is time to go for my Train. I bid the Senator and Junior a Distant farewell and Clarence a warm one and set off.

Actually I have 50 minutes before the Train which is just as well. In the rest room at the Station I discover I have not got my Reading Machine or the pouch of book reels. Clarence, having taken them over by Politeness reflex, is still carrying them.

No help for it I have to get them back even if I miss the Train. I start retracing my steps. These were quite numerous and I forget some, it takes me twenty minutes to find Rodent Environments: where I suddenly realize Clarence is now Somewhere Else.

This is the moment a Rat chooses to come out of a tunnel and Look at me; I begin to suspect they really are inimical to Man or at any rate to Me.

There is an Incom system, a series of communicator

boxes every 100 meters or so, maybe I can call somebody and ask where Clarence is.

I have gone about 3 Lunar paces when the most god-awful Wailing noise breaks out all round and I Jump so hard I literally hit the Roof.

When I descend the sound is starting to drop also, right down the scale like a Cosmic mucksucker lamenting the Dead; then it is replaced by a Voice.

"ATTENTION PLEASE.

"Those of you who work here will have recognized the Emergency Siren. We apologize to any of our visitors who were startled."

This Means Me.

"Because of a slight mishap, access to this Level is temporarily closed. If you will all go as quickly as possible to Room Seven See Twenty-three, following the illuminated arrows, a member of the staff will meet you there and explain. There is no cause for alarm, just a temporary local hitch in the arrangements for your tour. Please follow the illuminated arrows to room Seven See Twenty-three."

I would be glad to but there is a Temporary Local Hitch, viz. No arrows in sight. However the lights now start to dim and arrows gradually become visible on the floor. I start to follow them as fast as I can. This is not very because I have somehow forgotten all I learned about Locomotion in Low G; so I stop and take a deep breath and start Exercising as directed on board the Lift and presently I am proceeding in high gear touching the floor about once every three meters or so.

I have done this about 200 times and made several Turns when my foot touches something in mid-glide and I trip slowly over and land on top of it.

Who the hell left that here and what is it anyway—? I sort myself out and it makes a faint Moaning sound like a distant echo of that siren thing. Oh Stars it is someone lying here Hurt and Unconscious, now what do I do?

Illumination has got even dimmer, those damn arrows are glowing like crazy but I can barely see that what I fell over is long and skinny and wearing tight dark clothes; then I see there is something light on the shoulder blades and by peering close I make out the letters CINCINNATUS.

In short this is Ghastly Junior.

The hair at the back of his head has a dark patch on it that comes off on my finger.

Blood, I suppose. However the pulse in his neck is beating all right.

Head Injuries you should not move around but leave them to Professionals: I stand up and holler "Help!" half a dozen times.

No reply.

If only I knew what type of Emergency this is, for all I know Junior is as safe here as anywhere; but also for all I know some sort of Venomous animals kept for Antitoxins may be loose; or a horde of Mutant Rats; even the Plain sort have been known to Eat people who could not get away. But—

"ATTENTION PLEASE. ANYBODY ON LEVEL SEVEN WHO HAS NOT YET REPORTED TO ROOM SEVEN SEE TWENTY-THREE PLEASE DO SO IMMEDIATELY. FOLLOW THE ILLUMINATED ARROWS TO ROOM SEVEN SEE TWENTY-THREE. THIS HAS PRIORITY. DROP EVERYTHING AND COME RUNNING TO ROOM SEVEN SEE TWENTY-THREE AS FAST AS YOU CAN."

That settles it.

Junior's head has a lump on it but it does not feel cracked. I still do not know whether it is safe to Shift him but that also applies to leaving him where he is, so here we go.

I roll him over carefully, sit down alongside with my back to his head and haul him into Sitting with one arm and his head hanging over my shoulder, then I grip the arm and stand up.

Even in 1/6 G this is not so easy as it sounds, he is so damn long and I don't want to jiggle him, all the same I am not able to tote him more than a few steps without a Readjustment which provokes another painful-sounding groan. I say Is he all right? and Can he answer me? the answer in both cases seems to be No.

Well since I have Moved him now I had better get help quick; I turn and shuffle off following the Arrows as fast as I can.

I suppose Junior only weighs about 12 kg but I am not used to having even 12 kg of Person draped over my shoulder and dragging on the floor behind; presently I become aware of a Soughing of air, loud and rapid, which after a bit I realize is not the Ventilation system on the blink but just Me.

Later I find the distance gone is only about 150 meters but it feels More.

About 1/2 way there I become aware of Movement ahead: a dark figure crosses my field of vision and moves into a panel of brightness that opens up suddenly about 50 meters away. I try to shout but have not sufficient Breath: all the same, Excelsior! that must be Room VII C 23—

It is.

According to the label it is also *Mass Immunization Bay* but Who cares? I have hell's delight trying to get the door open without using Junior as a battering ram and in the end just kick it until somebody jerks it aside. They give an exclamation and I stagger in.

Inside is a positive Glare of light and I screw my eyes up: I get a confused picture of Things: and people, mostly standing in line alongside a glass-and-metal-covered trolley but there are a few in White coats scattered around. I select a large one and lower self and Junior to the floor at his feet.

Tell the truth I can't stand up any longer.

Somebody gives a loud exclamation and lifts Junior off me.

Somebody else takes my hand and hauls me to my feet.

Somebody yet else—a woman by the sound—screams at the top of her voice, "Blood! She's all over blood!"

I look down at myself.

It is true. The left side of my tunic has a great red patch and trickles have run down to the hem.

Have I killed him?

Then everything whirls into a sort of bright hazy cocoon and goes away.

Migod what a collection of aches. I am stiff all over and who raked an incinerator into my Mouth—?

Something touches my head lightly.

"Miss Lee. Wake up, Miss Lee."

Glad to oblige, so would anybody be who just had my dream.

There is a lot too much Light on my eyelids but through a slit between them I make out a smallish solemn-looking man with black hair brown complexion and a label on his white coverall reading DR. PATEL.

I try to sit up and discover the Stiffness is not all my own. I have been Zippered into one of those sleeping bags used in Free Fall and it is tied down to a cot or something; this particular bag also had wrist straps and some idiot has fastened them.

Soon as I realize this a Spot on my arm starts to itch like crazy.

DR. PATEL picks up a Free-Fall drinking bottle and sticks the spout in my mouth. It tastes so good I forgive him the Liberty.

When I have emptied it he frowns at me and says there

are some questions he must ask, do I feel well enough to answer them?

I reply Sure but let me sit up first.

He has a written list in his hand and now frowns at that. "First, can you explain how you came to be carrying Senator Gassett-Low's nephew and—"

Junior!

I give practically a yell; "Junior! How is he? Was he badly hurt? Have I damaged him?—He isn't *dead!*"

He jumps a little. "Dead? Certainly not. A moderate concussion only. It is yielding to treatment."

I say "But all that blood!"

"Oh, that? A nosebleed only . . . Now, Miss Lee, can you explain how you came to be carrying him and what caused his injuries?"

Sure I can, at least the first part, and I do.

"But you have no idea how he was rendered unconscious?"

None.

"Nor how he came to be lying in that particular spot?"

Even less.

"Miss Lee. I am informed that after lunch you accompanied Senator Gassett-Low and his nephew on their tour of the Rodent Environments, with an EF named Dalrymple as guide?"

Is he indeed, well Never mind whose tour it was: I agree,

"You left the other three at approximately 15:30 in order to catch the train to Lunarburg, which does not however depart until 16:20."

True enough.

"To walk from the point at which you left your companions to the point of departure of the train takes between ten and fifteen minutes if one does not linger on the way."

Well I stopped in at the Rest room—funny, feels like that was several hours ago.

"The Emergency Siren was sounded at 16:05."

I try to look at my chrono but can't.

"Miss Lee. How did it come about that when the Alarm sounded you were still within the confines of Level VII?"

I say "How long have I been unconscious, forgodsake?"

He frowns and repeats his question.

I frown back and repeat mine.

He coughs and glances at his chrono. "About—six hours. Now—"

"Then who drugged me, and why?"

I don't go around fainting; granted this is an Exception I would not have stayed fainted more than a few minutes; also I woke up with a Muzzy feeling, fast being dispelled by adrenaline now.

Dr. Patel fidgets briefly, then decides to reply.

"When you arrived at the Immunization Bay the police had not yet come. The tourists were much disturbed. The Director had ready a sedative hypospray in case of hysteria. When you collapsed at his feet he thought it better for you to be removed at once for medical attention along with the young man, rather than immediately become the focus of another hubbub. So he gave you a small dose."

I suppose I see his point but What bloody cheek all the same.

"Now. Can you explain—"

Well, he did answer my question, so I do.

When I have finished he Thinks, visibly.

"So your portable Reading Machine and the pouch of books should be among Dalrymple's possessions? I will see that they are at once restored to you."

I cry "Hey! Loose me, first!" but he Strides from the room through one of the five available doors—Actually this is hardly a Room at all, just a bit left over when they partitioned things off, it has more doors than wall and a lot of things plainly Left here till wanted—If he thinks *I* am going to be Left here till wanted he can think again.

Even with my hands on a three-inch tether, I can tell my tunic has been replaced by something loose and Hospitalish but I do seem to have my own trousers and there is a knife in the pocket if only I can get at it.

This takes some very fancy squirming; not only are my hands Restricted in scope but the sleeping bag was designed for an advanced case of Emaciation.

Or for somebody under Restraint.

Why the hell—?

But that is fairly Obvious: I am Suspected of something. Unjustly, of course—

Well it has to be unjustly, I haven't done anything since I came to the Moon. Not one single damn thing.

As to *what* I am suspected of, a moment's thought makes that Obvious too. Or does it? I mean if they think I hit Junior on the head why do they suppose I took the trouble to carry him half a kilometer afterwards? (It *felt* like that anyway).

Well whatever the Reasons if I want to escape I had better get on with it before Dr. Patel comes back.

After a couple of uncomfortable minutes my Hand gets together with my Hip pocket and I manage to tease the knife out to where I can get a grip; thirty seconds later I have a hand free and the first thing I do is Scratch the spot on my arm which is driving me Mad.

Not much satisfaction, it is covered with something slick and Scratchproof.

I can cut my other hand free at any rate.

I now find this sleeping bag is not regulation model even for Human Skeletons, the tab of the zipper is outside and the bag fits round my neck so close I cannot get a hand out.

Do I slash it with my knife now or do I Lie Low?

The latter, because Dr. Patel comes back.

"Miss Lee. No Reading Machine or books among Dalrymple's possessions. Can you explain this?"

I say No, Can't Clarence? and Dr. Patel frowns some more.

"It was thought better to put all EF personnel on this Level under deep sedation, because of the strain of this Emergency."

After a moment this translates as Clarence is Asleep.

"However I have questioned the medical personnel. None can throw light."

This sleeping bag leaves me no room to Shrug.

"Maybe he asked somebody to take them to the train for me."

"The Senator says nobody approached them before the alarm sounded."

This reminds me of something. "How did Junior get separated from them?"

Dr. Patel clears his throat.

"Some minutes after you left the young man expressed a wish to relieve himself. Dalrymple showed him to the nearest washroom and returned to the Senator, saying the nephew would catch up with them. He had not done so when the alarm sounded. Dalrymple insisted they should go to the Immunization Bay, saying the young man would also find his way there. We have not yet been able to talk to Mr. Gassett-Low Junior. Now can you suggest—"

There is a tap at one of the doors. Dr. Patel goes to answer it, presently he goes out again.

I prepare to cut my way out but have Second Thoughts; if I am already considered a Suspicious Character—

Something hits the nearest door like a minor Moonquake; there is a confused roaring and banging, then the Senator falls through.

He stands for a moment Swaying, then looks all round till he catches sight of me, registers Satisfaction and slams the door shut.

Unwillingly to Earth

"There you are, young woman! I want a word with you!"

Third Thoughts: I am Not going to lie here and be Loomed over. I insert the tip of the knife alongside the zipper and Pull.

There is a bit of resistance from the Hem at the top, then all of a sudden it gives way; the cloth splits like the rind of a melon and what with Effort and Elasticity I shoot out like the Pip.

The Senator takes a look at the knife and backs up a step.

"I'm not impressed by tricks, my girl. I want some answers and I want them Now!" He marches half a step away, then turns and shoots out a finger. "What were you up to with my Nephew? Why was he with you when the Alarm sounded?"

I say "He wasn't. I fell over him later on."

The Senator snorts. "And kicked his head by accident, I suppose!"

I say No, if I kicked him anywhere it was around the middle.

"Then how did it happen all his injuries were to the head?"

I say "Ask him!"

"Oh, yes, I'll ask him all right. I'll ask him how you lured him to that place so he could be hit on the head. I don't know what tale you spun him—"

Me? Lure *Junior*?

The Senator apparently takes Flabbergast for Conscious Guilt.

"I'm on to you, young woman! you're traveling under a false identity. That shakes you, does it? These hick policemen may not have caught on, but they'll react fast enough when I point it out, don't you worry."

I do not even have time to worry how I React myself

because at this moment another door opens and in comes a Pressure Suit with a man inside.

I mean it is the Transparent sort, the Plastic is half an inch thick and full of pipes and wires and the overall effect is to make it look a lot more important than the Man wearing it.

The Suit raises a transparent finger and lays it to the Transparent mask somewhere near the lips.

The Senator drops his voice. "I don't *have* to tell them, of course. Even if they finally work it out I think I can say I would be in a position to protect you to some extent. Provided you cooperate, naturally."

Pressure Suit is making gestures to say Go on, keep him talking! it has now been joined by Dr. Patel.

I say "Cooperate how?"

The Senator looks sly.

"I'm not interested in small fry. I want the man behind this. Tell me his name and I'll use my influence on your behalf. Who is he?"

Pressure Suit is still making go-on gestures but Where do you go from here? I reply truthfully that I have no idea what he is talking about.

He steps forward and grabs me by the arms. "Oh, yes, you know and you're going to tell me! The *name*! Say his *name*, damn you!"

I do not like being Waved in the air and am getting set to kick him on the shins when a voice behind me cries "Let her alone!"

The place is rapidly becoming a Circus; the Human Skeleton just walked in. Actually he has Skin as well as bones and I suppose some flesh betweeen them but I can see all his ribs, of which he seems to have Extra. He is wearing short pants and a large bandage round his head and no more, his skin is pale milk color, don't they have Sun-ray lamps on Cincinnatus? because this has to be Junior I suppose.

Unwillingly to Earth

The Senator swings round to confront him, this brings Pressure Suit and Dr. Patel into his line of sight and I think I heard his Jaw drop.

Dr. Patel hurries forward exclaiming that Mr. Gassett-Low Junior must immediately Lie Down, so I offer my vacated Cot; it seems the least I can do. The Doctor is inclined to Mourn over the damage but folds the cut bits back and persuades Junior onto it. He consents to lie down but states in a kind of creaky growl that if anyone starts Bullying little girls again he will get up and See to it; the last bit ascends suddenly to a kind of soprano. Evidently he has damaged his Larynx. I just hope it was not through being slung over my shoulder.

Pressure Suit now comes forward. Under the Suit he is in a dark green close-fitting uniform with various insignia on the sleeves; also an Embroidered translation of these which reads CAPTAIN LUNAR POLICE.

He says "That was most interesting, Senator," in a tired voice that comes from a diaphragm on his Chest, and the Senator turns Magenta and demands to know how long he was Eavesdropped upon.

"From the time when you were talking about your influence with the local Police," says Pressure Suit, "but we'll discuss that later."

Right now I would like to discuss What this nitwitted old whatnot means by alleging that I am traveling under a false identity: but Pressure Suit says wearily "If you please" and I remember that there is an Emergency. He walks forward to look down at Junior ans asks whether he is well enough to answer a few questions?

This is addressed to Dr. Patel but Junior answers for himself: "Of course I am."

Pressure Suit asks whether he knows how he came by his injuries.

Junior answers "Yes. Of course. When the bomb went

off I was just outside the entrance. It blew me across the corridor and I hit my head on the wall."

Dr. Patel and the Senator exclaim in perfect unison "Bomb? What Bomb?"

Junior looks astonished.

"It went off in that hall with all the big glass machines. Where they make disease antibodies. Surely you know about it?"

Pressure Suit asks "How did you come to be there?!" and Junior goes red.

"Well . . . I was looking for a short cut to Level IV, but I got mixed up."

Pressure Suit turns to the Doctor and says "Short cut?" and Dr. Patel answers stiffly that there is a Hoist in that area for Equipment and Supplies but strictly Not To Be Used for Personnel, let alone Tourists.

"Why were you going to Level IV?" is the next question. It makes Junior's voice run up to a Squeak. "I was . . . The EF man. Our guide. I was doing an errand for him."

The Senator snorts. Pressure Suit says "But what was that?"

"He found he had this *thing* . . . I mean he suddenly realized he was carrying Miss Lee's Reading Machine. He was showing me the way to the Men's Room when it bumped his hip. He wanted to go after her, but there was my Uncle waiting and *he* was, like it said on his armband, Exertion Forbidden. So I offered to take it for him."

He sounds like he was confessing to a Serious Crime and the Senator is scowling as though he thinks so, too. Pressure Suit remains calm.

"When you were blown across the corridor, was it still in your possession?"

"Sure. There was a sort of pouch full of spools, too."

"Didn't you see them when you fell over him, Miss Lee?"

I reply that it was so dark I didn't even see Junior.

"Did you hear the explosion experienced by Mr. Gassett-Low?"

No, but I was round a couple of corners and several hundred meters away.

"Did either of you notice anything whatever, during that afternoon, that seemed odd or out of place or might throw light on subsequent events?"

I say No and so does Junior, he has gone a nasty sort of Pale mud color and it occurs to me to ask "What sort of germ was it that got loose?"

Pressure Suit says "Nothing very lethal. A minor respiratory infection," but a second later Dr. Patel reacts in a big way.

"Captain Franklin! I did *not* tell Miss Lee the nature of the Emergency."

Well Who needs telling? I mean what else could it be? Air supply or power? the lights are on and we are breathing. Anyway that queue of people in the Immunization Bay were standing by a trolley just like the one where I got Immunized for going to Earth, and the itchy spot on my arm is just like the one I had afterwards, and why else would a Policeman be wearing a Pressure Suit in a room full of perfectly good Air? and if there really was a bomb in among all those glass tanks I should think it would loose enough Germs to kill us all seven ways each.

Captain Franklin says "One virus, only. As Explosions go it was quite small and local. Now, Miss Lee, if you'll come with me we will try to find out what has happened to your Reading Machine."

Naturally this was not his Main Objective; as we glide through the corridors he wants to know my Background and what I am doing on the Moon.

The corridors are now brightly lit and the area where I found Junior is Sealed off with screens and we have to go some way around to find one with a sort of glass-doored airlock. Captain Franklin stops and says something on his Radio I think. I see his lips move but don't hear anything; presently another Pressure-Suited Policeman appears behind the glass holding up a transparent sack which contains my Reading Machine and pouch of books.

I am glad to see it but turns out it has not been Disinfected yet and I cannot have it till Morning.

This brings to mind something else; I look at my chrono and find it is nearly 23:00. I ask How long is Quarantine?

Captain Franklin says "Three days" and I ask where we are all going to Sleep?

He says "Oh, the Lab people have fixed up some of the public rooms as dormitories. I'll call the girl in charge—"

I say I do not like dormitories, couldn't I use that little cubbyhole where they stashed me away? it has a cot.

He says thoughtfully that I would probably be more comfortable there under the circumstances, speaks to someone or other and tells me it is Okay.

When he has finished I ask Does he really think it was Sabotage?

He says "You heard that boy. He was blown across the corridor all right. Traces of blood and hair on the wall."

That does not prove it was a Bomb, I reply, the Egghead guide told us that during the filtration stages of the production cycle Pressure inside the big glass tanks went up to 100 atmospheres which would make quite a Bang if one of them burst, but I suppose they can tell what happened from the Bits.

He sighs so deeply that the Diaphragm of his suit rattles.

"Miss Lee, inside that sealed-off area are twelve employees of the Department of Health, busy destroying evidence in the name of Decontamination. A few of my boys are there too, trying to pick up glass splinters while wearing plastic gloves half an inch thick . . . We'll get the picture in the end, of course."

We are now among the Rodent Habitats and he wants to know all about the time I was here before, e.g. Did anyone pass us, Did we separate at all before I left, Was any of the others carrying anything?

I say Such as a Bomb? and he replies "Such as a spray can—a metal canister with a conical top?"

I know what they look like, No.

He says "Is Silicosol used on Excenus 23?"

I say What? and he repeats the question: I never heard of the stuff.

We are now returning and I ask something that has been Bothering me; if Junior hit the *back* of his head on the wall how did he injure his Larynx? without breaking his neck?

Captain Franklin stops and stares through his mask.

"Who says he damaged his larynx?"

I say "You could hear there was something wrong with it!"

He says "Is it any different from before?"

Come to think of it I never heard him Speak before, only mumble a bit; the Captain gives me a Look I cannot interpret.

"Stars' sake, girl! Didn't you ever hear a boy when his voice is breaking, before?"

Well the short answer to that is No.

The Pop. of my home planet has a restricted Age range, nearly all between 25 and 60; and at Russett they do not take pupils younger than 18 by which time the Male voice has mended itself.

However what I actually say is "But he's two meters tall!"

Captain Franklin makes a grunting noise. "One ninety-four and a half . . . Anybody who takes a growing lad into Space wants his head examined."

I know what he means; it is a popular idea that to experience Free Fall during the spurt of growth at Puberty makes it get right out of hand. Doctors are not sure it is true.

I ask How old is Junior? and am told he is just over fourteen; I suppose that accounts for a Lot.

We have now reached my Resting place. Captain Franklin points out the whereabouts of Showers and Toilets, tells me there is a picnic trolley set out in the room next to the Immunization Bay and wishes me Good Night.

I do not get one, however; though when I have showered and laundered my clothes—Dr. Patel gave me back my tunic, with the blood cleaned off, before I went with Captain Franklin—and compiled a sandwich I feel fit to Face the World again. But I should have asked for a blanket; that sleeping bag is Drafty now. However I must have got to sleep because I am woken in the morning by a Public Address System announcing Breakfast is Served in Room VII See Twenty-four.

A long table has been set up and about twenty of the Five Planets people, male and female, are sitting round it. There is also a serving table and I collect boiled eggs and toast and juice and coffee; as I finish I notice that Conversation which was general when I came in has now Stopped.

When I turn round they are all staring at me, even those seated with their backs to the service table. I have had plenty of people Mad at me but this is something else, a sort of stony refusal in their expressions to recognize that I am a Person.

What on Earth, or in the Moon—then I remember the Senator yesterday: have these Politicians and their spouses and attachments got it into their heads that I am a Sinister Character? or do they think I had something to do with letting the Virus loose?

The way it affects me, I don't know what to do with my

Unwillingly to Earth

Face: stare back or try to look as though I had not noticed them or What.

There is a sort of Break in the line: a head bobs up and then back: I see that Junior's uncle has a hand gripping his nephew's arm . . . I decide it would be No Kindness to say Hello to Junior. The end of the table is vacant so I take my breakfast there, and the nearest people shuffle their chairs sideways to get as far away from me as they can.

So when Tolly comes in there is a Gap. He marches over and swings a chair in beside me, says "Keep that for me," and goes to the serving table to pile up a plate or two.

The Silence has now Congealed till I wonder he can walk through it, but he sits down and says cheerfully "Miss Lee, your entrance yesterday was the most dramatic thing I've seen in years. Do tell me what led up to it."

The silence comes unstuck in a sort of Collective gasp and I start to tell him, he helps me along with questions now and then, and in the end I explain Junior's part as well as my own.

Tolly says thoughtfully "Police make a nuisance of themselves much?"

I say No, just ask questions, does he suppose the explosion was really a Bomb?

He shrugs. "What's the alternative? One of those hefty great tanks going Bang on its own? Never happened before, they tell me—one or two leaks in the past but always at a joint."

I say "But *why* let off a Bomb in a place like that? What would be the Point?"

I mean Terrorism as a way of getting what you want was discredited centuries ago and anyway nobody has Demanded anything, unless it has been Kept from us.

"No point I can see," agrees Tolly, "which doesn't

mean somebody else might not see one. Tell you one thing, if it was sabotage and the fella wasn't a complete lunatic—no reference to our hosts, of course—he won't be here now. Whole point of a Bomb is to get as far away as possible before the thing goes off."

I am very grateful to Tolly: I think perhaps the atmosphere has shifted from Hanging Judge to Suspended Judgment but maybe that is wishful thinking, anyway it is still far from Congenial; so I finish my coffee and mention that I must see how Clarence is this morning, and depart. However I only get as far as the Supervisor lady who informs me that Clarence has not been told I missed the Train, fortunately he was not present when I made my Entrance yesterday, it would have been very bad for him. All the EF patients—four of them—trapped on this Level are being kept away from the rest of us to avoid Undue Stress: Good morning, Miss Lee.

I go to look for Captain Franklin but am found instead by another Policeman who has my Reading Machine and books; so I make for the place where I slept—nobody seems to be using it—and try to think about my Essay.

I also try *not* to think about those faces round the Breakfast table; then there is a Bang on the door and I leap up ready to defend myself against a Mob.

However it is only Junior, in too much of a State himself to notice mine: he stumbles in and when he has collected all his legs under him announces in a soaring falsetto that he wishes to Thank me for saving his life.

I am Cross at having been frightened and tell him Not to be silly, I did No such thing.

His face firms up somehow and he says "But you did. Dr. Patel told me so."

I say "That Virus was quite mild and you'd have been found anyway in an hour or so."

Junior shakes his head. "It's quite mild if you only breathe it in. But I had cuts from the glass and my shirt was soaked in Virus suspension, so it got into my blood, and that's dangerous. In another hour or two it would have got to my brain. And nobody was looking for me because Mr. Dalrymple told them I was up on Level IV: I could have died of respiratory paralysis if I hadn't been treated when I was.''

Oh.

Junior says if there is ever anything he can do for me . . .

I am about to say Thanks I will bear it in mind, when it occurs to me that I do want something: I tell him All obligations will be canceled if he can find out what made his Uncle the Senator think I was Masquerading as Me.

Junior goes red and white by turns.

Then he says from the bottom of his chest that he knows the answer, his Uncle told him to prove I ought Not to be had anything to do with: but he does not care what his Uncle says and anyhow I ought to have a chance to Explain.

What made his Uncle suspicious is my Passport saying I was born on Excenus 23.

When I swooned (sic) the Director went through my pockets and read my Passport aloud to his Secretary and the Senator heard; later he looked up Excenus 23 in the Gazetteer of Habitable Worlds which he always carries; this says Excenus 23 Sole industry mining Areopagite, av. Pop. 3,200, 99% Male, av. period of res. 1 year.

Junior's Uncle says Nobody ever got *born* on a planet like that, no Women except—not the sort who have families, therefore Q.E.D. my passport is a Fake, presumably I picked an Obscure world without knowing anything about it.

Well what a—Here I remember Junior is an Adolescent and should be let down lightly over his Uncle's Unintelligence.

So I reply calmly "Well, the Gazetteer is nearly right, I suppose. But even a Mining planet can't be run with

Miners and nobody else. There have to be people to buy their ore and record claims and sell them food and equipment and Booze, and doctor them and so on. Not very many, but some. And the ones who are not Has-beens tend to be Up-and-coming young men on First Assignment with their wives along, and sometimes they do not wait to get home before having Kids, so I personally know at least seven people born on Excenus 23, not counting me.''

A voice behind us says "Forty-one, according to Central Register, since the Planet was opened up. You can tell the Senator that if there is anything wrong with Miss Lee's identification it's buried a lot too deep to be spotted by amateurs. I had it checked first thing.''

Junior is Blushing violently and to change the subject I inquire Has Captain Franklin found out whether the explosion was caused by a Bomb or not—? then interrupt myself to exclaim "But it wasn't! No smell!''

Junior Begs my Pardon and I reply that All explosives have By-products that smell, but when I fell over him within ten minutes of the Alarm I did not smell anything at all, hence there was no Bomb.

He says blankly "But that great thick tank couldn't have burst by itself.''

My memory has gone into high gear and I say Maybe *not* by itself, there is stuff you can buy that you paint on and it rearranges the Molecules of glass into a smaller space and kind of works its way through the Layers, when enough Molecules have been rearranged the glass goes all to pieces or if it is under pressure you get a Bang.

Junior says "Did you say you can *buy* this stuff?''

I say "Uh-huh. Not for Sabotage; it is used when you want to spray a large area. Like the time some of Dad's imported seed potatoes turned out to have an Imported disease, Sector Agricultural sent him some big glass bulbs half full of Fluid pressurized at about 20 atmospheres. He painted them with this Gunk and hung them from the main weathermast and about two hours later they went *poof!* and the liquid turned into Aerosol and was blown over everything right to the edge of the Weatherlid.''

Captain Franklin says in a tired way ''You don't happen to know the name of this 'gunk,' Miss Lee?''

I say it began Very-something but I forget the rest.

He fumbles a little booklet out of a pouch and spreads it open. ''Mm . . . You disappoint me, Miss Lee.''

Junior says belligerently ''Why?''

''She told me she'd never heard of Silicosol. Now any farmer's daughter on Earth knows that stuff. Sold in spray cans and acts as Miss Lee just described. I forgot that spray cans are not shipped to the Outer Planets—too many freighters in that volume have unpressurized holds. And now I see here in the small print that when the stuff is sold in ordinary cans they market it as Verracass. Another good clue gone to vacuum . . . And now, Mr. Gassett-Low, I believer your Uncle is looking for you: and I want a few words with Miss Lee.''

The Words he wants are in fact quite numerous and all about Clarence, and the only ones I have in answer are I Don't Know. Such as where he was born: I know it was a farm in a valley with a stream at the bottom, but I Don't Know which planet. Clarence was sent away to school at 14 and ran away to Space three years later. His passport was issued on Excenus 23 and says he has been an Effective Resident there for three years, which is longer than most Miners but not so long as some.

Political Views? he once said The good thing about Excenus 23 is that it has no Politicians.

And what happened during the thirty or forty years between leaving home and getting to Excenus 23? I just Don't Know.

Captain Franklin says ''And how did he seem when you

met him yesterday morning? Enjoying life? Happy to meet an old friend?"

Oh, Stars.

I reply that he seemed a bit quiet on the whole.

Captain Franklin tells me that according to Clarence's Supervisor he was Delighted to know that I intended to visit him; but next morning he was plainly Disturbed but refused to say Why.

I suggest he might have been having Second Thoughts about entertaining old friends in an Environment where he got supervised to that extent.

Inside all the plastic I see Captain Franklin nod.

"Not easy, being an EF. The whole place revolves round them but they've no privacy. Those armbands mark them as second-class citizens in some respects. Can't do without them, though. It's been tried. Some healthy half-wit yells to an EF for help with an awkward or heavy job and unless the EF is extra sensible and strong-willed he's apt to end up crash-frozen, with a thirty-percent chance that when his new heart is ready he won't revive.

"Of course the worst anybody will be to 'em is over-sympathetic, and most EFs take that as it's meant, but you get the odd one who can't adjust . . . Your friend Dalrymple is thought to have settled down quite well. He didn't give you any idea what was troubling him?"

I say I am damn certain he was *not* wondering How to get rid of me so as to go and spray Silicosol on an Antibody tank, if he meant to do that he would have called the Royal Cynthia and told me Not to come.

This seems a good moment to mention Tolly's theory that the Perpetrator if any would have got well away from Labsville; but the Captain waves it away.

"Sure, sure, he told me that. Sounds good but doesn't stand up. This was an inside job."

I say Why? Come to that does he know for sure it was Sabotage?

I guess he is getting Tired of this question but he does answer it.

"Miss Lee, those tanks get checked. Five days ago that one was pumped up to 150 atmospheres for 12 hours. Yesterday it blew at 85. Then there's the Silicosol. They use it right here. Stores on this Level have a couple of cases. There's a full can unaccounted for . . . Best guess is that to get through glass that thick'd take about twenty hours, so it must have been sprayed the night before."

I say Inside or Outside job, why would anybody want to blow up an Antibody producer, he must have been Mad.

Captain Franklin pulls a face. "One of those types who think they're appointed to administer the Wrath of God? We'd have heard from him by now. Then, only one in 20 of those tanks was in the high-pressure phase of the cycle—four of them, to be exact, and one of those was filtering off antibody, so blowing it wouldn't have made nearly so much fuss. Of the three at high pressure, two were culturing something pretty nasty. He picked the one with a mild respiratory bug in it. Assuming he knew—and if he knew which tanks were pressurized he knew what was in them, it's all on the same schedule—it doesn't seem like the Wrath of God to me."

I say I suppose the best hope of tracing the culprit is to find the Silicosol can, though I suppose he will hardly leave Fingerprints.

He turns with a Gleam in his eye I can see through his faceplate.

"Oh, we've found it. Complete with prints. In a locker belonging to your friend Dalrymple. Some of the prints are his. Just at the moment the Heart Foundation's Supervisor is defending him against all comers, but he's going to have a chance to explain it to me, quite soon."

It is not comfortable wondering whether Clarence can possibly be a quite different person from the one I imagined and I am almost glad when I get paged by the PA system to go to room So-and-so at my earliest convenience.

Here I find the Five Planets lot and we are all put through a sort of Computerized interrogation about the day before. I suspect this is Makework to keep us out of everybody's hair. I do my best but if the Answers have any significance the Computer is not telling; it goes on except for a Sandwich lunch until 16:00.

I am now in a mood to do some work on my Essay so I am not too pleased when Junior who has been sitting on the floor just outside jumps up as I am leaving and says he has to Talk to me. However all the Books say one must be Patient with Adolescents so I wait till he touches ground again and suggest he walk me to my Cubbyhole and tell me what is Eating him on the way.

He says What is Eating him is being under Suspicion. The Five Planets party have got it into their heads that we conspired to be Up to Something yesterday and that it has something to do with their Imprisonment now, and whatever his Uncle or Tolly or the Police say they will go on thinking it till the Culprit is identified.

I agree this is Tough on him and he says wistfully "Doesn't it bother you at all?"

Well Yes, a bit, but I needn't have anything to do with them; anyway I don't see what can be Done; does he?

He takes a deep breath and says "I think we ought to try to find the real Culprit ourselves."

Because of Tact to Adolescents I do not tell him he is Nuts. I just say "What could we do that the Police aren't doing already?"

Junior says "We can talk to the others. Informally. The Culprit might give himself away."

"Don't be silly," I reply, and I do not care if this is Tactful or not, "your party just happened to be visiting the place when the Tank blew up, why should any of them

Unwillingly to Earth

have anything to Give away? The real culprit is probably on another Level if not in Lunarburg by now."

Junior stops and anchors himself to an Incom box so as to Gesture more convincingly.

"Why should it be just Coincidence that the Sabotage happened when we were visiting Labsville? What it's done is to strand eleven of the Delegates here, while the conference in Lunarburg goes on. Today and tomorrow there'll be votes on four of the most important issues on the whole Agenda. And if you think Politicians would not try to strand Opponents where they can't cast their votes, you don't know what this Conference has been like. There have been enough Plots to sicken Machiavelli."

I never heard of Machiavelli until about six weeks ago so I am Impressed. I ask What Plots? and Junior hesitates.

"Well, my Uncle says a lot of it is ordinary Political Horsetrading—you know, swapping favors and support—only more open than usual because they are away from Home. He says on most planets you pretty well have to stay within the Rules because so many people are checking on you, but Off Planet the checks are mostly Off too and you can get away with a lot more. I mean the Lunar Police aren't going to be concerned about bribery, for instance, if it involves affairs on another planet. And the things that are illegal even here—like threats, for instance; my Uncle's sure one delegate's wife was Threatened and he changed his vote because of it; and one delegate from Lamartine made a fool of herself in open session and my Uncle says he's sure the woman was doped . . . well, there's no real proof, but that was why my Uncle wouldn't let me go and see the Rats on my own. He said he wouldn't risk anyone trying to put pressure on him through me . . ." He goes red again.

I say Could the Sabotage have been a Plot to stop his Uncle voting?

Junior kicks his feet about and says "Well, no . . . *He*

thought so at first. But it's pretty well known how all the eleven who got stranded here would have voted, and they just about cancel out on all four issues—five one way, six the other. And you must have a Majority of at least five to carry a motion."

I say What was the point of stranding this party if their Votes cancel out? Junior takes a deep breath and starts again.

"I think it was done to strand Mr. Tollinder. He was due to speak tomorrow about the Linder Valley, on Discus. He's the leading Conservationist and the best speaker in the whole Conference and my Uncle says his speech would probably have been good for twenty votes at least and that could cost Lamartine the motion."

I say What is the Linder Valley, if it is on Discus how does it affect Lamartine?

Junior tells me, at length. Shortened, it goes like this:

Mining on Discus is nearly all in one area so rich in minerals it supplies the whole planet. However some of the Mining Companies took out Concessions on other areas a long time ago, just in case. These have never been used. However again, one of the Companies swapped the Linder Valley concession for some machinery from Lamartine; a lot of interplanetary trading is like that because of Problems with Exchange.

But since the Concession was issued the Linder Valley has become heavily farmed and is also a Holiday area and the Inhabitants are claiming the Concession has lapsed; they have offered to pay off the cost of the machinery in Produce or something instead.

Discan law is not clear about the duration of unused Concessions so the Issue was brought to this Conference, and if Lamartine can get it tied in with enough deals so the Discan Gov. will lose something important by not Ratifying the final Vote they might get what they want.

If they win the Vote, that is.

Unwillingly to Earth

I ask whether Junior has passed this on to Captain Franklin, and he chokes.

"Yes. I did. He said Mr. Tollinder is the one Delegate stranded here who *hasn't* claimed the Sabotage was aimed at him personally and it would be a pity to spoil a Record like that."

I say all the same no doubt he will bear it in mind. And I think any scheme for talking to the Five Planets people is going to fall down because whoever fixed the Sabotage would have taken care Not to get caught himself.

Junior says he doesn't think so. Whoever did it would have wanted to make sure Tolly was on Level VII when the tank exploded and he couldn't do that from Lunarburg or even from anywhere else in Labsville.

Seems to me the person to talk to is Tolly. Junior says he has but Tolly says he was down on this Level because of an appointment to discuss Research funded by Discus and that was arranged several days ago.

Junior sticks to his opinion that the Culprit would have come, or sent a Representative, in case the appointment was changed or ended early, to try to keep Tolly on this Level; I see he has a point. But I do not think Talking to people will be any good because they will not Talk back, not to Junior or me.

To change the subject I ask if this conference is such a Snake Pit why did his Uncle bring him along?

Now I gather I have been Tactless again because Junior does his best to tie his legs in a knot.

"Well, he . . . my Uncle said it was a Historic occasion . . ." I would be willing to let it go at that but he goes on "Actually he put me down as his Secretary and gets an allowance for me, a lot more than the cost of the trip . . . Look, he really is pretty honest, but he said Somebody was going to pick up a handful of credits for this jaunt and it might as well be him . . . And he didn't *know* what it would be like."

It takes me nearly half an hour to Soothe him and I have just started to work on my Essay when that damn PA system requests All and sundry to come to good old VII C 23 for an early Supper.

When we get there turns out Captain Franklin is making a Speech first.

He uses a lot of Words but put briefly it seems the Lunar Gov. has heard Rumors that the Sabotage at Labsville was motivated by a desire to interfere with the voting at the Five Planets Conference, an Abuse of Hospitality and the Democratic Process that must not be allowed. Therefore the Gov. has persuaded the Conference to bend its rules enough for the Delegates now in Labsville to participate in tomorrow's meeting via life-size two-way Stereo, not just to watch but to Speak and Vote. The Equipment will be set up in this room at 22:30 tonight so please go to bed early. Meals tomorrow will be in the Waiting Room next door. Thank you for your Attention, Good Evening.

Well Good for the Lunar Gov. in my opinion but the Delegates look Taken Aback rather than Delighted. Junior who is in his Uncle's custody on the far side of the room starts giving me Speaking looks but I have seen enough of him for the moment. Supper is the Takeaway sort so I pick mine up and scram. Outside the door I run into Captain Franklin and ask whether he has been able to talk to Clarence yet?

Inside the mask I see his head go slowly from side to side.

"Asking awkward questions of EF subjects is by way of being a last resort, Miss Lee. I'll talk to him if I must."

I say Anyway if this theory of interfering with Voting has got anything to it there is no reason why Clarence should be involved.

Even through the plastic I can see he looks surprised.

"Dear me," he says, "so you really didn't know."

Know *what*, forgodsake?

"That your friend Dalrymple comes from Discus. It's on his medical record. Even the Supervisor admits that when he gets excited he has a Discan accent you could cut with a knife . . . Good night, Miss Lee."

I don't care. Clarence did *not* spray Silicosol on that tank, he is not such a fool as to leave the can in his personal locker if he had.

All the same I no longer feel like working and if I go to the cubbyhole Junior will come and talk to me again. There is a stereo show laid on after supper so I go and pretend to watch. Nobody pays much attention to me which is a Relief, maybe Tolly has been having a few words with some of them.

While Not watching the Drama I have thought of something; Captain Franklin has a lot on his mind and this is a point he may have overlooked.

At 22:45 I return to the Waiting Room full of smiles and apologies. I was using my Styler here earlier and now I cannot find it *anywhere*, I think perhaps—

Two Great Big Men take time off to help me find it and after a couple of minutes one of them produces it Triumphantly from the side of the chair where I put it just before leaving. I spread more Smiles around apologize a few more times and Go.

Twenty minutes later I return. More apologies but one of the Lady Delegates has to take an antiallergen pill and can't find it *anywhere* and I thought perhaps . . . The pills do not turn up even when two other men take a hand, after we have looked *everywhere* I start looking again, with enough Feminine Incompetence to make you sick; the Foreman calls my Helpers back on the job in a marked manner but nobody actually asks me to Leave, they seem to have decided that if they ignore me I will eventually Go Away.

So they are not looking when I slide the door open with a last flutter of Oh Dear Where Can It Be, then slide it Shut again and drop behind a convenient couch and lie still.

Half an hour later they have finished and Depart and What a waste, they do not even lock the Door. I get up and stretch and make for a more central hiding place, behind the solitary chair that has a cloth cover right down to the ground: I settle down as comfortably as I can.

I have had Worse waits, like the time Dad was in Hospital and I did not know whether he would Recover or not. But at least I did know Something would happen in the end, whereas this Foretaste of Eternity is not guaranteed to produce anything except Cramp. In face as Time drags on I get surer and surer I am making a fool of myself, until after about 100 minutes by my chrono something finally starts to occur.

The door slides open.

There is a dim light outside in the corridor and it casts a pale Parallelogram on the carpet. Then this is obscured, first by a human Outline and then by the Door being shut. A flashlight beam starts feeling its way around.

It flickers either side of my hiding place, then slides across it and Stays: I can see the light through the fabric: then I hear the sound of Breathing getting closer and the Light intensifies.

Then mercifully there is the sound of Contact as this person stumbles over a small table, and the light shoots away. I crawl very fast out from behind the chair and make for a free-standing bookcase about three meters away.

From further noises I conclude that the Intruder has settled down behind my former Refuge. I have a damn good idea who it is but daren't call out to him in case the next part of

Unwillingly to Earth

the Program chooses that moment to begin. It suddenly occurs to me to wonder what the Hell shall I do if the next person to come along is Clarence after all—?

I chew this thought for about twenty minutes and then there is a Repeat. Parallelogram, Silhouette, Obscuration and another Flashlight, a good deal more powerful than the first. It slides over the carpet and touches my Bookcase, but fortunately this Intruder is not looking for a hiding place; the light sweeps on to the mass of stereo equipment at the other end of the room.

It is all perfectly silent: I suddenly realize I cannot even hear Junior's breathing any more: I wonder how long he can go on holding his Breath.

Answer: Too long. The flashlight takes its time over the stuff: just as the Source starts to move towards it there is a sort of Rasping noise as Junior's lungs insist on their right to new Air . . . The beam swings towards his chair. I scramble up; there is a Bumping noise and I yell loudly and Junior's own torch lashes around throwing shadows all over the place and then the Lights come on and there is Captain Franklin's Pressure Suit in the doorway.

(With Captain Franklin inside it, of course.)

Junior is doing a slow descent from Mid Air. Low G has advantages, he and the new Arrival have collided with each other and the furniture but have done little if any damage, which is a Good Thing because to my total astonishment the said Arrival is Tolly.

He is Astonished too and maybe because of Political training he starts to talk first.

"*Junior?* And Lizzie Lee? Migod. Do you mean to say that my idiot colleagues were right all the time? You two really are conspiring to Sabotage—"

I say "Hold it!"

"Everybody hold it," says Captain Franklin irritably. "You. Mr. Tollinder. How do you come to be here?"

Tolly blinks.

"Well—I followed Junior. Must have been him, I suppose; at the time I didn't know who it was. Just woke up, about ten minutes ago, and heard someone moving around in the men's dormitory. When he went out it wasn't in the direction of the washroom but through the door nearest here. Well, this equipment is important, especially to me, and we all know there's a saboteur around. I came here, just in case. And—"

"Now you, Miss Lee," said Captain Franklin even more crossly.

I say "I didn't think the equipment ought to be left unguarded. So I hid in here. Junior must have had the same idea, because he came in about twenty minutes ago. I didn't tell him I was here, because—"

Tolly says "Talk about thin stories—"

Captain Franklin says wearily "Maybe. All the same, it happens to be true. The room has been under surveillance. We were hoping to catch the saboteur ourselves."

"Well," says Tolly blankly, and then again "Well . . . I'm sorry."

"Not half so sorry as I am," says Captain Franklin.

"Yes . . . I see. A neat little trap and we all sprang it, one after another. I apologize, Captain. And to you, Lizzie, and you, Junior . . . I really don't know what more I can do."

"You can tell me a little more about this person who sneaked out of the dormitory," says Captain Franklin. "I take it you saw him silhouetted against the corridor light when he went out."

Tolly seems taken aback.

"Oh, yes, of course . . . Average sort of build. Nothing outstanding about him."

"Well, sir, that eliminates several of your party, including young Mr. Gassett-Low here. Now would you say—"

I don't give a damn What Tolly would say. I am sick to death of the whole thing and propose to Mind My Own

Unwillingly to Earth

Business in future. The only thing I do give a damn about is getting to bed, and nobody else gives a damn what I do, so I depart.

Next morning after Breakfast I am waylaid by Junior who has got yet another Idea, viz., that the only way the Saboteur can now prevent Tolly from making his speech would be to damage Tolly himself.

I point out that if Tolly attends the Stereo session this morning nobody will have a chance to damage him.

"Yes," says Junior, "but he isn't going to. He says he needs to shake the fidgets out of his legs, so as soon as the corridors are open he's going for a walk to try over his Speech to himself. And I think somebody ought to go along with him."

We have been told that the final checks on the Decontamination process will be over by 11:00 and the barriers will be removed then.

I tell Junior that Captain Franklin seems to me competent to manage the Police work and in future I am going to leave it all to him: I am going to my cubbyhole to work on my Essay and do not wish to be disturbed.

By lunch time I have got about two thirds of it written.

At Lunch Junior sits next to me in a condition of Frustration: his Uncle insisted on his attending the morning session so he was unable to play Bodyguard. I point out that Tolly is there, plainly Undamaged, and that there was not much chance of anyone Getting At Him this morning because the corridors were full of Police.

When I return to my cubbyhole Captain Franklin is there.

He says "Coming to this Conference this afternoon?"

I say No.

"Pity. All the lab staff will be there—they don't often get a chance to see themselves on stereo. Incidentally your friend Dalrymple will be attending, and his friend Fitzroy—curious that two out of the four EFs trapped on this Level should be Discans, isn't it? I fancy several questions should be answered by the end of this session. Sure you won't change your mind?"

I do change it, half a dozen times, before 14:00 when the next session is due to begin; but in the end I go.

The Immunization Bay is now a miniature Conference Room with about 40 seats in seven rows: most of them occupied. The Stereo transmitters are at the far end beside a huge screen showing the transmission from the Conference Hall, and a smaller Monitor Screen showing what goes out from here. At the moment this is a view of the Audience. What does not show because of the way the cameras are angled is that round the walls are about 20 Pressure Suits containing Police.

The cause of all this, or so I suppose, is sitting on a sort of dais in yet another Pressure Suit: the Lunar Minister for ExtraSolar Relations, who has come to give proof of the Lunar Gov's interest in the Democratic Processes of their Distinguished Visitors: I know because he tells the stereo cameras so. Our view of the Conference Hall shows a big screen just like the one here and we can see him on that as well as on the Monitor; we can also see the Audience there, some of whom do not know they are on Stereo and are half Asleep.

Nobody could blame them: after the Minister's remarks the first part of the afternoon is taken up with some deadly dull business left over from the morning: I am sinking into a Stupor myself when Junior who has a seat just behind me leans forward and whispers "Mr. Tollinder's Gone!"

Tolly when I last saw him was sitting on the far side of the room. There has been a surprising amount of Going and a certain amount of Coming Back, throughout. However all the Delegates are now in sight except Tolly: I am about to suggest he has probably gone to the Bathroom when a Pressure Suit standing near the Minister steps forward and says in Captain Franklin's voice "Is anything wrong?"

Junior stands up. "Yes! There is! Where's Mr. Tollinder? I *told* you he was in danger—I told you they were trying to prevent his Speech! Now he's missing! Why didn't you look after him—?"

"Don't worry," says Captain Franklin, "we did. You want to know where he is? Switch to Mobile, Levinson."

I have just noticed something odd; the Monitor screen shows Junior and me sitting quiet and bored in our chairs. Then on the big screen the Conference Hall in Lunarburg disappears and we are looking down a long corridor at a back view of Tolly, plainly in a hurry but alive and well.

Somebody says "What the hell is he doing? He's due to speak in a quarter of an hour!"

The view is evidently being transmitted from automatic cameras near the ceiling. While we can see Tolly pull a bit of cloth from his pocket and start Doing something with it we cannot at first see what this is. Then he turns into a cross-corridor and we get a scan from in front and can see that he is twisting it into a sort of Rope.

He ties a half hitch in it and makes for the Incom box on the wall. He stands in front of this and puts the loop of cloth over his head.

Now Tolly does nothing at all for half a minute, as though he is working up to something or maybe just getting his Breath: then he flicks the switch and starts Bumping against the box, not banging it with his fist but jerking his elbows and shoulders so that they hit it and making a Panting noise.

Up to now it has all happened in dead silence but suddenly the Panting noises and Thumps start coming out of the PA speakers on the walls: still knocking himself against the Incom box Tolly gets hold of the ends of the cloth and pulls them tight; simultaneously there is a half-strangled yell from the speakers: "Help! Get the—Ahhh!"

Then a voice says politely "Can I help you? Sir?"

Suddenly there is Genuine scuffling as Tolly falls against the Incom box while trying to spin round and tear the noose off his neck simultaneously: then there is a switch to another scanner and we get a view of a Cop standing behind Tolly and two more, all of them in pressure suits, emerging from nearby doorways so that he is Boxed in.

The first one speaks again. "We wouldn't want you to think we don't take care of our distinguished visitors, Mr. Tollinder."

At which point the Minister for ExtraSolar Affairs leaps to his feet and screams "My god! You're not transmitting this?"

Captain Franklin points silently to the Monitor which shows a scene of people sitting quietly or Dozing off; evidently what is going out to Lunarburg is a tape taken earlier on.

One of the Delegates' wives says plaintively "What did Mr. Tollinder do that for?"

The Captain says politely "You'll be able to ask him in a minute, ma'am."

He looks at one of the open doors and Tolly is marched in.

That must have been a Recording we saw earlier, made at least ten minutes ago. The cloth noose has been loosened but is still lying on Tolly's shoulders, his Hair is on end and his face is a yellowish color and one corner of his mouth Twitches; he keeps rubbing at it but it won't stop.

Captain Franklin says "Nice timing, Mr. Tollinder. Just twelve minutes before your speech is due to begin."

Nobody says anything at all for about half a minute. Then before our eyes Tolly Straightens up and squares his shoulders and his color comes back to normal. He rips the cloth off and stuffs it in his pocket and smooths his hair with the other hand: then he walks across to the Minister and murmurs into the diaphragm of his suit.

Unwillingly to Earth

The head inside nods repeatedly; then I think the Minister says something to Captain Franklin over the suit radio, judging by the movement of his lips and the Captain's expression which is now one of Disgust.

Meanwhile nobody is saying anything except the speaker in the Conference Hall: I catch the words Linder Valley and suddenly realize he is a New one. Then Tolly walks back to his seat.

The next five minutes are queer because Nothing happens at all; nobody speaks to Tolly, not even the lady who wanted to know Why he did that: the Speaker on the screen is still Boring away and his audience going on being Bored.

Then three people come in through the door nearest the back . . . Clarence, another man in an EF armband—this one has Rodent-style teeth but looks more like a Rabbit than a Rat—and the Supervisor lady, wheeling a cart with a lot of clinical apparatus on top.

Of course she does not know what has been happening: I rise to tell her this occasion is Not suitable for men with bad hearts but a nearby cop touches me on the shoulder and tells me firmly to sit Down again.

The Speaker in the Conference Hall now announces that the next Speaker will be that well known champion of the Conservationist cause, currently in Labsville but enabled to be present in all but Flesh by the technological kindness of the Lunar Gov: The Honorable Randolph Tollinder, Congressman, Discus.

One thing I never expected was that Tolly's speech would turn out to be just another Bore.

I mean everybody who gives a damn must know the past history of the Linder Valley by heart, so why go over it now? Then I begin to recognize the note he is sounding, which is Inevitablity. There are minerals under the green grass of the valley and men need them—one could almost say Mankind needs them—so how can a few farmers expect their own wishes to prevail? The Lamartine corporation have promised that when it has quite finished with what's underneath it will put the Topsoil back and let the Valley be green again.

Then he starts talking about Generous Compensation; the final message is neither Loud nor Clear but has sort of seeped in: the Rape of the Linder Valley is going to happen and the inhabitants had better lie back and try to Enjoy it.

I twist round to look at Clarence but he is just sitting there: his companion is fidgeting and looking puzzled: I don't know whether they have taken it in or not.

Tolly goes back to his seat amid scattered Applause.

The moderator rises and clears his throat: "Mr. Tollinder being the last Speaker on this Motion, Delegates will now record their votes."

Here someone out of scan hands him a piece of paper. He reads it and nods.

"This is a message from the Lunar authorities. They fear that the transmission from Labsville may be interrupted before voting is complete. They ask that our colleagues stranded there be allowed to cast their votes first, rather than waiting for the turn of their particular Planet. Do I hear consent?"

Tolly has given a Galvanic jump that gets him half way out of his seat; but if he objects he does not say so, nor does anyone else.

"Very well. Delegates in Labsville will please come forward in alphabetical order to vote on the Motion; That in the opinion of this Conference the United Minerals Consortium of Lamartine has legal title to minerals underlying the Linder Valley on Discus and should be allowed to proceed without let or hindrance to the exploitation of the same. First delegate: the Congressman from Northland, Lamartine, the Honorable David Asante."

Unwillingly to Earth 123

Mr. Asante takes his place between the scanners and records one vote For the motion.

"The Senator from Exville, Cincinnatus, the Honorable George Gassett-Low."

Junior's Uncle takes the spot, glares at Tolly and records one vote Against.

The alphabetical listing leaves Tolly last. The next eight Delegates go up and record their votes (Four in favor, four against). Then the Moderator on the screen announces the Representative from Euchre, Discus, the Honorable Randolph Tollinder.

Tolly walks between the scanners and now there are Three of him; one on the Monitor, one on the screen within the big screen and one just Standing there. None of him looks really life-like; his color is all right now but his face seems to have changed its shape, Tension I suppose, and his eyes have gone back behind it and looking through holes. His triple Presence stares at nothing and says "Randolph Tollinder, Discus, casting one vote For the motion" then he goes back to being Single and walks to his seat.

The stir here is immediate; on the big screen it starts a few seconds later and the Moderator does a double take and looks sideways as though to ask what Tolly really meant to say. Then there is a shout from the back of the room.

"EF Emergency! Get a powered stretcher, quick!"

I jump up to see, but Clarence is still sitting upright; it is the little rabbity man who has keeled over.

During the next ten minutes whenever there is a Lull I can hear some other damn Delegate in the Conference Hall recording his vote; the Monitor is blank so I suppose transmission from Labsville has stopped.

I wonder whether the lady who wanted to know realizes Why Mr. Tollinder Did That.

I wonder whether he was just trying to cheat the people

in the Linder Valley, or the Lamartine Mining Consortium as well. Maybe when he sold out to them they agreed that he did not actually have to vote For them provided he could find a good enough excuse not to speak or vote Against.

Or maybe having sold his vote he was trying to get out of having to deliver, by staging the Sabotage: nobody could expect him to make a Speech when he was trapped in Labsville by Quarantine. So when Long Distance Participation was organized he tried to get out of it *again*: Nobody could expect him to make Speeches if he had been half strangled a few minutes before.

I wonder whether Captain Franklin knew it was Tolly all along, or not till he sneaked into the room where the Transmitters were, in the middle of the night.

At this point one of the cops comes and leans his diaphragm against my ear and says Clarence would like to speak with me. Elsewhere, please.

Junior rises to follow me and nobody objects.

Clarence is in a room that looks like a Hospital but he is not in bed, just sitting in a chair and looking Severe rather than Sick: I introduce Junior and he says he is glad I have found a friend in this place since he could not look after me himself, he did not know I had got Stuck here until a few hours ago.

He then looks at us both and says "Not much fun for you kids on this trip. I'm sorry."

I say It was not his fault anyway.

He sighs, then checks it as though even too much Breathing might be bad for his Heart.

"It *was* my fault, Lizzie, in a way. I could have put a stopper on before it happened if I hadn't believed that damn fool Fitzroy. I copped him about an hour before you got here, in the Antibody factory with a can of Silicosol. He hadn't any business there and he looked as guilty as hell, so I took it away from him and read the label; but he

Unwillingly to Earth 125

swore he hadn't used it yet. He'd only been there a few seconds, so I believed him. Actually he'd used the can the night before, and hidden it because somebody came. He was collecting it to sneak it back to Stores . . . I took it away and put it in my locker while I decided what to do. Didn't want to get him into trouble if I could help it, poor fish . . ."

Junior said "Did he tell you what he was doing? And why?"

"Oh, yes. I said I'd report it at once if he didn't . . . *He* thought the fella that put him up to it was going to herd twenty or thirty pro-Lamartine Delegates down into Level VII just before the tank was due to blow . . . Shouldn't have swallowed that one—me, I mean. *Or* Fitz, but he hasn't any brains . . ."

I say "Pro-*Lamartine*?"

"So they couldn't vote to mess up the Valley. Fitz used to go there as a kid. Loved the place . . . He read some guff about Tollinder in the *Lunar Times* and wrote to him saying Carry on the Good Work . . . Then some fixer came here to see him. Put him up to the sabotage . . . When Fitz found he'd bagged Tollinder himself he damn near passed out. Would have done if he hadn't been full of tranquilizers—we both were . . . When I caught him I made him clock in for full-time therapy all day—hell, he *needed* it after the shock of being caught—so he couldn't tell anyone he hadn't sprayed the production unit. I thought I'd neutralized the whole scheme; when the Alarm went off it never even occurred to me that Fitz was the cause . . ."

He sounds perfectly calm but the Supervisor arrives to say some Index or other has risen ten points and Junior and I are to Go.

We wish Clarence goodbye and start back the way we came.

I do not know what to say to Junior, he liked Tolly and admired him and Now look at him, shown up as a Phony and made to look Silly and now turns out he played the meanest trick I ever heard of on a man with a bad Heart.

However it is Junior starts the next conversation, he wants to know Do we have to tell Captain Franklin what Clarence said?

No need, I reply, he has obviously bugged the whole Level, not just the cameras that followed Tolly around: look how he always turns up at the Psychological moment.

At this Psychological moment a cop turns up and says Captain Franklin wants to see both of us please.

Judging by the Diagrams on the wall the Captain has taken over the office of a Xenophysiologist. I get the impression he has forgotten why he sent for us; but after a moment he fishes a Computer transcript out of a file.

"Here. Dalrymple's statement. You sign as witnesses, then we needn't bother him about it. Read it first."

Junior says "So you *have* bugged every room on this Level!"

The Captain puts his gauntlets together on the desk and says "No." Then he gives a kind of Shrug inside his suit. "I just used what's there. The whole of Labsville's monitored. Audio pickups every twenty-five meters, cameras every fifty. It's because of the EFs. They wear cardiorhythmic alarms, but transmission's poor through rock walls. With the cameras, an EF who wanders off to have a heart attack in private can be located within thirty seconds . . . Have you read that yet?"

The Transcript is quite accurate. I sign and so does Junior. Captain Franklin sticks it back into the file and says dreamily, "We retuned all the cameras in the Immunization Bay to infrared. When you went and sprang the trap I'd have traded the pair of you for a bent milli-credit: but today was much, much better. For nearly half an hour Mr. Randolph Tollinder really thought his number was up. He—"

Junior says "Isn't it?" and the Captain gives him a Look.

"Boy, you don't think anything will really happen to him, do you? A distinguished visiting statesman like him? You don't think we could ever be so crude as to bring him to court, say for damaging Lunar property and inconveniencing Lunar citizens and wasting the time of the Lunar Police?"

Junior says blankly "Why not? You've got all the evidence—"

"Evidence of what? Faking an attack on himself? No law against that."

I say "Surely there must be one against Sabotage!"

The look Captain Franklin gives me is very, very tired.

"Miss Lee, the Silicosol was applied to that tank when Mr. Randolph Tollinder was quite certainly two hundred kilometers away."

I say "Well, he—I forget the word—did something to that little man with the rabbit teeth—"

"He *suborned* him," says Junior sternly.

"They never met. Fitzroy hasn't left Labsville in six months and Mr. Randolph Tollinder never set foot in the place till the day you all came."

"He has two aides and a secretary back in Lunarburg," says Junior. "I can give you their names—"

"I've got 'em. I even know which one came here by train, the day it was decided to send a sightseeing group. I haven't found anyone yet who saw him with Fitzroy—"

"But surely," says Junior, "now he knows he was fooled, surely Fitzroy—"

"Fitzroy," says the Captain, "is dead. Temporarily, at least. They got his heart going a couple of times but couldn't keep it up. He may come out of the freezer alive in a few months' time when his new heart is ready, or he may not. By that time Mr. Randolph Tollinder and entourage will be back on Discus. In fact they're cutting their visit short. There's a ship day after tomorrow. They're booked on that."

I say "You could stop him, couldn't you?"

"Of course. All it takes is a warrant signed by the Minister of State for ExtraSolar Affairs. You saw how he reacted . . . No. Mr. Randolph Tollinder and entourage will be seen off with honors to get on with their political fence-mending back home. One thing I accomplished," says Captain Franklin broodingly, "I made the bastard record his vote while the issue was still doubtful, so that he *had* to deliver in the way he'd been bribed to do. That's one thing he'll find hard to explain . . . No. What am I saying? He'll get to whoever is due to feed that report into the printers back on Discus, and get it adjusted."

"But the rest of the Delegates know!" says Junior.

"Of course. The ones who matter to him are the ones from Discus. They'll have favors they want from him. Tomorrow they'll all get together and trade. He's doing it right now with the bunch *here*; none of them will mention that funny little act with the noose, when they get back to Lunarburg. Now if the other Discans at the Conference had seen *that*—"

"Why didn't they?" said Junior angrily. "Why wasn't that transmitted with the rest?"

"Because the officer in charge of the transmission chickened, that's why. He said if *I* wanted to throw away my post and my pension I could do it some other way . . . Hell, I can't blame it all on Levinson. I could have picked somebody who'd follow orders—if I put 'em in writing . . . But keeping foreign politicians honest is not my job."

I say "But *this* one destroyed Lunar property—and wasted the time of the Lunar police."

"If the Minister for ExtraSolar Affairs says to let him get away with it, who am I to argue?"

"But *why*?" says Junior. "Why does the Minister want him to get away with it?"

"Because interplanetary conferences are an important part of our tourist trade, that's why. At least he thinks they could be, but *not* if prospective conferers get to know that we had the discourtesy to show up a Distinguished Visitor before his fellow Delegates in the act of making a fool of himself."

I say "Did he really expect to get away with that act?"

"Course he did. It wasn't really a bad performance. If you'd only heard it, the way he intended, it probably wouldn't have occurred to you that it was a fake . . . He had a note in his pocket asking him to come to Room VII F 39 to learn who sabotaged that Unit, *before* making his speech. Thought of everything, he did. Except that we'd follow him by camera the whole way . . . The Minister took personal charge of that tape."

I say "But you kept a copy, surely?"

"What for? To cheer my old age?" Captain Franklin leans back and sighs. "Sure I kept one, but Space knows why. Maybe I'll wipe it after he's gone."

Junior is furious. "*I* witnessed everything. Nobody is going to silence *me*."

"Uh-huh. You won't get to talk to anybody, son. You're going home too."

"Who says I am?"

"Your uncle. First deal Tollinder cooked up was with him."

Junior turns clay-colored. "But that means I'll be on the same ship with that man. I won't travel with him. *I will not*. If—if they make me I'll tell everybody on board what he did."

"Then he'll make a fool of you some way. Man's a politician. Convincing people is his trade, and he's good at it. That's because he believes it himself—not the words, but the doctrine behind them."

"Doctrine? What do you mean?"

"*His* doctrine. What's good for Randolph Tollinder is good for Mankind."

There has been a Thought struggling at the back of my head for some minutes; now it suddenly pushes to the front and I say "It wasn't good for me."

They both turn and stare.

Captain Franklin says, "You don't look at it in the right way, Miss Lee."

Hell, do I want to do this? It is not *my* job to keep Politicians honest, either: unless it is Everybody's, maybe.

Tolly was kind to me and I liked him, and I don't suppose he *meant* Fitzroy to have a Heart Attack; he may not have known he was an EF when he picked him as a Tool . . .

But there is Junior. It is very Bad for the young to see their elders Getting Away With It and the people who ought to prevent it just Sitting Back; they have to get cynical some time but it Warps you to do it too soon.

I say "Tollinder got me stuck here when I wanted to go back to my Hotel. He caused me to be drugged and confined and Suspected by the Police. Those were offenses against me personally and I ought to be able to Sue him."

Captain Franklin gazes at me with wide-eyed wonder that changes to Hope, then back to Resignation.

"Stars, what a thought. Sue him, in the Piepowder Court. The *Lunar Times* would print *that*. Straight Court reporting, the Minister couldn't do a thing. And once it's in print . . ." He stops and sighs. "A lovely thought, Miss Lee, but it can't be done. What the *Handbook* doesn't tell you is that before the Bailiffs move they calculate the possible cost to the plaintiff if the case is lost; replacement tickets for defendant and witnesses, hotel bills, legal costs . . . on this case it could come to Cr. 10,000 you'd have to make available in escrow . . ."

I say My father has Cr. 500,000 in the Bank of Terra and I am empowered to draw up to Half of it.

Junior gives a sort of whistling gasp: Captain Franklin allows his Jaw to drop slowly until it touches his collar bone, then snaps it shut and reaches for the communicator.

"Well, it's a nice dream, let's stay with it for a little . . . Annie? Get me whoever is Consul for Excenus 23."

I doubt whether there is such a person, but Captain Franklin says Every planet with Pop. more than 2 has a Consul on the Moon, turns out he is right.

What is more the Consul is an Acquaintance, the fluffy lady from the Royal Cynthia Hotel.

She is surprised I am surprised and says Travel Agents always send Excenan citizens to her for that reason, she is Consul for half a dozen other Planets too; she then listens to a Summary of the situation, writes down the Relevant details including the number of Dad's bank account, and rings off after telling me to get a good night's rest.

There is a good deal to arrange first, but in the end I do.

Next morning is distinguished by an air of Total Unreality: Quarantine does not end till after Lunch and the morning is spent in elaborate personal Decontamination: Hair, Skin, Clothes, also Baggage which was collected from our respective Hotels and delivered here the day after the Emergency started. I don't believe any of it really happened nor do I believe it is ever going to Stop.

However I do eventually find myself on the Train. Junior is sitting two rows forward with his Uncle and Tolly four rows behind me but I have no urge to speak to either; or to read, watch stereo listen to music or even Think; but at very long last the journey wends to a conclusion, the train stops and we all pile Out of it.

Reality now appears in the shape of three men in crimson long-johns with a gold stripe down the sides, and flat circular black hats; the Leader who is carrying a clipboard makes straight for me and I sign a post-dated escrow check for Cr. 10,000. He turns and signals and one of the others approaches Tolly and hands him a summons to appear in the Piepowder Court, the third Bailiff is busy subpoenaing Witnesses.

Proceedings are interrupted by a Scream I have heard before: the Minister for ExtraSolar Affairs has come to greet the returning Delegates and one of the Bailiffs takes the opportunity to Subpoena him.

Tolly has his back to me and I do not get to hear or see his reaction because the Minister's is to charge straight across at me with the Subpoena in his hand.

"You. Young woman. Miss Lee. You can't do this. It's a misuse of the Court. Plain malice. I won't permit it. Intolerable! You must withdraw it at once. Do you hear me? At once!"

A very small very dry very ancient voice makes itself heard through the Uproar.

"I must ask that all communications to my Client be made through me."

The Lawyer whom the Excenus Consul found for me retired from active practice about 40 years ago and the Piepowder Court has been in existence for 2, but he proceeds to quote verbatim from the Act establishing it until the Minister exclaims "Not here! Let's go somewhere private, for heaven's sake!"

Where we end is some sort of Office not far away. The Minister has given up Blustering and demands to see my Passport.

Having got it he says in disbelieving accents "You are nineteen standard years old?"

The Lawyer says "Legally adult. Old enough to bring the action in her own name."

"But legally in tutelage as a Student." The Minister picks up the communicator and demands to be connected with Professor M'Clare.

Unwillingly to Earth

I don't know where on Earth they eventually find him except in a Time Zone where it is evidently Night. M'Clare is in a dressing gown and his hair is ruffled.

The Minister apologizes for disturbing him at this hour, but a young woman who is apparently his Ward is insisting on a Course of Conduct which will embarrass a Distinguished Guest of the Lunar Gov, will he please tell me to Stop.

M'Clare says "May I speak to her, please?"

The Minister says he would just like a minute to Explain—I stick my head under his arm close to the visual pickup and say Hello.

There is that three seconds of No reaction you are warned about but it is still Disconcerting; then he says "Hallo, Lizzie. Who are you persecuting, and why?"

I tell him . . . At the end is the Three seconds silence, then M'Clare's expression changes from Listening to Thought.

He says, "Lizzie, are you enjoying this?"

I say it is very nearly the nastiest job I ever undertook in my entire Life.

He says, "As your guardian I can legally forbid you to continue."

I say "Damn it, I am not looking for an Out! It is something that must be done."

He says, "Well, your methods seem ingenious. I'm not sure how foolproof they are. I'll give it some thought. When does this case come on?"

I say Next morning at 09:00: Tolly is not planning to leave till the following day so there is no point in having a session tonight.

He says "Yes. Right. Try to get back before the Semester starts, won't you? I'll see you then."

At this point the Minister seizes the communicator, demanding that M'Clare act like a Responsible Guardian and make me Stop, but he is too late: M'Clare has switched off.

It has been arranged I am to sleep at the Lawyer's Hotel for convenience in conferring with him. We confer. The Lawyer is not happy about such an important part of the Material evidence having been entrusted to so young a person.

I say Junior is very Reliable for his age.

"Yes. Quite. But he will have to be very careful with his words in order to convey the right impression without committing perjury, or involving this policeman whom you say you have undertaken to protect."

What Junior has charge of is a Camera, fifth-hand, purchased by me from Captain Franklin's son and sold to Junior for Cr. 0.1 so that he can truthfully say he Owns the thing. He can also truthfully say he took the Tape contained; it was his finger on the button. The lens was aimed at a screen showing the session in the Immunization Bay, including closeups of the screen with Tolly's performance as a Self-Strangler and his arrival between two Policemen; the tape has been intercut with scenes Recorded but not transmitted to Lunarburg, such as the row of pressure-suited Policemen round the walls, so as to look as though he took it while the Session was on.

Tolly may Suspect its origin but it will do him no good to say This is not an amateur stereo but an illicit copy of the official Police tape; Captain Franklin seems fairly sure he can get away with it.

I also have a tape of Clarence's Remarks played onto the Notes section of my Reading Machine.

Finally the Lawyer is satisfied that he has covered all the arrangements and allows me to go to Bed.

The Piepowder Court is held in an ordinary Lunar room, cut square not tubular, with benches for Spectators and the Press. There are chairs at the far end for the Principals and the Lawyer and I make our way to them. I see Junior on the front bench looking Tense but Determined and the Senator next to him.

Court should open in five minutes but does Not.

Presently the Lawyer whispers to me "The Minister should be here. He can't afford to be seen neglecting his obligations as a citizen. I don't like this."

However after about ten minutes a door slides open behind the Judge's chair and In comes a man in gray with purple braid, followed by the Minister and Tolly and a fat man with Lawyer written all over him, the last three go to the chairs opposite ours and sit down.

A red-and-gold Bailiff steps up and announces The court is now in session to hear and judge the complaint of Miss L. Lee, Excenus 23, against Randolph Tollinder, Discus, both being Transients.

Tolly's lawyer immediately stands up.

"Your Honor, this case arrises out of the recent Emergency at Labsville, in which the plaintiff and my Client were both involved. *Innocently* involved. The plaintiff claims that she suffered inconvenience and unpleasantness, and my client concedes this. She has made the further claim that this was caused by the action of my client, and this he emphatically denies. However in view of the weighty and urgent affairs that have brought him to Luna he does not wish to expend his own time, or take up the time of this Court, by arguing the matter. He has therefore paid into Court the very considerable sum of Cr. 20,000 to cover all possible claims on Miss Lee's behalf. May I say, Your Honor, that the time involved was only three days and the inconveniences suffered by the young lady were not of a nature to cause lasting harm. Therefore this is a generous settlement. In return, we ask that the young lady be enjoined against making public statements which might be injurious to my client's reputation."

My Lawyer says softly "Damn. I was afraid of this."

I whisper "I don't have to accept."

"Oh, yes, you do," he whispers back. "This court was designed for the financial settlement of personal grievances, not for the exposure of political corruption. If you try to pursue this further the Judge will rule you out of order and have you restrained. I hoped Tollinder would not be able to get hold of a sufficient sum in the time available, but—" He shrugs.

Two minutes later he has accepted a draft from Tolly's lawyer on my behalf.

Tolly has bounded back on top of the World and is looking More than Life Size: his voice rings out from the far side of the Court: "M'dear fella, I don't grudge it to her, she really did have a nasty time and no doubt she needs the Money—"

He and the Minister and his Lawyer are processing towards the door: it opens just ahead of them and a Bailiff in gold and scarlet and black is standing just beyond.

He hands Tolly a paper and begins "Randolph Tollinder, you are summoned to appear at the Piepowder Court today at the hour of 15:00 to answer the complaint of the New League of Delos, to wit, that you did unlawfully cause one Derek Fitzroy to be procured and suborned to damage and destroy an Antibody Production Unit at Labsville, said Unit being the lawful property of the New League of Delos. Plaintiffs ask for Actual Punitive and Exemplary Damages in the sum of Cr. 500,000."

The Judge has leaped to his feet as suddenly as a Tourist just off the Lift and is hanging on to the edge of the Table to anchor himself while crying "What? What? What?" One of the Bailiffs is approaching me, my Lawyer is murmuring "Beautiful. Beautiful!" Junior has been stopped by another Bailiff and looks totally Bewildered. What the hell is the New League of Delos anyway?

Then I remember.

Unwillingly to Earth

When all the Planets got together to fund Reserve Antibody Production they did not want to call themselves Association of 423 Planets or whatever; about 4000 years ago Delos was a Sacred Place where sickness and death were Not Allowed and there was a League of it then, so this was the name they picked.

A tall dark distinguished man who is Lawyer for the New League of Delos steps forward and tells the Judge that the Local Police Chief at Labsville has been Subpoenaed and should be here by 15:00; it is understood that he has handed certain records to the Minister for Extra-Solar Affairs (here the Bailiff hands a subpoena to the Minister who looks fit to combust) so as the Defendant has presumably got his case together already there seems no reason for Delay after the Policeman arrives.

The Senator does not object when it is suggested that Junior, who is now looking Totally Confused, should wait with me at the Lawyer's Hotel till the next hearing starts. On the way the Lawyer explains matters to Junior in a long dry quiet soothing statement that reduces it all to something that happened a long Historical time ago, maybe History has its uses after all.

He says The New League of Delos has been inactive for many years since there was nothing much for it to do, but it still has Representatives and all the Political Pull it could possibly require. Junior then asks a question I have been Pondering: "How did they know what Tolly did at Labsville? Who tipped them off?"

The Lawyer coughs. "I have no information on that score."

Nor have I but I can guess: M'Clare.

This Hotel is the sort that gets the *Lunar Times* in Printout as well as Spool; Junior and I are given a stack of them and left in the Lounge. Presently I mutter to Junior that I was not just trying to get Tolly's money, anybody can have that money, I will give it Back: the point was—

Junior says "Yes, I know. You were using the Legal Machinery available and so was he. I quite understand."

Later I ask if his Uncle is very angry at having his deal with Tolly upset. I suppose now it has fallen through?

Junior puts down his paper and says earnestly "Lizzie, my Uncle hates corruption. But one of his constituents who's in interstellar trade has got into trouble on Discus over Import rules and Mr. Tollinder could have been a big help. Uncle says he has a Duty to help his own people any way he can and the Linder Valley is none of his business—"

I say Okay, okay, I quite Understand too.

Nothing else happens till Lunch; after that we go back to the Lounge and wait some more. I wonder what Tolly is doing now.

Then somebody comes in and walks straight towards us, a stocky man with nothing in particular in the way of Face but vaguely familiar; then I realize that when I saw him before it was under Glass.

Captain Franklin in fact.

Not in uniform, he traveled in tunic and trousers like anyone else but will change before the Hearing I suppose—

He stops in front of us and says "Well, it's all over. You can go home."

Junior says "What?" and I say The Hearing is not due to start for an hour yet.

The Captain says "No Hearing. Tollinder's dead."

There is a sort of wordless noise from Junior at the same moment I say "How?"

"Cyanide. Pinched it from one of our labs, I suppose; just in case."

I can feel the Shock right down in my guts but somehow

I am not surprised. I could not imagine Tolly going back to Discus in disgrace and I suppose neither could he.

Captain Franklin sits down opposite Junior and me and says "There's a proverb in one of the old languages—Spanish, I think—that says 'Take what you want and pay for it, says God.' Tollinder took, all right—according to his secretary, Lamartine Minerals paid off debts of nearly Cr. 1,000,000 for him—and then tried to get out of paying. You could say he's bilked his creditors one last time, or you could say he's finally met the bill: either way, it was his choice. Don't let it ride you . . . Miss Lee, you're booked on the Lift at 18:00. Your Lawyer felt you wouldn't want to hang around. Mr. Gassett-Low, I believe you're going home tomorrow. You'll both be back, I expect. Everybody but a born ground-hugger goes through the Moon once in a while . . . If you ever need anything, get in touch."

I have some Tidying-up to do and make the Lift with only fifteen minutes to spare and find a Surprising number of people seeing me off. The Lawyer shakes hands—he is going to take his fee out of the Cr. 20,000 and split the rest between Clarence and Fitzroy when they are ready to leave—but the Consul for Excenus 23 kisses me and so to my surprise does Captain Franklin. (I asked the Lawyer if he was liable to lose his job for disobeying the orders of the Minister of ExtraSolar Affairs and was told that the Minister was more liable to lose *his*, as things turned out.) For a moment I think Junior is going to kiss me too but he loses his Nerve and just asks for my address. There are also several people from the Five Planets Conference but I am not sure whether they are Seeing me Off or just making certain I actually Go.

In the Lift I don't feel good.
It is not that I think I have done the Wrong thing, but I

wish Tolly had been a Repulsive character with eyes too close together and a Reptilian coldness of disposition, instead of somebody who took the trouble to be Nice to me when he didn't have to. Of course if Politicians do not want to be held Accountable they should stay out of the Kitchen and of course if you find one has done something—not necessarily Absolutely Evil but Wicked or just very Bad—you should Take Steps about it if it so happens you can, but it must be a lot easier afterwards if you could count them Inhuman instead of All too much so.

This reminds me of my Essay which in a way was the Start of the whole thing. I get it out and read it through and conclude whether Right or not it will just have to do. I cobble an Ending onto it.

Meanwhile Weight has been going up in graduated stages, am I really as heavy as this? however I am more or less used to it by the time we land.

There is Nowhere else I want to go so I return to Russett a day early.

Hardly anyone seems to be around. B has not arrived of course and neither have the rest of my class. M'Clare is still wherever he went and so are most of the other Instructors, however I learn Priority Catford is on campus so I stick my Essay in her pigeonhole. At least I did *one* thing I intended to do.

All the same I don't know why people go on Vacations, I wish I'd stayed home.

Since I have nothing else to do I decide to make a start on the Reading Lists for the next semester. They are on my desk and I take one over to the Library console.

There is a spool in the receiver already. Can B be here after all—? No, the label is coded to me.

My portable Reading Machine was waiting for me at the Lift Terminal and I picked it up (I gave my Lunar one to the fluffy lady to be given to a Deserving Cause) so I drop the spool in.

Title: *Mask and Truth: an Examination of Fictional Themes of the Twentieth Century in Relation to Contemporary Thought and Experience* by Cecil Cudfield.

I switch to the Index and see it includes the Topics of at least eight people's Vacation Projects: one chapter is called "Evil, Horror and Alienation" and when I skim through there is the Argument of my essay with lots of Historical tie-ups I never thought of and plenty of examples, some of them better than mine.

But if it has all been written already Why tell me to do it again? it does not make Sense.

To Hell with Education.

Part Three:
FATAL STATISTICS

I WISH SOMEBODY WOULD TELL ME WHAT THE HELL IS GO-ing on.

Seeing the one and only reason why *Cutty Sark 527* has gone into orbit around Figueroa is to land me so I can start on my Field Work, and

Seeing M'Clare arranged it through Influence with the Directors of the Frontier Line and it adds 2 days to the journey and Captain Maddock is fit to be tied, and

Seeing I was instructed a couple of hours ago to get my bags packed and my goodbyes said ready to jump into the Lander the minute we returned to phase,

Why am I still sitting here, although this Superannuated space scow dropped out of hyperspace fifty minutes ago?

The Captain is *not* maneuvering for landing, because *Cutty Sark* has been in synchronous orbit over the Space Field since five minutes after dropout. I can see the Field on the repeater screen they have given me; a plain whitish ragged-edged patch like they all are except on the half-dozen oldest planets of Civilization . . .

This reminds me that three out of the five Reports on Figueroa which formed the main part of my briefing started off something like *Figueroa's current problems are illustrated even before landing by the first view of the Space Field*; I don't see what they mean by that, it looks pretty much like the Field at Home.

Then I remember that my home planet Excenus 23 has Pop. 3,500 or thereabouts, whereas the last best guess at Figueroa's was 3,500,000; not yet self-sufficient for anything except basic foods, they must have at least ten times as much traffic; Where does it all go?

I am distracted from this question by the observation that the Captain is getting some sort of Bad News over the Intercom, complicated by Custard Dawes who is acting out his Anxiety Complex into the other ear.

I spend perhaps thirty seconds wondering what Custard is Disturbed about *this* time and then go back to the Repeater screen.

The controls on this cannot change what the big scope in *Cutty Sark*'s belly is actually looking at, of course, but I can call up some magnification; I enlarge the view of the Space Field until it starts to fuzz up and begin looking for Clues.

Now I can just see a regular pattern of Marks which must be the Landing-and-Launching pylons and their shadows . . . There are twelve in the pattern, four sideways by three down; (Excenus Field has two rows of five) . . . There seems to be bare ground around the Field, very dark . . . Then suddenly a Pattern jumps out at me; not a new one but the pattern of the pylons, the same spacing exactly continued on into the Dark. Shadows do not show on this ground, but there are the pylons themselves like little straight silvery dashes, rows and files of them extending practically forever . . . well, nearly up to the top of the screen at this magnification . . . and up at the very top are big sharp-edged shapes, oblongs and Ls with something rounded in the middle . . .

I call to mind a picture of the Space Gate, Figueroa, from the earliest of the Reports, which still had a good deal in it about *This rapidly developing new member of the Community of Planets*; Yes it could be: Yes it certainly is, I remember the Rotunda in the middle . . . The Dark stuff is almost up to those buildings; What the hell has been *happening* to this planet?

Not an outflow of lava, I don't think, the pylons would have Melted . . . anyway it would not have stopped like this at a square Perimeter with the Space Field or part of it untouched in the middle . . . but *something* has certainly engulfed a lot of the landscape—

"If I may have your attention, Miss Lee—!"

Great Godalmighty . . . I hurriedly haul myself back into my Skin and give my attention to the Captain; he evidently reverts to being an Authority Figure when Disturbed, seeing he started calling me Lizzie more than two weeks ago.

He says "Did you come across any mention of Figueroa's Ionosphere while you were doing your homework, Miss Lee?"

This is Not what I expected; after a second or two for adjustment I come up with a possible answer: "Hyperactive, isn't it?"

"Exactly," says the Captain, and gets stuck.

I say "Are you having trouble getting in touch with my friends down there?"

Which Ought not to be the case; I now remember that Figueroa's Space Gate has an extra-heavy-duty transmitter punching signals through the Ionized layer and a Relay satellite beyond to unscramble Interference.

The Captain says "Trouble!" and pushes his hand through his hair to Illustrate; then he remembers this is not Captain-like behavior and hurriedly smooths it down again.

"Look, Lizzie—" I think the change in approach is Diplomacy not Forgetting—"something's wrong down there. Very wrong. Old Sparks has been trying to get an answer from the Gate ever since we came out of phase, but not a whisper. Not even a carrier beam, the transmitter's dead."

I think carefully how to put it and then say "Did you have any luck on Laydon's call number?"

Captain Maddock does something funny to his Mouth, not exactly a snarl or even a Pout . . .

"We tried that, of course . . . In fact Sparks put out a call on automatic repeat. He did get something, once. Solar wind let up for a minute or two, a few words came through. Pretty garbled, at that."

I say "But Laydon's still on the planet?"

"Someone answered on that wavelength, yes."

So at least my friend B Laydon's elder brother has not been Swallowed up without a trace . . . I say "So how soon can I get down?"

The Captain heaves a great Sigh and drops on to the seat opposite.

"Look, Miss Lee . . . Lizzie. We don't know what's happened on Figueroa. The latest news I have of the place is nine months old. Place was no worse than usual then. But something's wrong now—badly wrong . . . Planet's been going downhill for years, looks as though it's *gone* . . . Better come on with us to New Peru and fix up a passage back to Terra from there."

And spend God knows how long planet-hopping—no shipmaster goes straight from the Outer Reaches to Terra—while *Pedagogue* lands on Figueroa 4 weeks from now and picks up Douglas Laydon and the others and takes them back to Russett College to report No Lizzie Lee . . .

Like Hell I will.

The Captain says persuasively "We can get a message

to Laydon—our transmitter punches through the ionosphere clean as a laser. It's just that *his* transmitter hasn't enough power when it comes to replying. He'll tell your Professor what happened when he gets picked up."

Tell M'Clare I came out here, five weeks' travel, and then hadn't the guts to do my Field Work after all? No way!

Everything went wrong with my Field Work right from the start—or before it; two days before I was due to take ship, I broke my wrist. I could have perfectly well finished the Forceheal treatment on board ship, but M'Clare said No; the first twenty-four hours of any voyage are spent in Free fall while getting far enough away from the Solar system to go out of phase; Bones need Gravity to knit properly and I am *not* going to return you to your Father with a crooked arm, nor do I propose to let you waste time next semester going back to the Hospital to have it broken and re-set, Stop arguing with me, Lizzie! and try telling me how you *really* came to break it, instead.

I did it Fooling about on antigrav, which is strictly forbidden and I ought to have had more sense. I changed the Subject; but I was still not allowed to go.

So *Pedagogue*, which was taking the Field Study party to Figueroa, went without me and I had to proceed by Commercial carriers with two changes on the way, arriving nearly a month after everybody else.

I spent most of the time *en route* studying up on Figueroa but it looks as though my Information is out of date.

Not that I expected to find the place in good shape. It has notoriously been going downhill for years, but fairly slowly; so far the Sponsoring planets have always been able to claim there was Light around the corner, Immigration/Emigration about to stop being too fast/too slow and Production becoming greater/more varied/better balanced, nobody really believed that sort of thing but it would have been a worse sign if it had Stopped.

Something has definitely Stopped now.

However if Douglas Laydon can survive down there sufficiently to answer radio calls, then So can I; Captain Maddock finally gives up arguing and accepts that this is the case.

I then discover why Custard Dawes is in more than his customary State of perturbation; it is his turn to operate the Lander and the Captain refuses to let him off.

Poor Custard confides in me on the way down that he could have got someone else to do it for a quite trifling sum, if he had been allowed to. Actually this rule was made in the first place because taking down the Lander is one of the jobs the crew usually *want* to do; it is a bit ironic that Custard is Stuck with it now. He spends the first half of the descent trying to convince me we had better both turn Back to the ship.

He spends the second half grumbling, while I alternate between trying to raise Doug Laydon personally and keeping an eye on the screen. I don't have any luck with the radio but *Cutty Sark*'s Communications Officer is putting out a continuous message telling Doug where and when to pick me up—Talking of which, Custard is making for the whitish area not engulfed in whatever has overrun the rest of the Space Field and I remind him that Captain Maddock said we should land North of the Space Gate, off the Field itself, because the dark stuff has covered the access roads and if it is something Impassable Doug may not be able to bring his Transport to pick me up.

Custard does not like this reminder. Custard does not like anything about this trip, but if he has any reasonable reason for objecting to the chosen spot he is not going to explain it; I insist on sticking to Plan.

During the last half-kilometer of the Descent I discover what the dark stuff is on the Space Field.

Unwillingly to Earth

Huts. Or, seen from space, *roofs*; thousands and thousands of them, made of sheet-plastic and sheet-metal and old doors and planks nailed side by side. They are mostly dark, but as we get lower I can see light-colored bits here and there, also assorted Shadowed interiors where the roofs have fallen in.

No people in sight, whoever put the huts there have Gone.

Custard finally consents to land in the place Captain Maddock told him to, which is presumably where Doug Laydon will come to find me. I am not going to tell him, but the sight of those acres of empty huts has Shaken me quite a bit and I wish very much I could call Doug to confirm that he is coming, but all I get out of the radio is Noise.

I request Custard to Open up so I can get out and take a look around.

His reply is something like as follows: "Look, Lizzie, I mean Miss Lee, I mean, this place is *bad news*, that's what it is, why don't you just sit where you are and let me lift you back to the ship?"

I have learned over the last three weeks that it is absolutely No use getting cross with Custard, but I do. The fact is, this Landscape is getting on my nerves and for one craven moment I was tempted to follow his suggestion and go back to the ship.

So Custard's feelings get hurt and when he finally operates the switch to open the door he is gazing Straight ahead so as Not to have to pick me up if I catch my foot in the doorsill and fall on my nose, I suppose this also avoids Disappointment when I don't.

Outside, it is nearly noon of a really beautiful day. I have stepped out onto well-shaved bright green lawn edged with flower beds; was all that Desolation seen from orbit some kind of Delusion? then Common sense comes back and I turn my head.

Getting out of the Lander I was facing *behind* it; when I look towards its nose there are the Ruin and Desolation as before.

Worse, because now I can Smell it as well.

I got taken to see the remains of a Forest fire once, part of my Orientation; it had been put out by rain (one of the things for which Terrans *do* use Weather satellites) and smelled just like this.

Figueroa has large forests, it says in the Reports; for a moment I think one of them must have Burned, then I remember that they have been Extensively cut down for building; in fact, what I am smelling is burned Hut.

So that is what made the Dark patch.

Just as I grasp this, Custard lets out a Yell.

"Lizzie! Get back in here! Lizzie! *Now!*"

I look quickly into the Lander but nothing is Biting him that I can see; I take a couple of steps toward the rear of the Lander, meaning to see What if anything is on the other side, and something hits me in the small of the back and knocks me flat. Then there is the *whoosh!* of the doors closing, and when I roll over the Lander is six feet up and retreating rapidly into the sky.

In the Course of my life I have learned a number of Words for situations like this and people like Custard but none of them seems adequate. I just sit up, feeling a bit dizzy, and look to see what Hit me.

It was my baggage. I expected to be six months on this trip and therefore brought nearly 7kg of clothes and stuff; it is now Lying on the grass at my feet.

Thank goodness my Reading machine was fastened to my belt instead. Then I look further and see what frightened Custard into hysterics.

* * *

Unwillingly to Earth

People. Just people, about six of them . . . No, more bob up out of the flower beds or somewhere; ten. Or twelve. Probably sixteen . . . To hell with counting. They are various shades of Dark, some as black as my friend Likofo Komom'baraze, others more like Maui Smith.

Anyway they all look perfectly harmless. Only a bit odd. They are dressed mostly in bits of cloth wrapped round them and tied; and not much above the waist, except one old lady who is wearing what looks like a Uniform jacket six sizes too big.

Then I see that Two or three of the Recent arrivals have long shafts with metal bits at the top, and one has a knife about two feet long.

On the other hand at least half of them are half-size or less; two of them on all fours. And the one with the knife has been chopping down bushes; there is a pile of them on a flower bed nearby—

One of them steps forward; the old lady. She only comes a couple of paces, then calls to me "Young lady! You take that radio, tell that man make he come *back* here! This planet is a *bad* place to be!"

That was what Custard said.

The rest are all making sounds and Signs of agreement; the ones with the long sticks thump them on the ground. The small ones look solemn . . . I do not think I am going to make any impression on Custard even if my Wrist radio can get through, but the advice seems well-meant and I do not wish to be Uncooperative, so I set it to the Lander's call frequency and try.

After six tries and Silence except for static I try Doug Laydon instead; this time I think I get an answer, at least the interference noises at one point sound rather like *Lizzie*, but I can't be sure.

By this time the people have come closer and I decide to stand up. It is Odd to find myself looking down on half a dozen heads; being 5 ft. 1 in. I don't think I ever before found myself partly surrounded by People shorter than me.

The old lady addresses me again. "That man is a *bad* man!" she says.

The rest shake their heads and agree. I know Custard is not really a bad man, but so far as the present situation goes he might just as well be; I shake my head too.

The old lady says, practically, "What you go do?"

I explain that I have some friends on the planet who are going to pick me up any minute now; evidently they are all Doubtful of this, but polite.

I say "What has Happened to this place?"

They all look round, rather as though they never saw it before.

I look round too. At second glance, the big buildings of the Space Gate are showing signs of battery as well as wear. Several of the big windows are starred here and there and one has a crack right across. There are gaping holes where the doors used to be; through them I can see stumps where the counters in the foyer have been broken off, and if there were chairs, they have gone.

The grass is probably taken care of by some sort of automaton; but not the flower beds, I now see that the ones that still have flowers also have Weeds. The nearer ones have been dug up and planted with Green things in orderly rows, like crops.

I am about to ask whether they all Live on this spot and if so, *why*, when my radio suddenly springs to life.

"Get ready to jump, Lizzie! Here we come!"

This is said in my Earpiece; I guess the old lady has one too, relayed to by a broad-tuner somewhere, because she Jumps and says something startled to the others and they start to back away from me. Which is Just as well, because a few seconds later there is a suddenly-approaching Whizzz! and here comes a Floater a lot faster than is safe in these surroundings. It seems to be heading straight for me, then swings sideways at the last minute as someone leans over the side and makes a Grab for my hand.

I Jump as instructed and get hauled aboard, landing on the floor of its tray-like back end, in an Undignified Huddle with the Astral Cad.

A. C. Van Hatton is not a person I would choose to be Tangled with if my Preference had been consulted; I Sort myself out with more Haste than Care and lean over the side to wave Goodbye to my recent acquaintances. Some of the grownups look as though they are in two minds about Shaking their fists, but several of the children wave back.

The Vehicle is swinging round in a half-controlled halfcircle that brushes its underside against the remains of several Huts. It then starts streaking down a broad highway between Trees, most of which have had branches untidily lopped off. I cling to the side and yell "Why the hell did you do that?"

The Astral Cad raises a long thin hand, hooks it over the side of the Tray and languidly hauls himself sitting up.

"Lizzie, my sweet," he replies, "why the hell didn't *you* do as you were told?"

I reply that I was Told to come to Figueroa to do my Fieldwork and that's what I have done.

"I am referring, my poppet, as you very well know, to the message sent by Our Gallant Leader to *Cutty Sark*, telling you *not* on any account to land."

Oh.

I say, "The ionosphere is acting up. The only message we got was too garbled to read, except for a few words. It showed Laydon was still here and that was all."

This is Perfectly true, if it sounds unconvincing it is because since landing I have Deduced that the message probably said something of that sort.

"Well," says the Astral Cad, "that's your story and no doubt you'll be sticking to it. Hold tight!"

The Vehicle suddenly does a 95° turn down what I suppose is a Side street. It is lined with skeletons of houses, made of wood. I mean the Skeletons are made of wood and probably the houses were wood throughout; tag-ends still attached to the upstanding members indicate that the spaces were filled with Wooden planks. All the doorways are gaping empty; I suppose this is where the materials for all those Huts came from; but What has been going on?

I say "What *happened* to this planet, forgodsake?"

The Astral Cad might or might not have been too Tired to answer, but the vehicle goes into a series of loops and twists around and between Houses that threatens to throw both of us in a tangle again and puts a Stop to conversation.

Evidently we are Dodging something, but *what*?

The Alternation of straight spurts and bouts of twisting goes on for some minutes, taking us beyond the area of houses; then we turn up some sort of Forest path and go hellforleather a couple of minutes far too close to a lot of trees. Then a row of Dilapidated houses appears and the vehicle hurtles straight at the near end and dives in.

I mean the End wall shoots upwards, leaving a gap, and a moment later we have stopped dead inside. The wall drops rapidly but quietly behind us and apparently we have Arrived.

"Welcome to the Hulk," says the Astral Cad.

I look round the space enclosing us and say *"This is a Ship!"*

The walls are Gray-painted metal with ridges of welding and curve up into the Roof without a break.

"Top marks, poppet," says the Cad. "It stopped going places yea these many years ago, but it *is* a ship."

Unwillingly to Earth

"It *used* to be," says the driver of the Vehicle, climbing out of it.

Just as I suspected, it is Blazer Weigh.

When I first saw the Astral Cad I thought he was an Absolutely Typical Terrie, bored at ten, cynical at six and *born* looking down his nose; then I discovered his family had been on Alpha Centauri 9 for seven generations.

Some time in the next semester I heard M'Clare say, "If a person, or an institution, seems to be absolutely typical of a particular planet, or nation, or group, then he, she or it is probably a fake. Or, to put it more charitably, aware of the stereotype and self-designed to match."

A. C. Van Hatton has deliberately Designed himself to match an Outsider's Stereotype of a Terrie, you could hardly be more Peculiar than that.

(Actually I have yet to meet a genuine Terrie, on Terra, who is even a half-way match for the Type; the ones who go *off* Terra are probably the Originals for it)

Blazer Weigh, on the other hand, has deliberately Designed himself as a match for the Astral Cad; somehow this is Obvious although the final Result has little if any resemblance. I mean the Astral Cad talks all the time and believes himself to be witty, Blazer hardly opens his mouth and is Visibly under no delusion as to what comes out of it.

All the time, though, you can see poor old Blazer trying to be as Arrogant Blasé Callous Decadent Enervated and Etc. as his Model and Chum, and not coming within a Mile of it.

But Where the Cad goeth there is Blazer, and when Priority Catford gave out the Assignments for Field Study she seems to have decided Not to fight it; here they both are.

"I stand corrected," says the Cad, giving his Friend and admirer a weary look. "This *used* to be a ship."

Well I have seen disused Spaceships converted into Dwellings before now, there are several on Excenus 23 providing accommodation at Outlying mining areas. There are obvious advantages to it, you get a Weather-tight shelter with all necessary Life-support such as water recycling, sewage disposal, air regeneration, and so on. I can see it being Particularly useful under circumstances like now, since you can Hole Up inside and completely avoid whatever is wrong with the Environment.

But I *don't* understand how it got *here*. Russett has only been using Figueroa for Fieldwork for about three years. How was the Ship put in place and camouflaged, within a quarter of a mile of a fairly large town, without the Inhabitants being aware of it?

I presume they weren't because I don't see the point of the Camouflage if they were.

I climb over the side of the Tray and drop to the ground, taking my baggage with me; Blazer makes Half a movement to take it over but I hang on. Then a door irises open at the far end of the Hangar and Doug Laydon walks in.

This Brother of my friend and roommate B was a Third Year student when I first arrived at Russett and therefore Graduated just over a year ago; he has been doing Postgraduate work on Figueroa for nine months.

The Astral Cad droops over the side of the Tray and says languidly "Here she is, Laydon. Your message forbidding her to land got garbled. So she says."

"Since you went to fetch her, we've had signals from *Cutty Sark* saying the same thing," says Laydon. "They only got an occasional word of ours."

He sounds calm, courteous, efficient and in charge. Also he *looks* ten years older than when I saw him last, and Tired to death.

I say "Doug, if it was wrong to land here I'm sorry."

He musters quite a good grin.

"It's all right, Lizzie. I'm afraid you're stuck, though.

Unwillingly to Earth

Pedagogue won't be back for four or five days. Fieldwork's off. You're going to be bored to death.''

I say "Look. Can somebody explain what the hell *happened* to this planet?"

Blazer Weigh says, "The population's been evacuated." Nobody laughs.

But—the *population*? Three and a half *million*? How? and what *for*?

Don says, "It's a long story. Come on into the living quarters and we'll try to explain."

The door through the back wall of the Hangar leads straight into a little House belonging to somebody else.

The room is Ethnic but stiff. Walls covered with sheets of wood, heavy wooden furniture with no upholstery, only cushions, and one big square dark-colored rug in the exact middle of the floor.

Then I realize it is all rather clever Camouflage; door and window are built into the open Main Hatch (but with nothing to stop it being shut in an Emergency) and the rest is just a decorated Box fitted into one compartment of the ship, so if some Official or Passerby decides to investigate this Row of houses in the middle of nowhere at least one of them will give a fairly convincing impression of being somebody's Home.

We walk straight through and out through a door on the other side and are back in the Ship.

I am offered a meal, a drink, and a Bathroom, accept the last two and after a short Interval settle down with a glass of reconstituted fruit juice to hear what Doug Laydon has to say.

At first this seems to be Nothing and I fill in by asking where Kirsten and Mishi are?

All three of the men exchange Glances and Don says heavily, "Yes. Well . . . They aren't here, Lizzie. In fact, they never landed. They went back in the *Pedagogue*."

The Astral Cad drawls "Carlotta and Mei Lin left too."

Which makes me the only Female member of the Study group left.

Doug Laydon pulls himself straighter in his seat and says "Buren and Hsuan left as well. They were injured in a riot and the medical services here were swamped—what was left of them. Van Hatton and Weigh gave up their places on the *Pedagogue* so that they could be taken for treatment."

Maybe my eyes Widen or something. He adds hurriedly "That sort of thing's all over, of course."

"Nobody left on the planet to riot," says Blazer Weigh helpfully.

I say "Forgodsake, how *could* they evacuate three and a half *million* people?"

Doug rubs a hand over his face and starts to look *twenty* years older now.

"Look, Lizzie, just listen and I'll try to explain . . . Nobody really intended to evacuate *all* the population, they just . . . Look, I'll have to start from the beginning . . ."

Figueroa is unique two ways.

One, when it was found thirty-seven Standard years ago, it was already terraformed. Theory is that one of the Generation ships built before the Breakdown found the planet and planted a complete Terraforming package, with different units designed to become effective one after another as Conditions became right for them.

Two, Figueroa is at one end of a Wormhole, one of these Structures in space that you can travel in for light-weeks and end up light-years from where you started; and the other end is quite close to not one but *three* inhabited Star systems.

Naturally a Terraformed planet belongs to the people who Terraformed it. But Who does it belong to when the

Unwillingly to Earth

people who did the work have gone over the horizon most of a millennium before?

When news of Figueroa got back to the Known volume it set off a free-for-all no one was in a position to control. Some immigrants were sound Pioneering groups. Most weren't. Some landed with just a Wad of cash and asked the way to the nearest Hotel.

Most of them came from the planets near the other end of the Wormhole: New Nassau, Rosemary, Baliloa. Soon Stories started to come back of Planetary nationals starving, farms robbed, people selling themselves into slavery for enough to eat . . . The kind of things everybody thought were Long gone from the Human scene.

The three planets sent in Aid and got things more or less straight; then they set up a Corporation to manage the place.

The Corporation did some work on finding Cash crops, exportable minerals and so on, but the Payingest line they came up with was to build houses with local Timber, bricks and tiles and sell them for the offplanet cash new residents brought along. When locally produced Food got inadequate they used some of the cash to import more.

Okay, as a System it teetered, getting nearer Ruin with every shipload of immigrants who didn't bring money (they tried to enforce a Minimum but they couldn't keep the ships long enough to send the poor ones back) and swinging Back when they got in a load of comparatively well-to-do or Cash crops had a good year. Nobody trusted it to Last forever but it was expected to hang on for some years yet, maybe till some Local group worked out something better and managed to make it Stick whatever the Corporation said. Nobody and Nothing had predicted a sudden total Catastrophe.

I say "I read the Reports up to eleven months ago."

* * *

Doug nods slowly. "It started to crack a couple of months after that. No time for the news to get back to Earth yet."

No chance for M'Clare to learn the score and Reroute us.

"The Corporation didn't do the Terraforming here," Doug says wearily. "They got it ready-made. And most of the immigrants came from planets terraformed several generations ago. They didn't know how it was done or how fragile the ecology was. So they cut forests down all round the main settlements and didn't do much to protect the exposed soil, and just after I got here we had a long drought, and forest fires, and then the winds started."

He sounds unutterably depressed about it and no wonder. "The topsoil started to blow away. A lot of crops were ruined. The planet started the winter with about half the food needed to get through it, and no cash crops to pay for imports.

"The Corporation would have had to go light-years into the red to keep things going. Instead they decided to fold . . . Rosemary sent in a team to investigate. They recommended lifting out part of the population, instead of sending in food—it actually worked out cheaper, in transportation terms.

"What they *meant* to do was to evacuate the least productive part of the population. What *happened* was that some of the people in key jobs decided the Corporation was leaving them stuck with the baby. So *they* left. Services began to break down. People panicked. They took off any way they could. Rushed freighters and wouldn't let them take off till they were packed to the bulkheads with people. Presently no independent shipmaster would land on Figueroa at all.

"People on the three planets who had relatives here started to raise a major stink. In the end the governments were just about forced to arrange a mass evacuation for those who wanted to go. You've never seen anything like the ships that put down on the Space Field; big old arks that had been mothballed in orbit for a couple of centuries, some of them. Most of the passengers traveled under narcosis, so food and water and services could be minimal. The first estimate was, they'd have to take another half million; only once again, a lot of the ablest people pulled out.

"Within three months of the first evacuations just about everything had gone heisenberg. Dominoes falling over. If people in towns wanted food they had to trek out to the country and barter for it, with whatever they'd got. There are barns out there half full of knickknacks from a dozen different planets. A lot of those farms have been deserted, now. Farmers panicked, in the end, like the others, and came pouring into town looking for a ship. They were so afraid of being left behind, they wanted to be right on the Field. Those that could, camped in the Space Gate buildings; the rest grabbed materials from anywhere they could and made huts on the Field itself.

"God, it was a mess. The sanitary facilities in the Gate buildings held up pretty well, but water was always running short. They had burial parties at first, but for the last few days if somebody died in a hut—the ships wouldn't take anyone very old or very sick—anyone else there just moved . . . After the last ship took off someone set the huts on fire; cleaning up, I suppose."

Doug closes his eyes and shakes his head violently, as though to get rid of Memories; he is looking exhausted. After a moment, however, he opens them again, and says "The last ship left about three weeks ago."

"Just after we arrived," drawls the Astral Cad. "*Pedagogue*'s skipper wouldn't land—quite rightly, she'd have been mobbed. He put us down by Lander, hard by, and Our Leader here came forth with a portable flashlight to lead us in. Fortunately, there was a code designation for this place and they both remembered it."

I say, "Yes, but where did you *get* it from? Even M'Clare couldn't get this Ship in, and hidden this close to a town, without people spotting it."

Doug says "Oh . . . Yes, of course. It was planted a long time ago, soon after colonization started. Not by Russett, of course. The Terran Bureau of Interplanetary Affairs put it in. They kept an eye on things, quietly, for a good many years; just making sure the planet didn't become a pirate's hideout or anything of that sort. Then when the Corporation took over they pulled out."

I say "Why?"

"Corporation didn't want 'em," says Blazer Weigh.

Doug starts to object; then changes his mind.

"I suppose that's true. Anyway, maintaining an Embassy when requests for information and instructions can't be answered in less than four months is a bit of a liability . . . They withdrew. Then when things really started to go sour on Figueroa they wanted a source of information, so they pressured M'Clare to set up the Study Group here. He refused point blank unless there was a safe place we could withdraw to if it all turned vicious, and they offered him this."

"Safe as houses," says Blazer Weigh.

A grounded Ship is a lot Safer than houses, of course, provided the Life Support system is intact. You could undergo Siege in one indefinitely if you were prepared to live on Recycled water and food; plenty of spacemen do, for months.

"Cheer up, Lizzie," says the Cad. "The larder's quite well stocked. We shan't be reduced to processed algae and yeast; provided *Pedagogue* keeps to her schedule, of course."

That is Not what is bothering me, and I say so.

Doug says, "The Hulk really is safe, Lizzie. Some of the characters who stayed on after the Evacuation are pretty odd, but they can't get in here."

Unwillingly to Earth

I say "Yes, but what about Fieldwork?"

Doug heaves a sigh. The Astral Cad heaves another, and gets his Remarks in first.

"Lizzie, love, are you still expecting to sally forth with your little Recorder and find a Typical Figueroan to interview? As Doug said, those that remain are thoroughly *un*typical—at any rate round here."

"You really can't expect to carry out your assignment under these conditions, I'm afraid," says Doug. "Probably all three of you will be given new ones, when you get back to Russett—unless the Assessors decide to waive that requirement."

I say "Don't try to tell me you have all stayed Cooped up in here for nearly a month."

"Not completely, of course," says Doug uneasily.

I say "Right. What have you found to do?"

They look at one another.

"It's quite true," says Doug at last, "that we've been recording certain data, which may or may not turn out to be useful in the future. But we've done nearly all that we can in that line."

"What line is it?" I inquire.

The Astral Cad takes up the thread.

"Part of the Satellite Survey system is still working—two units out of three, in fact. The relay beam's tight enough to punch through the ionosphere and so far the pickup system hasn't failed. We've been going through the recent data to locate settlements still showing signs of life. The data are all fed into computers, of course, direct from the antenna, but there's every chance of the computers' being down-powered before this planet gets back on its feet, if it ever does. So we've been getting the info into our personal recorders and onto printed maps and so on. As Doug said, we've pretty well finished. And, no, you can *not* join in."

I say Nothing, as Pointedly as I can.

"The man in charge doesn't like girls," says Blazer Weigh.

"Or to put it in his own words, the ladies are delightful in their proper place," says the Astral Cad.

"Sorry, Lizzie, but that's a fact," says Doug. "We can only get at the computers by permission of the man in charge at the Space Gate—"

I say "In *charge*?"

"Yes, well . . . the Corporation still have a lot of gear on Figueroa. I suppose it still belongs to them. Anyway they left a . . . sort of caretaker here."

I say, "All by himself?"

Doug nods.

"There is some doubt," says the Astral Cad, speaking to the far horizon, "as to the formality of the appointment."

"I've told you before," says Doug, "and I'll say it again, since you make it necessary—we've no grounds for questioning the Custodian's authority. He may have been officially put in charge and he may not. *We* weren't. He has the keys and he knows the codes to access the data. If he chose to shut us out we couldn't work at the Gate any more."

The Astral Cad performs a sort of Salute.

"As you say, worthy leader. There'll be no more to do there after tomorrow, anyway. We'll have covered the whole planet."

I say "But have the Corporation just *left* him here? How long for?"

The Astral Cad shrugs. "We haven't asked him."

"It's his own choice, Lizzie," says Doug. "If he'd chosen to pull out during the evacuation there was nobody to stop him."

Well I think it's a shame. However there is Nothing anybody can do about it at the moment, I suppose. I say "What are you going to do next?"

"Eat lunch," says the Blazer, getting to his feet. "My turn to cook."

It makes very little Difference who cooks; the food is prepared by emptying powders into the Rehydrater and setting the heating controls to match what it says on the Packet and the result is just like I have been eating on *Cutty Sark 527*. Not even the desire to keep me from asking Questions can dispose my Colleagues to Linger over the meal.

When we have put the Dishes in the cleaning slot I ask "Did you find many Settlements still active, in that Survey you did?"

Doug says, "Some."

"Most of them," says the Astral Cad, "on Continents other than this one."

I say "Independent Firsters, do you think?"

Doug takes me by the elbow and leads me to a chair, so he can Loom over me. He then makes the following Statement.

"Lizzie. I remember that your Assignment was something to do with the Firsters, but you are not, repeat *not*, going out after them."

I say "Certainly not."

Figueroa has five main land masses. When the one with the Space Field on it began to fill up the Real Pioneers mostly sold the farms they had established and used the money to move to one of the others. Some had settled there already: I suppose they were the *Original* Independent Firsters, but the name got applied to the others as well.

My Assignment was to inquire into the Knowledge Beliefs Attitudes and Opinions of other Figueroan citizens concerning the Firsters, with a view to seeing whether, *One*, Hostility towards them might lead to Trouble in the future; *Two*, their Example will be any use in trying to guide other Figueroans into making better use of the Planet.

I explain this and inquire about groups remaining on *this* continent, preferably nearby.

Doug utters a Groan.

The Cad says, "Lizzie, dear. People who chose to remain on this continent can all be classified as *Eccentric*, to say the least. Some probably did so because they had acquired or built up something they couldn't bear to abandon.

"Some, on the other hand, almost certainly took advantage of the general confusion to collect all the loot they could. Both groups are now holed up with whatever supplies and weapons they could gather, ready to beat off anyone who might try to take their possessions away from them."

"Look," I say, not bothering about tact, "is there any *evidence* that these Looters exist, or do you just think it would be Logical if they did?"

"Oh, they exist," says Doug rather grimly. "We ran into one bunch, before *Pedagogue* arrived. That was how Buren and Hsuan got hurt."

"Since then" says the Astral Cad to his fingernails, "we have approached inhabited houses, twice; and got shot at, twice. Whatever their motives, the people remaining in this area of the planet are *not* in a mood to make the acquaintance of strangers."

I say, "What about those people at the Space Field, then?"

Not having been present, Doug inquires What People and I explain. He glances at the Cad.

"New to me,' says that Individual, shrugging. "They were round on the South side, nowhere near the entrance we've been using. Nothing to show how long they'd been there."

I say, "I think they are living there now. Farming there, anyway. They had vegetables planted in the flower beds.

Unwillingly to Earth

They didn't try to scare me away. I suppose that Smash and Grab approach was in case they tried to Shoot at you; but they hadn't any guns."

"No way to tell that," says the Cad. "Lizzie, dear, that Smash and Grab approach as you put it is mandatory when picking up anybody on this planet. Not so much for fear of getting shot at as to avoid giving anyone a chance to steal the floater."

That does not seem to make sense: I say "There must be thousands of floaters around for the taking."

"No doubt; but their fuel cells are gone. After the power station was shut down, any portable power sources were cannibalized."

I say, "I would like to talk to those People again."

Doug looks as though he might start Tearing his hair, in a restrained sort of way. The Astral Cad throws his hands towards the ceiling and lets them flop.

"Lizzie, do get it into your head that M'Clare won't expect you to carry out your Assignment after all the potential subjects have gone."

This of course is perfectly True.

All the same I am damned sure M'Clare would not expect me to spend nine weeks Getting here and then spend most of a week Sitting in a contained environment making no attempt to do anything at all.

I say "You've still got some work to do with the computers at the Space Gate. Drop me wherever you go in. I'll walk round and see if those people are still there. You won't risk losing the floater any more than you'd be doing in any case."

I am *not* going to run my Life on the assumption that anyone I run into is More apt to be dangerous than not even if I am a girl.

It is a Rule that someone always stays in the Hulk and next day it is the turn of the Astral Cad. Blazer and Doug and I set out in the floater. The Route so far as I can tell is different from yesterday's and the last section goes past a sort of fenced-in Park full of enormous Machinery, draped with thick transparent plastic and looking like Ghosts of itself.

Just after this we come to a double Gate in a high concrete wall. I can see the buildings of the Space Gate sticking up behind the wall. The gate is locked.

Doug leans over from his seat and says to the gatepost "Laydon and Weigh to see the Custodian, please."

There is a sudden rasping noise and a voice says quite loudly "Laydon? Laydon, is that you?"

"Yes, sir," says Doug. He glances at me sideways and adds "Reporting for duty."

"Good . . . Check Security, Laydon. Suspicious characters. Lurking."

Doug gives a quick and Harassed glance around and says "Nobody in sight. Sir."

After which somebody steps round a nearby bush and says gently "Excuse. I have needing to speak with the In-Charge."

Two other people step round the bush after him and just Stand.

They are some of the people I met the previous day. I don't recognize them personally, but they have the same range of skin colors and the same sort of clothes.

The voice says "Laydon? Laydon! Report!"

Doug swallows and says "Yes, sir. I have to report that three visitors are asking permission to see you."

"Get rid of them," says the voice.

Doug and Blazer exchange Looks; then Blazer says in the best imitation of the Astral Cad's voice I have yet heard from him, "Should I ascertain the subject of the visit, Sir? It could be relevant."

The voice says, "If you want to come in today, come now," and something goes *click!* in the door.

Unwillingly to Earth

Blazer and Doug hold a hurried Whisperation and Doug mutters to me that I had better come with them, perhaps.

I say No, when shall I come back to meet them here?

"Three hours," says Blazer, before Doug can argue; and shoves open the two parts of the gate. The three people come out from behind the bush again, but the door opens just enough to allow the Floater inside and closes around its back end without ever leaving space for them to get through.

I say "I am sorry." Which is true, and I think the Incharge or Custodian or whatever he calls himself has lousy manners, I suppose he is afraid of Hijacking but he could at least have refused politely.

By the time I get to the place where I met the People yesterday I am good and sick of the smell of Burned wood, and I could do without setting eyes on anything Black again for a year or two, and when I find the place where the Lander flattened out the Lawn there is nobody there.

While I am wondering where to look I feel something Poke the back of my arm.

I turn fast and don't see anything for a moment; then I look down and there is one of the little People looking up at me about six feet away.

Correction, there are three of them. No, five . . .

I am just not Used to being Waist-high in human beings . . . Okay, I know about Kids, but I never met this many all at one time.

I do not know whether to Pat their heads, or what.

Seems they have their own Ideas, a couple of them get hold of each hand and start to Pull, and we all set off the way that I came.

We seem to be about to Plunge into the nearest cluster of burned-over Huts when it moves into Focus and I realize it is not Huts at all but a Ship.

* * *

I never saw anything like it, not even in a Museum, probably because it is too big; I am told later the Ground plan covers about an acre and a half, and most of it is three decks high.

The Height I suppose should have told me straight off it was not a mass of Huts, but it is black all over; anyway whatever the Reasons the fact is I didn't see it till now when it suddenly Looms above and the Shock nearly knocks me over.

There is an enormous oblong Gape in the metal wall and we have arrived in front of this. The children Swarm round me and the tallest girl calls something I don't understand; and a moment later the Elderly lady who spoke to me yesterday appears from round an outside corner and says "You are welcome."

I say "Thank you."

After this there does not seem anything else to say; I meant to start with Apologies for having been so Rudely kidnapped in the middle of a conversation but I am not sure this would be understood.

She comes to a conclusion and says "We will go on the grass." After which she proceeds towards the Lawn at a brisk toddle, calling something in the strange language as she goes.

A moment after we reach the grass the three tallest girls arrive panting, two carrying folding stools and the third a woven mat. They put the mat on the grass and the stools on the mat, Bob up and down a little with one knee bent, and run away.

The old lady says "Sit," and we do.

The Instructions for interviewing possible informants say Let *them* set the style of conversation, especially where you do not know local manners and customs, which God knows I don't; that is, I have had some Briefing about it where the average Figueroan is concerned but these people are evidently Something Else.

However when we have been silent five minutes or so I say "Has your ship been on this planet long?"

The old lady thinks this over and says "Too long."

At first I suspect this is a Snub but after another minute or two during which I think she is doing some Translation she says "Nine days."

Now I suppose it is My turn and she already knows that I arrived yesterday, so I say, "My friends have been here for three weeks."

She blinks slowly and says "Your friends talk to the In-Charge."

The people at the Gate must have been wearing Radios. I say, "The In-Charge has allowed them to use the Space Gate computers."

Suddenly all the creases on her face fold shut and she looks Furious. She says "Chief has asked to talk to the In-Charge. The In-Charge says No!"

I say, "I know he did, but I do not know why."

"Four time," says the old lady. "Chief begs the In-Charge for appointment. *Four* time."

I say, "When I came here I did not know the people of the planet had gone away. Other planets have not been informed."

The old lady nods sharply.

"*No* informing. *Msilikatse* in orbit, the In-Charge does not inform. Chief says, Okay to land? The In-Charge says, okay to land. Permission granted. No inform! *Msilikatse* lands. No Customs. No Immigration. Nothing."

What the hell was the In-Charge, I mean the Custodian, trying to do? It does not make Sense. Bringing that enormous ship down on an empty planet . . .

When he saw it I bet he was scared Stiff, which might explain how he is Behaving now.

I say, "You have a very large Ship."

The old lady looks sharply at me and I suspect she knows what I am thinking. She says "Hero class, rated for three hundred active, seven-fifty narcotized."

I feel as though History opened a large dark Mouth and Yawned at me. Hero Class ships were built six or more Centuries ago, for the second wave of Colonization; ferrying people from the Central Stars out to the next batch of newly-terraformed Worlds. When the ferrying was over they were cut up for Construction materials; nowadays even the Constructions have mostly been melted down for scrap.

They were not built to land on planets at all; but I suppose if you fitted one with large enough Antigravs and came down slowly, the heating and Aerodynamic problems could be overcome. It would certainly take a Hell of a wind to push that Monster off course.

I say, "I never saw one before."

The old lady says "Come." She gets up and toddles briskly back towards the Ship.

Being shown over that Enormous iron City is no doubt an Experience, but there are several moments when I could do without it. For one thing, I can hardly See; the old lady has not switched on any lights but carries a Lamp, and every five minutes or so it flickers and she turns it off for a moment; till the Fuel cell revives I suppose, but I am never perfectly certain it will Do so.

All the hatches and air locks are wide open, so there are sudden patches of Daylight. The chief impression is of Size and Decrepitude and the thought of people going to Space in the thing makes me Cold all through.

When we finally get outside I thank the old lady for a most Interesting tour and take several deep breaths; despite the open hatches the ship smells Musty. Actually I suppose they have just shut down the Auxiliary power supply for Maintenance or Repairs; with the Life Support systems running maybe it is more Homelike.

Unwillingly to Earth

I then look at my chrono and discover it is High time to go.

I did not try to Question the old lady during my Sight-seeing Tour; she might think it Bad Manners which would mean it was Bad Technique; but she did mention some things in passing, and on the way to meet Don and Blazer I try to sort out what I learned.

Viz:

Msilikatse and her people come from a place called Yeji-Dagomba.

The people of Yeji-Dagomba, or some of them, have a Tradition of long voyages; a whole Tribe or Sept or Kinship or what have you will take ship together and make the rounds of half a dozen planets, setting down for half a year or a year to work—all Planets in the Outer Reaches are short of manpower for big Construction jobs and such—taking most of their pay in local Products, to be Traded at later ports of call. They get home ten or twelve years later, increasing the Planetary stock of Wealth and Experience and bringing a few dozen kids to get acquainted with the home World.

This current voyage has lasted more than ten years and they are on their way Home. They have about three weeks' journey to go.

When I get in sight of the Gate I find it is shut, with the Floater already outside. Blazer is sitting at the wheel but Doug is standing beside it talking to one of the three People, probably Chief.

I slow down and start to catch my Breath. Blazer is looking cross, Doug as usual looks Worried and Responsible and Wishing he knew what to do for the best. As I get within earshot he says "I can't promise anything. Tomorrow I will ask to speak to the Cus—the In-Charge. I will tell him your problem if he allows me to. I can't do any more than that."

Chief puts his hands together and makes a little bow and says "I thank you."

Doug makes a sort of Not-at-all gesture and climbs into the floater and Blazer yells, "Hurry up, Liz!" As I reach the floater he says, "I've just been told that we picked you up within a hundred meters of a Hero Class transporter and never noticed it was there."

He sounds Disgusted, Disbelieving, and Disgruntled. I say, "I've just been shown over it."

"This I have to see," says the Blazer, and the Floater screams off before I am properly inside and nearly throws me Out again. I sit up and yell to Slow Down, there are Children around.

However he slows down of his own accord as the ship comes in sight and Edges up to the metal walls as though he has gone shy . . .

The Ship is made up of broad rectangular Bays alternating with deep narrow niches. That method of construction has not been used for several Centuries but it is the Metal which really shows that the ship is *old*. It has been struck by Micrometeorites so many times that there are Pits overlapping Pits, with Knobs between. It has been covered with Black-body paint so often the Knobs have a cap of it several millimeters thick, but the latest coat has a fair collection of new bright Pin-pricks and scratches already.

Blazer moves the Floater past a couple of bays at Minimum Cruising Speed, then before we reach any of the open Hatches he whirls it round and streaks for Home.

We pass the three People sitting patiently under their bush; Blazer does at least swing wide enough not to Blow their clothes off but otherwise his driving is completely Hog. We shoot past the compound full of machinery and arrive among streets of houses without, so far as I can see,

Unwillingly to Earth

going through the usual Twists and turns, and finally slam into the Hulk when the door is just barely open, and Flounce to a stop just short of the far wall.

When we troop into the main Living Area the Astral Cad is trying to sit on the back of his neck in a Chair not designed for it, and resting his heels on the back of another; he remarks to the air, "Judging by the way you rattled the furniture, I gather the old man has finally gone off his head."

"Never on it," grunts Blazer Weigh.

Doug heaves a sigh up from the Bottom of his chest and says, "Yes. I suppose so."

I say, "Why? What has he done?"

Blazer has dropped into a chair, trying to imitate the Cad's posture, but as there is no second chair within reach he has to haul himself up and just plain Sit. He says "Oh, he only switched the Radio Relay Satellite off, that's all."

The Cad is so Moved his heels slip off the chair-back and he also bounces into a normal position. He says "Why?"

"Usual reason."

"Oh." The Cad turns towards me with exaggerated grace. "This will interest you, Liz my dear. It's a pity you can't interview our friend the Custodian, who is, after all, the one Inhabitant of this planet that we know of who has remained within reach; he has definite views on the subject of your Assignment. Very definite."

I had just about forgotten my Assignment; it takes me a moment to say, "The Independent Firsters?"

Doug has sat down, still frowning heavily. He looks up and says, "He's using them as an excuse."

I say, "What for?"

"Oh, for shutting down every facility on this benighted planet," says the Astral Cad.

Doug says, "He claims he's custodian, of all the Corporation's property on Figueroa, and he claims to believe the Original Firsters are going to try to take it over, now everybody else is gone."

Blazer says "Actually the Relay Satellite isn't Corporation property; it was installed before they took over."

"They've maintained and repaired it," says Doug. "Legalistic arguments aren't apt to get us anywhere."

"Especially," says the Cad, "since the old lunatic is no more official Custodian than I am. He just took the chance to grab power when all his seniors pulled out."

Doug sighs again. "We don't *know* that. He does have the keys and the computer codes . . . which makes the question of his appointment irrelevant."

I say "How does shutting down the Relay Satellite help to keep other people from taking it over? The controls are on the planet, aren't they?"

Blazer says "I told you, he's mad."

"Only nor'-nor'-west, in this case," says the Cad. "Shutting down the Relay Satellite reduces the chance of interference from outside. Distress calls aren't likely to get through the ionosphere to be picked up by passing ships, for instance."

I say "What about the people from the old Ship?"

They all speak at once. I think Doug says "Oh, hell, yes," the Cad says "*What* old Ship?" and Blazer says "*What* about them?" and then immediately begins to tell the Cad about the Hero Class Ship. The Cad listens with an expression of patient bewilderment and finally says "Yes, yes, very exciting, but what has this got to do with the Relay Satellite?"

I say "I think the people were in Distress."

Doug says "Yes, poor devils. I promised to help if I could, but I doubt very much—"

"Oh, Stars," says the Astral Cad. "Our Worthy Leader in his pose as Protector of the Poor, encouraged therein by our latest recruit in *her* pose as Little Friend of All the World. Get thee behind me, Pollyanna, and *don't* push."

I say "What did the Chief want to see the In-Charge so badly for?"

"He needs fuel for his auxiliary generator, and—"

Blazer says "*Fuel?* The Hero Class have *four* proton monopiles—"

"This is for the life-support systems," says Doug.

"The power for that is drawn off one of the monopiles."

Trust Blazer to know that.

"Yes, I *know*. The Chief Engineer told me all that. Trouble is, the connection between the monopile and the life-support power system has broken down somehow—damn it, the thing's six hundred years old. To get the ship home he's got to use an auxiliary power supply. The only one available runs by oxidizing some chemical or other. He says there ought to be a supply of it here. That's why the ship put down. They can't take off again till they've got some."

Blazer is frowning. "Could be bradynitro, I suppose. That's used for—"

"Does it matter?" inquires the Cad wearily. "I take it we haven't got access to any. I take it the self-styled Custodian does have it. I take it your self-imposed duty is to persuade the old loony to part with some of it and I wish you luck, I really do. Now can we talk about something else?"

However the Blazer's interest in Machinery apparently outweighs even the influence of his Friend and Model and he continues to speculate on the fuel required for *Msilikatse* and its possible uses around the Space Gate until the Astral Cad rises in a Marked manner and drifts out of the room.

Next day Doug agrees I can travel with him to the Space Gate and take the floater on to *Msilikatse*. I want to talk to the old lady again if she will let me. Doug does a bit of rather half-hearted Dodging—I think everybody has lost Faith in possible predatory Watchers—and the route takes us past the Machine Park again. I get the impression out of the corner of my eye that one of the upstanding Crane-type things moves as we go past; I suppose the Custodian(?) is amusing himself with the Remote controls.

I think Doug was expecting, perhaps hoping, Not to be allowed in any more, but when he mutters to the speaker in the Gatepost the valves of the door move open.

When Doug is inside and the gates shut I back the Floater and find the Chief Engineer standing there, with only one attendant this time.

He says "Your friend has gone to see the In-Charge."

I say "Yes. He wants to ask him about fuel for your generator."

The Chief says "He is a good man."

It occurs to me this is probably True. I wrote Douglas Laydon off as a Stuffed Shirt the first time I met him but under present Conditions he is showing up rather well.

When I reach *Msilikatse* there seems to be No one around; I walk along the side of the ship till I come to one of the open hatches and hear faintly a kind of Groaning somewhere inside.

It does not sound quite like somebody being ill but it is a good enough Excuse for going in to see.

After fifty meters or so I realize it would have to be an Enormous somebody to make as much noise as this and after another twenty the Deck is shaking under my feet, finally I arrive at a glass door with the Noise coming from the other side.

There is light in there but it is faint and Flickering, all I can make out is a row of people standing with their backs to me and Stamping their feet up and down.

Unwillingly to Earth

Then they all stand back a pace and four others jump in front of them and start Stamping instead. After a moment the lights go brighter and I see the four who have been replaced are dripping with Sweat; one of them turns towards the glass door and sees me standing there.

He turns back and I suppose Says something, because a moment later the old lady comes into view and opens the door.

She is scowling and says "Eh! Girl. Why you come spying like this?"

I say "Sorry. I heard the noise and thought somebody might be ill. I'll go."

Fortunately she thinks this is Funny, she bursts out laughing and turns to yell something to the others, who also start laughing and calling out in their own language; after a moment a man in overalls appears waving a big oil can and says something to me which is plainly a Joke, but I don't understand.

The old lady gives him a playful Clout on the rear and explains "He say the Machine old and get Rheumatic like me."

All this time the new four are solemnly stamping up and down and I can now see that they are treading down Steps on a kind of rolling cylinder. The man with the oil can goes back to work on it and after a bit one of the components in the Noise dies away. There are a lot of yellow-looking Plants around.

Suddenly I realize what all this is about.

Okay, I have heard of Treadmill generators, some of the remotest communities on Excenus 23 have one as an Emergency standby; what shocks me is not the Idea itself but that anybody should have to use human labor to make electricity to make light to run Hydroponics on a *Space ship* of all places.

Besides, what Good can it be? Energy usage is never 100% efficient. They must use up a lot more Calories to make the light than the plants can possible store as Starch; and they must generate more CO_2 than can be absorbed.

The old lady says, "Fuel is for Power. We get power ourselves also."

I say "Enough for a *voyage*?"

She thinks for a moment and then says "Re-charge-able stor-age ac-cum-u-lat-ors."

Oh.

But surely to store enough Life Support Power for a three-week voyage will take months and months, even if they run all systems at a minimum level. Even if the Treadmill is kept going by relays of people who run themselves to exhaustion, which they seem to be doing—

Right then, in fact, somebody steps Backwards off it, swaying. Somebody else replaces him before the Treadmill's note has time to alter, while he takes two more steps and Crumples quietly to the floor.

Nobody seems surprised, let alone Dismayed; two women are bending over him feeling his Chest, then they carry him briskly to a Mat in the open hatch and lay him out on it.

I say, "Does that happen often?"

Which I guess was Tactless, anyway the result is a Resounding silence and the old lady goes over to take a look at the Collapsed man.

I decide to take a quick look around . . . Behind the Treadmill I come on four men sitting in a row, with big helmets over their heads like the hood of a Library-style Reading machine.

Beside them is a control panel with the usual Dials and things. I am still looking at that when the four men get up and change places with the ones on the Treadmill. Four others move under the helmets and sit down.

On some of the dials the needles are in the Red.

There is a touch on my arm and I find the old lady

Unwillingly to Earth

beside me. She says "The Manpower is set for mean average response."

I say "Is that safe?"

She blinks at me and repeats, "It is Mean Average."

Before I can answer—anyway I cannot think what to say—the old lady gives a little jump and her eyes widen; then she cries "The Chief will speak with the In-Charge!"

There is an immediate Buzz and everybody except the four Stampers and the man with the oil can gathers round her, talking.

If Doug has been successful in his Mission he will be wanting the Floater shortly; I tell the old lady I must go back to him. When I reach the Floater I find that she has come too.

Well Why not? She climbs in beside me, shouts Negatives at the crowd of children who want to come for the ride, and I drive away.

As we approach the gateway we can hear Voices; the old lady puts a hand on my arm and points to a place where the floater would be Hidden from the gateway by a bulge in the wall. I park it there and we walk on, quietly.

The gate is open just enough for one man to stand in the opening, and he is doing so. The In-Charge, I presume; but I did *not* imagine he would be a cherubic little man with curly hair combed down with water so that it looks like a Baby's; or that he would be looking so remarkably Pleased with himself.

Then I see Doug standing just behind him, unable to pass, and not looking Pleased at all.

The In-Charge is saying "Two thousand liters? You said two thousand liters, is that right?"

The Chief says, very carefully "Two thousand liters. That is correct."

"Oh, yes," says the In-Charge happily, "we could supply ten times that amount. Pump, or in drums?"

The Chief says "We will take it from your pump. We have transporter."

"Good. Good. Excellent. Now. How do you propose to pay for it?"

He is Twinkling all over with enjoyment. Doug looks thunderous.

Interstellar payments are tricky, especially here in the Outer reaches. But, damnit, the People must have been prepared to pay for the stuff when they put down here . . .

"We have guaranteed drafts on Banks of Latimer, Garuda, Mercutio, Rosemary."

Rosemary should be foolproof, at least, as one of the Three Sponsoring Planets—

"Sorry," twinkles the In-Charge, "no banking facilities here at the moment."

Stars!

The Chief looks perfectly impassive; but he has come to a Halt. Then he says, "We have also Dagomba scrip—"

"Never heard of the place," says the In-Charge happily.

"We have also scrip from New Nassau."

Another of the Sponsoring Planets; surely that will do it—?

"My dear fellow," says the In-Charge, switching suddenly to pathos, "whatever use is that going to be *here*?"

"You could keep it and hand it over to the Corporation," says Doug abruptly from behind him. The In-Charge throws a look of Venom and vinegar over his shoulder and says "At the moment liquid assets are liable to be confiscated. Bankruptcy proceedings. I'm afraid that won't do."

During this the Chief's back, which was straight to begin with, has been getting even Straighter. He now says, one word at a time, "We carry trade goods. Also cargo."

"No market for them now, I'm afraid," says the In-Charge with undiminished cheerfulness. "It looks as though we can't do business. A pity."

Unwillingly to Earth

The old lady has been silently Fermenting beside me; now she steps forward and screams something which is obviously a Curse, and the In-Charge jumps backwards and loses his Smile.

"Get that woman out of here!" he exclaims.

"Why?" says Doug. "She isn't on Corporation ground. It presumably belongs to their creditors in any case. In fact as Custodian you should be considering the interests of the creditors, not—"

"Get out!" yells the In-Charge. "Traitor! Ungrateful! Get out! Go!"

"Get out of the way, then," says Doug, and grabs him by both shoulders and Spins him backwards out of the doorway. He dives through himself just as the valves clang Shut.

I do not want to look at the Chief or the old lady. I can't help seeing Doug who is standing with his Back to the gates and his head up in what looks like an attitude of Noble Defiance, a lot too late. For some reason the In-Charge has deliberately and elaborately humiliated all of them and it makes me feel Apologetic about also belonging to the Human Race.

What I want is to get right Away from everybody for a bit, so I walk round behind the Chief and his Attendant and go on walking. They don't notice me and neither does the old lady; I don't know about Doug. As I go I hear the Chief say "I thank you, sir."

Doug answers, "You have nothing to thank me for. I haven't helped you at all."

The old lady says, "You *try*."

I wish the In-Charge was here so I could kick him; what Makes anybody behave like that, Mad or not? I would offer to pay for the Fuel myself, but I suppose his excuses would work just as well against my Universal Credit Card . . . I wonder how hard it would be to break in and Steal the stuff, but I don't know where it is and I don't suppose Doug does either.

There is a sudden Shout from up ahead and a sort of clanking and creaking noise. I look up and one of the Cybercranes from the Machine Park is just stepping over the fence, waving its shovel-head to and fro on the end of a Neck ten meters long.

The telescopic legs seem to move slowly but they are so long that they cover a lot of ground. It takes a Stride away from the fence. The head does one side-to-side traverse, Dithers for a moment, then settles down pointing straight at me. The left front leg and the right back leg Telescope up, swing, and come down, having moved the Crane several meters closer to me.

I don't know what the Hell this means but I think it is time to Run. I turn to do so and there are a whole bunch of the Kids from *Msilikatse*, I suppose they have Followed me.

I yell "*Shoo! Run!*" and make appropriate Gestures; then I turn and Run the other way. Not towards the Crane but Away from the machine park towards a cluster of the burned-over Huts which are about fifty meters away.

I can hear the thing coming after me, shaking the ground every time one of its Legs comes down. Just as I reach the first Hut there is a sort of *Whish!* behind me and I jump sideways and the Shovel-head comes down on the Hut wall and knocks it to splinters.

I dodge in among the Huts, trying to get out of the thing's Line of Sight; which means I can't see where its Head has got to. Then suddenly as I Squeeze between two of the walls there it is right over me; I can see the red gleam of its eyes which means it has got me Registered and all I can do is dive inside the Hut and hope its brain is not Bright enough to work out where I must have gone.

Some Hope, there is a rending Crash as the roof is knocked sideways and I am left crouched in a corner

Staring up at the thing, oh Damn this is a stupid way to die—

The head suddenly jerks back and I hear the sound which means it is Readjusting its legs, I suppose this is where I should Review my past life but all I can think of is, I can't help closing my eyes but I am *not* going to Scream . . .

Then there is a Flare that burns dazzling white even through my eyelids and a most godawful Bang! and then nothing happens and goes on happening until I realize I am not Dead after all.

Just the same it is quite difficult to get my Eyes open; when I do, all I can see past the broken edges of the roof is the Sky.

I don't know how long I just crouched there Enjoying it, but suddenly there is a lot of Shouting going on and I can hear my name: "Liz! Lizzie! *Liz! Forgodsake, Liz!*"

I try to get up but my legs don't Feel like it, so I shout "Here!"

This leads to a lot of Trampling and noises as though some of the Huts are being broken down: more Shouts, which I answer; then the Back wall of the hut is suddenly smashed in and Doug is falling through the Hole.

He is so covered in Smuts I didn't realize at first that he is bare to the waist; then I see red beads trickling down the Black smudges and realize he is covered in Scratches as well; I don't think my mind is working too well because it does not occur to me to Question this phenomenon until later. Meanwhile Doug Lurches to his feet and takes two strides across the Hut floor and Hauls me into his arms.

I don't know how long we remain at an Angle propping one another up and I can't remember a word either of us said, which is probably just as well, but in the end Doug gets back to his Senses and pushes me through the hut door to face the Chief and the old lady and three or four others who are waiting outside.

There is some Handshaking and the old lady suddenly darts forwards and Kisses me, then we all go to look at the Cybercrane which is standing on its two front legs with the hind ones flat on the ground, and its jib bent backwards at an angle with what is left of the Shovel pointing straight up at the sky.

Some of the Shovel has melted and is hanging down in Blobs, and there is more Melting at several points on the Jib and a big hole where it joins the Body of the thing.

Something has happened so that everything around me seems to be wrapped in Invisible padding about two inches thick; it takes Time for ideas to get through; but I gradually realize everybody is waiting for me to Comment on the thing.

I say "How did you Stop it?" and then, "What made it Start?"

Doug says, "This is the man who stopped it; Second Engineer Emmanuel. He managed to short the power-pack through the thing's brain, just in time."

Second Engineer Emmanuel seems to have got rather Battered in the process, his arm is in a rough Sling and half his face is puffed up round a big patch of dried blood.

I feel around in the Padding to find out what I ought to be doing, and say, "Thank you very much."

He shuffles his feet about and grins, showing a missing tooth on the Puffed side. Then the old lady pokes him and says something sharp, and he shuffles again and mutters "Is nothing, Miss Sir." Doug has a grip on my Elbow which indicates something Not to be said right now, so I do not repeat the rest of my question.

There is a lot of talking in what I suppose is Dagomba language; it begins to seem to me as if it is going on for Ever, and then suddenly we are all walking back towards the floater. Then I see the Gate open and the In-Charge appears, shouting, "I told you they were thieves! I said they were all thieves!"

Things stop for just a heartbeat, before everybody starts for him at a Run and he disppears inside and the Gate slams shut.

Some kids have appeared from Nowhere, the way this lot do. One of them is carrying Doug's tunic. He puts it on, wincing as it goes over his scratches, and I ask what he took it Off for.

"It got caught in the gate," says Doug irritably.

So when I thought he was Posing he was just Stuck, maybe I ought to apologize.

When we return to the Hulk our colleagues are lounging in the Lounge, but our entrance causes them to sit up sharply and then Rise simultaneously to their feet.

I think the Cad is searching for an Epigram when Blazer Weigh exclaims "Forgodsake, what *happened* to you two?"

We stopped at *Msilikatse* and some of the children brought us water and towels and soap and a comb, and our clothes are Evercleans and all the Dirt has shaken off them long ago; but I can feel from inside that there is something wrong with my Face and the Padding stops me getting in touch with my Muscles so as to put it right.

Doug shoves me gently into a chair and drops into one himself and says "Give me five minutes' peace and something to drink, and I'll explain."

Blazer goes over to the Dispenser. The Cad has just thought of a Remark when Doug says "Leave Lizzie alone. She's getting over a shock. Just over an hour ago she was very nearly killed, and it was *not* the result of anything she did herself, so no smart remarks, please."

The Dispenser has never produced anything but Reconstituted fruit juice since I first encountered it, and that's what we get now. Doug drinks his slowly, puts down the glass, and says, "All right . . . You know that yard full of machinery we pass on the way to the Gate? The Custodian has programmed some of the machines to attack people who interfere with them."

There is a blank silence; then Blazer Weigh says "Crap. Those things don't *have* attack circuits. He can't have done."

Doug says, "They respond to objects and movements around the business end. They can move suddenly as well as slowly, over a long distance as well as a short one . . . I don't know how he did it exactly; maybe they have some kind of burglar-alarm circuits and he managed to link those in to the ones that control movement. Anyway, he did it. The Second Engineer from *Msilikatse* was prowling round one of the machines and a cybercrane next to it started thrashing its jib around. He dodged it and hid, and the thing walked across the compound wall and saw Lizzie with a bunch of kids from *Msilikatse* and started chasing *them*. Lizzie broke away and got it to chase *her* among those burned huts. The Second Engineer managed to climb up on the chassis, somehow, and just before it smashed the hut she was hiding in he succeeded in shorting the auxiliary power cell. It blew with enough of a bang to fuse all the brain centers and knock the thing over backwards."

So that's what happened . . .

Blazer Weigh says "How the hell did he manage that?"

"Never mind," says Doug severely. "The point is, the old man's paranoia is dangerous. He got it into his head that someone was going to try to steal the machines—"

"It sounds as though he was right," says the Astral Cad.

"The man wanted to see if the power cells were removable. The Chief Engineer was perfectly willing to pay for the fuel he wanted, or any other usable power source; but he suspected the old brute wouldn't let him, and he was right."

"I don't see what good the power cells could have been," drawls the Cad. "They don't run on bradynitro."

"They could be used to re-charge storage batteries. I gather *Msilikatse* has a big stock—enough to run the Life Support system all the way home."

"Oh," says the Astral Cad thoughtfully.

I have a feeling I ought to Say something at this point, but the Padding is still getting in the way.

Maybe I make some sort of Noise, because Doug looks across at me.

"Lizzie, you look terrible. Why don't you go to your cabin and sleep it off?"

I can't even manage to Resent the suggestion; I just Go.

I don't know how long I slept because I don't know what time in the afternoon I went to sleep, but when I wake up it is Breakfast time, the Padding sensation has gone, and even that reconstituted Glop that the robo-kitchen turns out at this time of day smells attractive. I shower and dress in a hurry and join my Colleagues around the table.

Breakfast in the Hulk is never a Sparkling occasion, this morning it is extra Glum which I attribute to the events of Yesterday as described by Doug to the other two. I stoke up pretty quickly—one thing about Reconstituted food, you can swallow it fast—and inquire whether anyone else is going out to the Space Gate this morning.

This produces a sort of Tripartite explosion of toast crumbs, then for once it is Doug who finds the words first.

"Forgodsake, Lizzie! What's the point of going there? What do you think you can do? or the rest of us, if it comes to that."

Wouldyoubelieveit, just for a moment I have completely forgotten what it is I have to do; I woke up remembering there was *something*, not *what* . . . However the Cad sticks his oar in before I have time to Reveal this.

"Speaking for myself, No. We have gathered every last

available statistic that could conceivably have any value for future work, and—"

I say, "That's It!"

Okay, I don't really Blame them for thinking I have gone mad and anyway I have no Time to act insulted, I just go on "It's a statistic that's lethal, when you get down to it. Did you know *Msilikatse* has a Mesmeric Equalizer on board?"

They all have approximately the same Expression on their faces: however Don says "No," Blazer says "Where?" and the Astral Cad says "What in the name of sanity is a Mesmeric Equalizer?"

Blazer Weigh says, "They were used quite a bit a couple of Centuries ago. Mostly in the Outer Reaches, of course. People in the Central Planets would never have stood for them . . . One of the main elements was an Enforcement Unit—on the same lines as the Concentration Unit in a Reading Machine, bu this one was concerned with manual labor. The other was the Equalizer. It worked out the effort required for a given job and then shared it out equally between the group who were to do it."

The Astral Cad inquires wearily "What the hell *for*?"

"Oh, it was designed to simplify industrial relations. The amount of work to be done could be agreed on at the start, and then performance could be enforced; but there were a lot of drawbacks."

"I should damn well think so," said Doug. "But what use would a thing like that be on *Msilikatse*?"

I say, "On my home planet it was used another way, once."

How it got to Excenus 23: a bunch of young men from wealthy families decided to come and prove they could make their own Fortunes. One of them was always Fussing because he claimed he worked harder than anyone else, and imported an Equalizer to try and Even things. But the others refused to use it and soon after they decided to make do with the Fortunes they had inherited, and left the planet.

Then another bunch with *no* Fortunes found a rich seam three weeks before their Lease expired and were frantic to dig out as much as they could. The Equalizer was still where the others had left it and one of them had the bright idea of using it to increase their Work output by taking out the Governor circuit and setting it to enforce Maximum effort the whole time. For nearly a week they were Ladling the stuff out and then one of them fell down dead. No resuscitator nearer than 250 miles so he stayed that way.

I explain the Relevant part of this and Don says, "You think that's what the people on *Msilikatse* have done?"

I say "I know it is. I saw the Control board."

"What I don't see," drawls the Astral Cad, "is what Statistics have got to do with it."

Slowly and carefully, I Explain.

"What the Equalizer does is to measure the Working Capacity of each member of the group, then take the Average. Or Mean. The Controls are set for a percentage of this, usually about 85. The Governor stops it going higher than 90% but if you disconnect that circuit it will go to 100% and that's how the one on *Msilikatse* is set."

"In other words," says Doug, "the people whose capacity is a bit below the mean of the group are going to be forced to do More than they can."

"Anybody can manage more than their normal capacity for a bit," says the Blazer, whose liking for Machines seems to impel him to defend every Aspect of them.

I say "I know that. But forcing people beyond their normal limits is dangerous. Sooner or later they're going too far and somebody will Die of it."

I don't quite know what I expect: not Shock and horror because they would see the punchline Coming, but I do expect *something*.

After a bit Doug says heavily, "I expect you're right, Lizzie, but what do you think you can *do*?"

Well, obviously, go and Tell the people on *Msilikatse* that what they are doing is dangerous, and get them to set the dials back . . . I say "I suppose you think they won't Listen."

The Astral Cad straightens a trifle in his chair.

"My dear, dear Liz. You've been studying Cultural Engineering for two years, and you can still think there's any probability they *will* listen?"

This is Not the end of the argument but I finally wear them down. Blazer Weigh gives me a rundown on the controls of the Floater and I set off.

There is no sign of militant Machines or the In-Charge or any other Enemy around *Msilikatse*; only some children, who appear Pleased and excited to see me and run for the old lady, who for some reason Bows and starts thanking me. I eventually grasp that this is because I led the Cybercrane away from the children yesterday and she thinks this was somehow Heroic, which was not the case. I would have been no safer if I had run in among them.

I try to explain that I just ran towards the Huts because there was nowhere else to hide. But not very hard, because it occurs to me they may Listen more if they go on thinking like that. I ask to speak to Chief and am conducted to him, sitting on a folding chair alongside the main hatch. There are several people lying on Mats, two of them women.

Chief rises and bows to me and the children bring a chair. I explain very carefully why I have come and he Listens very carefully and says nothing for a long time. One of the people lying down calls something and a woman comes out and spreads a blanket over him.

Finally Chief says "You are good to be concerned. This thing I know. The power-wheel has been not used for

Unwillingly to Earth

many-many years, never in my time of voyage, but I was told by the Chief before me. But now we need power to leave this planet."

I say "But you only need to set the dial back 5% and it will be safe enough!"

He says "Five percent means one day in twenty. To recharge the accumulators will take forty days. Five percent is two days. All days on this planet are danger for *Msilikatse* people."

I cannot Argue with that.

I say "I wish I could get fuel for you. I wish I could help."

He says "Already you are our friend."

When I start to leave I am mobbed by the Children who take me to see the Old Lady, I want to say Goodbye to her anyway. We exchange a few rather Ceremonious words and I mention I would like to see the Second Engineer to thank him for saving my life yesterday; however I gather he has gone into the remains of the Town with two other men to look for some Wiring and stuff. I ask just how he put that Thing out of action yesterday; apparently she does not Hear but the children do and start to Giggle into their hands.

When I have said Goodbye they grab me and pretend to be showing me the new Plants being grown for the Hydroponics section. What they really want is to rub dirt on my Evercleans when I am not looking and watch it Fall off, seems some of them saw this yesterday and the others will not Believe until shown. I ask them how Second Engineer Emmanuel managed to blow up the Cybercrane and they giggle a lot more, finally the eldest girl whispers in my ear "Second Engineer break open the engine box and Piss inside!" and I say Goodbye in a positive Explosion of giggles, and drive away.

Damn lucky for me he thought of it, anyway.

* * *

I am halfway back to the Hulk when something on the control board comes to life with a sort of Pop and Blazer Weigh's voice Yells at me "Lizzie! If you copy, say so!"

I say "I copy, where's the Volume control?"

"Never mind," he yells back. "Take the next turning Right and then Left and then Report."

I turn Right and then Left, which Heads me back towards the Gate, and say I have done so.

"Good. Now Right at the garden with the big pine tree and third Left after that."

Now I am headed for the Hulk by a track parallel to the usual one.

"Okay. Look at the control board. See a switch colored green? When the moment comes, slam that down and jam the accelerator full on, understand?"

I say "Understood."

"The Hulk's under siege, we think."

For a moment I take this to be more Instructions, then I realize what he said. I say "Does the Moment come when I contact the Besiegers?"

"Hope not. With any luck you'll have dodged them. If you do see any just barge through and the anticrash field will shove them sideways. No, the moment comes when—"

At that instant I *do* see the Besiegers, or anyway three men with what look like Stunners; I shove the accelerator home and bang the Hooter and the floater Charges through them and a moment later Blazer yells *"Now!"* and I throw the Green switch—the Accelerator is jammed on already—and something Snaps round the whole of my body leaving just a small opening for my Nose. There is a Swooping sensation and a *Crash!* and I get the impression of being Compressed into a container much too small for me, and then the goddamn Safety Cocoon shrinks back into the seat of the Floater and I can see where I am.

* * *

Unwillingly to Earth

Which is inside somebody's House after a Hurricane, furniture in Bits blown into the corners, pictures hanging askew . . .

The Camouflage room in the Hulk.

The Floater has come through the Main Hatch at full acceleration and Stopped with its nose three feet from the back wall and I can't understand why I am not Dead.

Then Doug bursts through the door and states at the top of his voice that I am Not, not even stunned, not a scratch on me, I do not feel so sure of this myself but I suppose he would know.

I get out while he is babbling about Crash Cocoons and Energy Absorption Fields and Automatic Homing, and take a look at the Floater. The front end has been kind of Consolidated for about six inches which may or may not mean it will never Float again.

Then it occurs to me to ask Who the hell is besieging us, and Why.

"Come into the Control Room," says Don.

I hadn't realized this place was still Functioning at all, but Blazer and the Cad are inside bending over various installations and a series of screens are lit up, showing Trees and houses in various directions but nothing else I can make out.

The Cad says "The Enemy have gone to ground."

I say "Who *are* the Enemy?"

"Oh, there you are," says Blazer Weigh, fiddling with some knobs.

"Lizzie, dear," says the Cad, "prepare for a delightful surprise. The Enemy, as you ungratefully call them, are the subject of your Field Work Assignment, the Independent Firsters in person."

"Listen," says Blazer Weigh.

"You Terrans in the old ship," blares the Recorder he has been adjusting. "You're surrounded. Show sense and you won't get hurt, not by us anyway. What's on this planet belongs to the people of this planet, the ones who got here by their own efforts and been working all along to make a place for themselves and their children. You got a lot of stuff in there that we reckon is rightly ours. There's been a damn sight too much taken out of Figueroa for the benefit of outsiders and we reckon something's owed to us for that. You're getting picked up tomorrow or day after, we don't want to interfere with that, but we aim to see nothing else goes off planet and we're staying here until you've gone to see that it don't. We know there's one of you out in a floater. When we take possession of it we'll let him in to join the rest of you. Signing off, acknowledge please."

"Plainly an optimist," says the Astral Cad. "Though I think we might acknowledge reception now that we have Lizzie back among us."

Before anyone can Do so another Speaker comes abruptly to life.

"That wasn't so damn smart," it says. The voice is a different one, gruffer, and not making any attempt to sound Reasonable. "If you banged up that Floater we just might decide to take it out of your hides, before we let you go."

Before anyone can Intervene the Astral Cad has flipped the Switch of an Outside Speaker and retorted "And we just might decide to fix a few booby traps, or arrange to blow this installation, before we depart!"

There is a Yell of rage from the inside Speaker, cut off suddenly as though someone out there had thrown a switch. Blazer Weigh has already thrown the one inside, and he stands silently while Doug and I combine to tell the Astral Cad what we think of him.

I get tired of it sooner than Doug, who has been Putting up with the Cad 3 weeks longer than me. I switch on the radio, while Doug is pausing to think of another Insult, and speak.

"You Figueroans out there. What are you talking about?

Unwillingly to Earth

We aren't going to take any of this equipment with us. We don't want to, and we couldn't, anyway, it's too heavy."

There is a Pause, during which I hear someone saying "Damnit, that's a girl!" and then the first Voice speaks again.

"Your friends at the Space Gate could, and they're not going to. We need that monopile as much as they do, and it's staying where it is."

Blazer Weigh leans over and switches off our mike, and I hear Shouting start a moment before somebody outside switches theirs off too.

"How the Hell did they get to know about that?" he says.

When I have time I will get together and Kick myself for not realizing that the existence of Light and Automatic gadgets and so on in the Hulk *have* to mean that it has an Independent power supply. I have got too used to Large-scale Utilities, two years ago it would never have occurred to me that it worked by anything Else.

I will add an extra Kick for not thinking that *any* sort of Power supply could be tapped to recharge *Msilikatse*'s accumulators.

Doug says "What could have made them think we had any idea of transferring the pile to *Msilikatse*?"

"It's a crazy idea," says Blazer. "The pile's over a century old, and if we tried to shift it the casing would probably crack. Let alone it weighs over three tonnes and we've no transport that would take it."

Doug says thoughtfully, "You and Van Hatton went outside together this morning. What did you talk about?"

"There was nobody around," says Blazer Weigh quickly. "We checked before we went out."

Doug looks at the Cad, who shrugs.

"I forget the exact words. We discussed the Dagombans' problems and Lizzie's overreaction to them. I seem to remember saying that if it happened to occur to Lizzie that the Hulk had its own power supply she would infallibly decide that their need was greater than ours, and demand that we disconnect it and carry it along to the Space Gate and hand it over . . . Your eavesdropper, if any, didn't know a joke when he heard one."

"I don't imagine that the average Firster has much acquaintance with monopiles," says Doug coldly. "Nor do I feel he has to be blamed to failing to recognize your humor as such. However, that seems to explain the present situation . . . Just *let it go*, Lizzie, discussing Van Hatton's mental peculiarities won't improve them and we've got other things to think about."

Which is obviously True, but at the end of about ninety minutes' loud and acrimonious Thinking we are left with the following Facts:

One. If the Firsters choose to keep us In we have no safe way to get Out. *Two*. *Pedagogue* is due any time after twelve hours from now. She will presumably drop a Lander. This will have to be some way off because of the Trees and we have to get out of the Hulk in order to make rendezvous.

What I think we ought to do is Call the Firsters again and try to convince them that (a) we have no plans to remove the Monopile or other equipment (b) the Cad's remark about Boobytraps was spoken through the top of his head and got tangled in his Hair.

Doug gets to his feet.

"Look," he says, "we don't want to leave the Hulk until *Pedagogue* gets here. So far as I can see, there's nothing we can usefully say to the Firsters before that, so forgodsake let's have an end to all this talking and concentrate on getting all the data ready to take with us. Pack it so that it can be easily carried if we have to run for it. You two do it, Lizzie isn't familiar with the material. I'm going to make out my final Report."

Unwillingly to Earth

* * *

However when the Precious Pair have departed he does not get out his styler but slumps down in his chair with his chin on his chest and his eyes shut.

I am damn certain *he* realized that our pile could have juiced up *Msilikatse*'s accumulators and didn't choose to say; What do my colleagues take me for? but I suppose there is no point in raising the matter; we can't even tell them about the pile over the radio without touching off a War between them and the Firsters now.

I am sitting there Repressing some very good Remarks when Doug makes a sound possibly to be classified as a Laugh.

"Lizzie, do you remember what people said about Figueroa when it was first discovered? Bonanza planet. A new free self-sufficient life for millions. The biggest free gift ever handed to the human race. Damn it, it *should* have been all that. Yet you can see the final mess coming practically from the start."

I say "If you study Cultural Engineering, you can. When Figueroa was discovered, nobody did. Our Department wasn't founded until twelve years after colonization had begun. Next time—"

Doug makes the Laughing noise again.

"Lizzie, next time there's a find rich enough to touch off the kind of greedy, headlong rush that ruined Figueroa, the same thing will happen again. Dammit, I bet it'll happen again *here*.

"You know, the Firsters have got a right to be aggrieved. They're the one group who set out to colonize this planet by their own hard work, and they've been swamped by people who expected to have everything handed to them on a plate and the others who expected to make a profit by doing the handing. I think they do have a right to take over anything they can use. But if they make a go of it and Figueroa is ever in running order again, there'll be another rush of would-be colonists, half of them claiming that they've inherited property here or bought the rights to it from the previous occupants. The Corporation will sell their rights to some other damned group, probably the same people under another name, and they'll descend on Figueroa with a regiment of lawyers and a battalion of goons, and the Firsters will be worse off than they are now."

I say "It doesn't have to be like that."

"Maybe it doesn't have to be, but it will. The Firsters won't even know what rights they have, in that situation, and there won't be anybody to tell them. They'll be chased out; or they'll stay and fight and be accused of piracy, which means the Three Planets will more or less have to intervene and the Firsters will be lucky if their home settlements aren't bombed out."

No Government in the Outer Planets can afford to overlook Piracy, because the Populations they govern are quite aware that it could be their turn next.

I say, "The Firsters may not know what's likely to happen, but *we* do."

"What good is that? We're leaving."

"We can leave a Warning behind. The Firsters aren't fools. They feel they've been done down by outsiders; they won't have any difficulty believing it could happen again."

"All right, you could trigger off planet-wide paranoia, but what good will that do?"

I say "*Not* Paranoia, just Awareness that certain Consequences will follow certain Acts. Specifically, that if they try to take over installations on this Continent there is a big risk of losing them again; so they shouldn't invest more Effort and Materials than they can afford to abandon. Where is the Paranoia in that?"

Doug sighs heavily. "Lizzie, people aren't reasonable. They don't pay attention to warnings, either. The Russett Research Unit has been firing off dire warnings as regularly as a traffic beacon for three years, and nobody took a blind bit of notice."

I say "And look what happened. If we leave them a few of those old Reports the Firsters can see we know what we're talking about, because the warnings have come true.

"It doesn't have to be all Warnings, either. You said the Firsters wouldn't know what rights they have. We can tell them. There are quite definite Rules about property abandoned on planets still in course of colonization; the Hulk computer's bound to have it all. We can leave the Firsters printouts, with a summary to explain what it's got to do with them."

Doug says "How much use is a printout of the Law when you're dealing with a goon squad?"

I say "It can help to deter people from sending goon squads. But mostly it can warn people which things lead to trouble, and how to avoid them—"

Somebody says, "Stars and Nebulae, has Lizzie found some new Cause to hold forth about?"

The Astral Cad, of course. He and Blazer have just returned with four smallish compact heavy-looking packs.

"We've checked everything," says Blazer. "Shall we stick the extra copies in the destructor?"

Doug says thoughtfully. "No . . . We might have a use for them."

"Don't tell me," says the Cad. "We're going to make little paper kites with them and fly messages to *Msilikatse*, to let them know—"

"No," says Doug in a tone of abrupt Decision, "we're going to run an exercise in Cultural Engineering."

At first the Point is only to fill in the time until *Pedagogue* arrives, which cannot be in less than 12 hours and might not be for a couple of days; but before long it has turned into a real Project. Blazer takes charge of Finding and printing out relevant Articles of Interplanetary Agreement, Doug drafts Explanations of why they are relevant and Astral Cad and I Criticize, surprisingly often in Agreement with one another. The stack of Documents gets thick and the Time approaches midnight. There are empty cups on every ledge and discarded food containers on the floor, Dad's housekeeper Buffalo Cole would be Shocked and horrified but I am *not* going to drop out of the Argument to tidy them away.

By now we have got on to Government; it is generally agreed that the Firsters are going to need one, for Outside Relations only. The Cad and I are arguing about What title or description is least likely to convince the Firsters that they are handing somebody a Mandate to interfere with Personal Affairs when there is a sudden buzz from the Control Room alarm, followed by a shout from Blazer Weigh.

"It's *Pedagogue*! She's come!"

Pedagogue is transmitting Print not Voice; by the time we get to the control room Blazer has acknowledged the first call, and the second installment is just coming through on the screen;

PEDAGOGUE TO GROUND PARTY. WILL PICK YOU UP IN TWO HOURS SAME PLACE ACKNOWLEDGE.

Comment is immediately Drowned by a blare from the speakers.

"You in the old ship! Tell your friends with the funny name you're not leaving until we check you haven't set any booby traps. Open the main hatch, or we'll open it for you."

By way of Illustration there comes a Thump! that shakes the whole Hulk.

I had not exactly Forgotten that we were Besieged, but I certainly had not been thinking about it. We had been discussing the Firsters for twelve hours as though we were all on the same Side, and the Reminder that this is Not how they see things comes as a distinct Shock.

"They've rigged a battering ram," says Doug grimly. "*Now* what do we do?"

Pedagogue's Com officer is feeling Neglected and a message appears on the screen saying Do we copy, Acknowledge please.

Blazer glances at Don for Instructions, gets none, shrugs, and taps out GROUND PARTY TO PEDAGOGUE. SNAGS HERE DEFER DESCENT.

Thump!

The Cad says irritably, "Haven't we anything to Discourage that?"

"They'll discourage themselves in time," says Doug briefly.

"Hull's armor-plate, not standard," Blazer explains.

Pedagogue comes through with a request for details on the Snags and sets off an argument: the Cad wants to send SURROUNDED BY HOSTILES, SEND HEAVY SQUAD, in the hope this will Frighten the Firsters off.

Doug says there is No sense in such an obvious bluff and dictates a brief statement of the Facts; Blazer wants to put it in Code, but Doug says the Firsters know the Facts already and Code will simply increase Mistrust of which we have already more than enough.

I say "Look. In fact we have *not* booby-trapped anything so why not let them come in and See?"

This sets off another Argument, in the middle of which the next message from *Pedagogue* arrives. I wonder why they have not used Code, despite the Mistrust factor, because it runs;

PEDAGOGUE TO GROUND. INFRARED SHOWS ABOUT FIFTY UNITS IN YOUR VICINITY. CAN BESIEGERS BE TRUSTED NOT TO HIJACK LANDER, IF SO ADVISE PERMIT SEARCH.

I suppose John Li Chu in *Pedagogue* knows really that he has set us an Insoluble question because the next message comes a few minutes later:

PEDAGOGUE TO GROUND. IF NO GUARANTEE LANDER SAFE MUST SEEK MILITARY ASSISTANCE.

Now I see why they are sending in Clear; it is intended as a Deterrent to the Firsters. I just hope it does not work the wrong way.

Blazer Weigh is thinking of another Consequence and makes it known in a shout of horror: "Military Assistance? That means we'd be Stuck here for another week!"

This leads to Uproar and a series of plans for driving off the Firsters long enough for us to reach the Landing ground. I am trying to decide whether in fact we could Trust the Firsters, supposing they promised to let us go to the Lander without trying to Capture it; I think we probably could, but Probably is not apt to be good enough for John Li Chu . . .

I become gradually aware that the Floor has started to Vibrate; and just as this Registers clearly the Vibration rises up the scale and turns into Sound. It is the most Enormous, Earth-shaking, Ear-boggling Rumpus that ever invaded my Consciousness, and while it is going on I cannot Think or do anything else; then after about thirty eternal seconds it suddenly Stops.

There is one second of echoing silence, and then a voice from the radio; *Landing Alert.* Msilikatse *landing alongside row of houses at Coordinates* (a string of numbers which Blazer feverishly starts to check). *Clear the area. Warning. Clear the area Coordinates* (Numbers again) Msilikatse *landing in ten minutes. Clear below.*

Not even Blazer notices for some moments that *Pedagogue*'s Com officer has come through again.

PEDAGOGUE TO GROUND. VERY LARGE OBJECT YOUR VICINITY, TWO KILOMETERS UP AN DESCENDING. HOT SPOTS DISPERSING. SUGGEST YOU EVACUATE.

The question is, Do we trust *Msilikatse*'s Navigator or not . . . In the end it more or less goes by Default, before we have Settled anything there is that appalling Noise again for a few seconds, then a great Wallowing tremor in the ground underneath; then the radio again.

Msilikatse *landed safely*.

Then a minutes later: Msilikatse *to Terran Friends. The wicked ones have run. Tell your Lander to come quickly before they return.*

When the Lander eventually comes down it is on *Msilikatse*'s two acres of upper deck, which is a much bigger open space than the one where they landed Blazer Weigh and the Astral Cad. However that is not for several hours. Meanwhile there has been an Emotional meeting in *Msilikatse*, which turns into a Celebration when the Chief Engineer has grasped that the Hulk has a Proton Monopile capable of recharging his Accumulators in four hours flat.

The Dagombans learned of our Situation by way of the radio traffic with *Pedagogue*, in which the Monopile was not mentioned; the Firster's messages were too roiled by Interference to be understood.

Another Item has been added to my list of Things I Never Thought Of, namely Space Ships Fly. But it did not occur even to Blazer that a ship the size of *Msilikatse* could take off to fly 14 kilometers and then land again. (Of course in any properly Settled planet a ship putting down anywhere except on the designated Space Field would be landing in very hot water indeed.)

And it certainly would not have occurred to any of us that *Msilikatse* might Take off and Land just to make our Besiegers run away, simply because we had once tried to help *them* and therefore they considered us friends.

It is not till we return to the Hulk to show the Chief Engineer and his staff the kind of connections he will need to make to the Monopile that we discover a string of plaintive Messages from *Pedagogue*, wanting to know What goes on; and John Li Chu is not Happy when informed that we shall not be ready to take off for several hours. However we point out he would lose a lot More time if he had to go to Rosemary in search of Military Assistance and that we are finishing a Professional Job.

Of course there is no way to know that the Firsters will use our Recommendations and Reports for anything but Kindling; but we have also put out the Manuals on all the more important pieces of equipment, with Notes by Blazer on the various Peculiarities they have developed over the years; which ought to show that we really do mean well by them, at least. Also a Document stating that the equipment in the Hulk is now the Lawful property of the people living on Figueroa at the date of our departure, which might be Useful if anyone tries to take it away.

We have to Leave before the Dagombans have finished Recharging, and then they have to go back to the Space Gate to take on board plants they will need for Reoxygenation, also some equipment that got left outside when they Took off to the rescue; but after the Lander docks in *Pedagogue*'s garage space and just before we break orbit the Radar shows a massive Shape floating slowly up from the ground. The Com officer comes in with a Message, badly garbled, but with enough Redundancy to be sure that it is saying Goodbye, they are going Home.

So are we. Back to Russett, that is.

If M'Clare says I have not done my Assignment and must Repeat Field Studies I shall go on Strike and also Strike him, Field Studies are mainly for Experience and I consider I have Had Enough.

Anyway I have certainly Learned a lot; some of it I will not know I have Learned until later on, but one important thing I am sure of Now.

With Mankind Expanding in all directions and new planets being colonized every decade, people *need* Cultural Engineers.

Part Four:
THE LOST KAFOOZALUM

I REMEMBER SOME BAD TIMES, MOST OF THEM BACK HOME on Excenus 23; the worst was when Dad fell under the reaping machine but there was also the one when I got lost twenty miles from home with a dud radio, at the age of twelve; and the one when Uncle Charlie caught me practicing emergency turns in a helicar round the main weather-maker; and the one on Figueroa being chased by a cybercrane; and the time Dad decided to send me to Earth to do my Education.

This time is bad in a different way; no sharp edges but kind of a desolation.

Most of the people I know are feeling bad just now, because at Russett College we finished our Final Examination five days ago and Results are not due for 2 weeks.

My friend B Laydon says This is yet another Test anyone still sane at the end being proved tough enough to break a Molar on. She says also The worst part is in bed remembering all the things she could have written and did not; The second worst is also in bed picturing how to explain to her parents when they get back to Earth that *someone* has to come bottom and in a group as brilliant as Russett College Cultural Engineering Class this is really no disgrace.

I am not worried that way so much. I cannot remember what I wrote, anyway, and I can think of one or two people I am pretty sure will come Bottomer than me—or B either. I would prefer to think it is just Finals cause me to feel miserable, but it is not.

In Psychology they taught us The mind has the faculty of concealing any motive it is ashamed of, especially from itself; seems unfortunately mine does not have this gadget supplied.

I never wanted to come to Earth, I was sent to Russett against my will and counting the days till I could get back to Home, Father and Excenus 23, but the sad truth is that now the longed-for moment is nearly on top of me I do not want to go.

Dad's farm was a fine place to grow up, but now I have had four years on Earth the thought of going back there makes me feel like a three-weeks' chicken got to get back in the shell.

B and I are on an island in the Pacific. Her parents are on Caratacus researching on local art forms, so she and I came here to be miserable in company and away from the rest.

It took me years on Earth to get used to all this water around, it seemed Unnatural and dangerous to have it all lying loose that way, but now I shall miss even the Sea.

The reason we have this long suspense over Finals is that they will not use Reading Machines to mark the papers for fear of cutting down Critical Judgment; so each paper has to be read word by word by three Examiners and there are forty-three of us and we wrote six papers each.

What I think is I am sorry for the Examiners, but B says they were the ones who *set* the papers and it serves them perfectly right.

I express surprise because D. J. M'Clare our Professor is one of them, but B says He is one of the greatest men in the galaxy, of course, but she gave up thinking him perfect *years* ago.

One of the main attractions on this Island is swimming under water, especially by moonlight. Dad sent me a fish-boat as a birthday present two years back, but I never used it on account of my above-mentioned attitude to water. Now I got this feeling of Carpe Diem, make the most of Earth while I am on it because I probably shall not pass this way again.

The fourth day on the Island it is full moon at ten o'clock, so I pluck up courage to wriggle into the boat and go out under the Sea. B says Fish parading in and out of reefs just remind her of Cultural Engineering (crowd behavior) so she prefers to turn in early and find out what nightmare her subconscious will throw up *this* time.

The reefs by moonlight are everything they are supposed to be, Why did I do not do this often while I had the chance? I stay till my oxygen is nearly gone, then come out and sadly press the button that collapses the boat into a thirty-pound package of plastic hoops and oxygen cans. I sling it on my back and head for the chalet B and I hired among the coconut trees.

I am crossing an open space maybe fifty yards from it when a Thing drops on me out of the air.

I do not see the Thing because part of it covers my face, the rest is grabbed round my arms and my waist and my hips and whatever, I cannot see and I cannot scream and I cannot find anything to Kick. The Thing is strong and rubbery and many-armed and warmish, and less than a second after I first feel it I am being hauled up into the Air.

I do not care for this at all.

I am at least fifty feet up before it occurs to me to bite the hand that gags me and then I discover it is Plastic, not alive at all. Then I feel Self and encumbrance scraping through some kind of aperture; there is a sharp click as of a door closing and the Thing goes limp all round me.

I spit out the bit I am biting and it drops away so I can see.

Well!

I am in kind of a cup-shaped space maybe ten feet across but not higher than I am; there is a trapdoor in the ceiling; the Thing is lying all around me in a mess of plastic arms, with an extensible stalk connecting it to the wall. I kick free and it turns over exposing the label FRAGILE CARGO right across the back.

The next thing I notice is two holdalls, B's and mine, clamped against the wall, and the next after that is the Opening of a trapdoor in the ceiling and B's head silhouetted in it remarking Oh *there* you are, Liz.

I confirm this statement and ask for Explanations.

B says She doesn't understand all of it but it is all right.

It is not all right, I reply, if she has joined some Society such as for the Realization of Fictitious Improbabilities that is her privilege but no reason to involve *me*.

B says Why do I not stop talking and come up and see for myself?

There is a slight hitch when I jam in the trapdoor, then B helps me get the boat off my back and I drop it on FRAGILE CARGO and emerge into the cabin of a Hopper, drop-shaped, cargo-carrying.

There are one or two Peculiar points about it or maybe one or two hundred, such as the rate at which we are ascending which seems to be bringing us right above the

Unwillingly to Earth

Atmosphere; but the main thing I notice is the pilot. He has his back to us but is recognizably Ram Gopal who graduated in Cultural Engineering last year, Rumor says next to top of his Class.

I ask him What kind of melodramatic shenanigan is this?

B says We had to leave quietly in a hurry without attracting attention so she booked us out of the Hotel *hours* ago and she and Ram have been hanging around waiting for me ever since.

I point out that the scope-trace of an Unidentified Flying Object will occasion a lot more Remark than a normal departure even at midnight.

At this Ram smiles in an inscrutable manner and B gets nearly as cross as I do, seems she has mentioned this point before.

We have not gone into it properly when the cabin suddenly shifts through a right angle. B and I go sliding down the vertical floor and end sitting on a window. There is a jolt and a shudder and Ram mutters things in Hindi and then suddenly Up is nowhere at all.

B and I scramble off the window and grab fixtures so as to stay put. The stars have gone and we can see nothing except the dim glow over the instruments; then lights go on outside.

We are looking into the hold of a Ship.

Our ten-foot teardrop is sitting next to another one, like two eggs in a rack. On the other side is a bulkhead; behind, the curve of the hull, and directly ahead an empty space, then another bulkhead and an open door, through which after a few seconds a head pokes cautiously.

The head is then followed by a body which kicks off against the wall and sails slowly towards us. Ram presses a stud and a door slides open in the hopper; but the new arrival stops himself with a hand on either side of the frame, his legs trailing any old how behind him. It is Peter Yeng Sen who graduated the year I did my Field Work.

He says "Gopal, dear fellow, there was no need for the knocking, we heard the bell all right."

Ram grumbles something about the guide-beam being mis-set, and slides out of his chair. Peter announces that we have only just made it as the deadline is in seven minutes' time. He waves B and me out of the hopper, through the door and into a corridor where a certain irregular Vibration is coming from the walls.

Ram asks What is that tapping? and Peter sighs and says The present generation of students has no Discipline at all.

At this B brakes with one hand against the wall and cocks her head to listen; next moment she laughs and starts banging with her fist on the wall.

Peter exclaims in Mandarin and tows her away by one wrist like a reluctant kite. The rapping starts again and I suddenly recognize a Primitive signaling system called Regret or something, I guess because it was used by people in situations they did not like such as Sinking ships or Solitary confinement; it is done by tapping on water pipes and such.

Someone found it in a book and the more childish element in College learned it up for Signaling during compulsory lectures, Interest waning abruptly when the lecturers started to learn it too.

I never paid much attention not expecting to be in Solitary confinement much; this just shows you; next moment Ram opens a door and pushes me through it, the door clicks behind me and Solitary confinement is what I am in.

I remember this code is really called Remorse which is what I feel for not learning it when I had the chance.

However I do not have long for it, a speaker in the wall requests everyone to lie down as acceleration is about to begin. I strap down on the couch which fills half the com-

Unwillingly to Earth 217

partment, countdown begins and at Zero the floor is suddenly *down* once more.

I wait till my stomach settles, then rise to explore.

I am in an oblong room about two and a half meters by four, it looks as though it had been hastily Partitioned off from a larger space. The walls are prefab plastic sheet, the rest is standard fittings slung in and bolted down with the fastenings showing.

How many of my classmates are on this ship? *Remorse* again as tapping starts on either side of me.

Discarding such Hypotheses as that Ram and Peter are going to hold us for Ransom—which might work for me as my Dad is a millionaire, but not for B whose parents think money is Vulgar—or that we are being carried off to found an Ideal Colony somewhere—any first-year student can tell you why that won't work—only one idea seems plausible.

This is that Finals were not final and we are in for a Test of some sort.

After ten minutes I get some Evidence; a Reading Machine is trundled in.

I prowl round it looking for tricks but it seems standard: I take a seat in it, put on the headset and turn the switch.

Hypothesis confirmed, I suppose.

There is a reel in place and it contains background information on a problem in Cultural Engineering all set out the way we are taught to do it in Class. The Problem concerns development on a planet got settled by two groups during the Exodus and been isolated ever since.

Well while a Reading Machine is running there is no time to think, it crams in data at full speed and Evaluation has to wait. However my subconscious goes into action and when the reel stops it produces a Suspicion full grown.

The thing is too tidy.

When we were First Year we dreamed up Situations like this and argued like mad over them, but they were a lot too neat for real life and too Dramatic as well.

However one thing M'Clare said to us, and every other lecturer too, just before Finals, was Do not spend time trying to figure out what the Examiner was after but answer the question as set; I am more than halfway decided this is some mysterious Oriental idea of a joke but I get busy Thinking in case it is not.

The Problem goes like this:

The planet is called Incognita in the reel and it is right on the edge of the known volume of space, it got settled by two groups somewhere between three and three and a half centuries ago. The rest of the Human Race never heard of it till maybe three years back.

(Well it could happen that way, inhabited planets are still turning up eight or ten a century, on account of during the Exodus some folk were willing to travel a year or more so as to get Away from the rest.)

The ship that spotted the planet as inhabited did not land, but reported to Central Government, Earth, who shipped Observers out to take a look.

(There was a rumor circulating at Russett that the Terrie Gov might employ some of us on that kind of job, but it never got official. I do not know whether to believe this bit or not.)

It is stated that the Observers landed secretly and mingled with the natives unobserved.

(This is not Physically impossible but sounds too like a Field Trip to be true.)

The Observers are not named but stated to be graduates of the Cultural Engineering Class.

They put in a few months' work and sent home unanimous Crash Priority Reports the situation is *bad*, getting worse, and the prognosis is War.

Unwillingly to Earth

Brother.

I know people had Wars, I know one reason we do not have them now is just With so many planets and cheap transportation pressure has other Outlets; these people scrapped their ships for factories and never built more.

But.

There are only about ten million of them and surely to goodness a whole Planet gives room enough to keep out of each other's hair?

Well this is not Reasoning but a reaction, I go back to the data for another look.

The root trouble is stated to be that two groups landed on the planet without knowing the others were there, when they met thirty years later they got a disagreeable Shock.

I cannot see there was any basic difference between them, they were very similar, especially in that neither lot wanted anything to do with people they had not picked themselves.

So they divided the planet along a Great Circle which left two of the main land-masses in one hemisphere and two in another.

They agreed each to keep to its own section and leave the other alone.

Twenty years later, trading like mad; each has certain minerals the other lacks; each has certain agricultural products the other finds it difficult to grow.

You think this leads to Cooperation Friendship and ultimate Federation?

I will not go into the incidents that make each side feel it is being Cheated; it is enough that from time to time each has a scarcity or hold-up on deliveries that upsets the other's Economy; and they start experimenting to become self-sufficient; and the exporter's Economy is upset in turn. And each thinks the other did it on purpose.

This sort of situation reacts internally leading to Politics.

There are troubles about a medium-sized island on the dividing line, and the profits from interhemispherical transport, and the laws of interhemispherical trade.

It takes maybe two hundred years, but finally each has expanded the Police into an army with a whole spectrum of weapons *not* to be used on any account except for Defense.

This situation lasts seventy years getting worse all the time; now Rumors have started on each side that the other is developing an Ultimate Weapon, and the political Parties *not* in power are agitating to move first before the thing is complete.

The Observers report War maybe not this year or the next but within ten, and if neither side was looking for an Ultimate Weapon to begin with they certainly are now.

Taking all this at Face value there seems an obvious Solution.

I am thinking this over in an academic sort of way when an itchy trickle of sweat starts down my vertebrae.

Who is going to *apply* this solution? Because if this is anything but another Test or the output of a diseased sense of humor, I would be sorry for Somebody.

I dial black coffee on the wall servitor and wish B were here so we could prove to each other the thing is just an Exercise; I do not do so well spotting proofs on my own.

Most of our class exercises concern something that happened, once.

After about ninety minutes the speaker requests me to write not more than one thousand words on any scheme to Improve the situation, and the Equipment required for it.

I spend ten minutes verbalizing the basic idea and an

hour or so on "equipment"; the longer I go on the unlikelier it all seems. In the end I have maybe two hundred words which acting on instructions I post through a slit in the door.

Five minutes later I realize I have forgotten the Time Factor.

If the original ship took a year reaching Incognita, it will take at least four months now; therefore it is more than four months since that report was written and it will be most of a year before anyone arrives and the War may have started already.

I sit back and by transition of ideas start to wonder where this ship is heading? We are still at one G and even on Mass-Time you cannot juggle apparent acceleration and spatial transition outside certain limits; we are not just orbiting but must be well out of the Solar System by now.

The speaker announces Everyone will now get some rest: I smell sleep-gas for one moment and have just time to lie down.

I guess I was tired, at that.

When I wake I feel more cheerful than I have for weeks; analysis indicates I am glad something *happened* even if it is another Exam.

I dial breakfast but am too restless to eat: I wonder how long this goes on or whether I am supposed to show Initiative and break out: I am examining things with this in mind when the speaker comes to life again.

"Ladies and Gentlemen. You have not been told whether the problem that you studied yesterday concerned a real situation or an imaginary one. You have outlined measures which you think would improve the situation described. Please consider, seriously, whether you would be prepared to take part yourself in the application of your plan."

Brother.
There is no way to tell whether those who say No will

be counted Cowardly or those who say Yes Rash Idiots or what, the owner of that voice has his inflections too well trained to give away anything except on purpose.

D. J. M'Clare.

Not in person but a Recording, anyway M'Clare is on Earth surrounded by exam papers.

I sit back and try to think, honestly: If that crack-brained notion I wrote out last night was going to be tried in dead earnest, *would* I take a hand in it?

The trouble is Hearing M'Clare's voice has convinced me it is a Test, I don't know whether it is testing my courage or my prudence in fact I might as well Toss for it.

Heads I am crazy, Tails a defaulter: Tails is what it is.

I seize my styler and write the decision down.

There is the slit in the door.

I twiddle the note and think Well nobody asked for it yet.

Suppose it is real, after all?

I remember the itchy, sweaty feeling I got yesterday and try to picture *really* embarking on a thing like this, but I cannot work up any lather today.

I begin to picture M'Clare reading my decision *not* to back up my own Idea.

I pick up the coin and juggle it around.

The speaker remarks When I am quite ready will I please make a note of my Decision and post it through the door.

The coin slips and falls to the floor: it is Heads this time.

Tossing coins is a pretty Feeble way to decide.

I drop the note in the disposer and take another sheet and write "*YES*. Lysistrata Lee." Using that name seems to make it more binding.

I slip the paper in the slit and poke it till it falls through.

Suddenly I am immensely hungry and dial breakfast all over again.

Just as I finish M'Clare's voice starts once more.

"It's always the minor matters that cause the most difficulty. The timing of this announcement has cost me as much thought as any aspect of the arrangements. The trouble is that however honest you are—and your honesty has been tested repeatedly—and however strong your imagination—about half of your training has been devoted to developing it—you can't possibly be sure, answering a hypothetical question, that you are giving the answer you would choose if you *knew* it was asked in dead earnest.

"Those of you who answered the question in the negative are out of this. They have been told it was a test, of an experimental nature, and have been asked to keep the whole thing a secret. They will be returning to Earth in a few hours' time. I ask the rest of you to think it over once again. Your decision is still private. Only the two people who gathered you together know which members of the class are in this ship. The list of possible and available helpers was compiled by the computer. I haven't seen it myself.

"You have a further half hour in which to make up your minds finally. Please remember that if you have any private reservations, or if you are secretly afraid, you may endanger us all. You all know enough psychology to realize this.

"If you still decide in favor of the Project, write your name on a slip of paper and post it as before. If you are not absolutely certain do nothing. Please think it over for half an hour."

Me, I had enough thinking. I write my name—just L. Lee—and post it straight away.

However I cannot stop thinking altogether. I guess I think very hard, in fact. My Subconscious insists afterwards that it did register the plop as something came through the slit, but my Conscious failed to notice it at all.

Hours later—my watch says twenty-five minutes but I guess the Mass-Time has affected it—anyway I had three times too much Solitary Confinement, when will they let me *out* of here?—there is a knock at the door and a second later it slides apart.

I am expecting Ram or Peter so it takes me an appreciable fraction of a moment to realize I am seeing D. J. M'Clare.

Then I remember he is back on Earth knee deep in Exam papers and conclude I am having a Hallucination.

This figment of my imagination says politely "Do you mind if I sit down?"

He collapses on the couch as though thoroughly glad of it.

It is a strange thing; every time I see M'Clare I am startled all over again at how good-looking he is; seems I forget it between times which is maybe why I never fell for him like most female students do.

However what strikes me this time is that he looks tired, three-days-sleepless tired with worries on top.

I guess he must be real, at that.

He says "Don't look so accusing, Lizzie, I only just arrived on this ship myself."

This does not make Sense; you cannot just *arrive* on a ship twenty-four hours after it goes on Mass-Time; or can you?

M'Clare leans back and closes his eyes and inquires whether I am one of the Morse enthusiasts?

So that is the word; I say When we get back I will learn it first thing.

"Well," he says, "I did my best to arrange anonymity for all of you; I suppose if I deliberately assemble a collection of ingenious idiots I can't complain if I find myself

Unwillingly to Earth

circumvented. I had to cheat and check that you really were on the list, and I knew whoever backed out *you'd* still be on board."

So I should hope he might: *Horrors*, there is my first answer screwed up on the floor and Writing uppermost.

However he has not noticed it; he goes on, "Anyway you of all people won't be thought to have dropped out because you were afraid."

I have just managed to hook my Heel over the note and get it out of sight. M'Clare has paused for an Answer and I have to dredge my Subthreshold memories for—

WHAT—?

M'Clare opens his eyes and says like I am enacting Last Straw, "Have some sense, Lizzie." Then in a different tone "Ram says he gave you the letter half an hour ago."

What letter?

My brain suddenly registers a small pale patch been occupying a corner of my Retina for the last half hour; it turns out to be a letter postmarked Excenus 23.

I disembowel it with one jerk. It is from my Dad and runs like this:

My dear Liz,

Thank you for your last, glad you are keeping fit and so am I.

I just got a letter from your College saying you will get a degree conferred on you on September 12th and parents will be welcome if on Earth.

Well Liz this I got to see and Charlie says the same, but the letter says too Terran Authority will not give permission to visit Earth just for this, so I wangled onto a Delegation coming to discuss trade with the Department of Interstellar Commerce. Charlie and I will be arriving on Earth August 24th.

Liz it is good to think I shall be seeing you again after four years. There are some things about your future I meant to write to Prof. M'Clare about, but now I shall be able to talk it over direct. Give him my regards.

Be seeing you, Lizzie girl.

*Yours affectionate Dad
J. X. Lee*

Dear old Dad, after all those years farming with a Weathermaker on a drydust planet I want to watch his face the first time he sees *real* rain.

Hell's Fires and Shades of Darkness, I won't be there!

M'Clare says "Your father wrote to me that he will be arriving on Earth on 24th August. I take it your letter says the same. I came on a Dispatch-boat; you can go back on it."

Now what is he talking about—? Then I get the drift.

I say "Look. So Dad will be on Earth before we get back. What difference does that make?"

"You can't let him arrive and find you missing."

Well I admit to a Qualm at the thought of Dad let loose on Earth without me, but after all Uncle Charlie is a born Terrie and can keep him in line; Hell he is old enough to look after himself.

"You met my Dad," I point out. "You think J. X. Lee would want any daughter of his backing out on a job so as to hold his hand? I can send him a letter saying I am off on a Field Study or a Test or whatever you say, and Hold everything till I get back: what are you doing about people's families on Earth already?"

M'Clare says we were all selected as having parents *not* on Earth at present, and I must go back.

I say like Hell I will.

He says he is my Official Guardian and Responsible for me.

I say he is just as Responsible for everyone else on this ship.

I spent years trying to think up a remark would really get Home to M'Clare; well I have done it now.

I say "Look. You are tired and worried and maybe not thinking so well just now.

"I know this is a very risky job, don't think I missed that. I tried hard to imagine it like you said over the speaker. I cannot quite imagine dying but I know how Dad will feel if I do. I did my level best to scare myself sick, then I decided it was just plain worth the risk. To work out a thing like this you have to have a kind of Arithmetic, you add in everybody's feelings with the other factors, then if you get a Plus answer you forget everything else and go ahead.

"I am not going to think about it any more, because I added up the sum and got the answer and upsetting my nerves won't help. I guess you worked out the sum too. You decided ten million people were worth risking twenty, even if they do have parents. Even if they *are* your students. Well, that was the right answer, and you did give us all a chance to say No.

"Nothing has altered that, only the Values look different to you because you are Tired and worried—and probably missed breakfast, too."

Brother some Speech, I wonder what got into me? M'Clare is wondering, too, or maybe gone to sleep Sitting there, it is some time before he answers.

"Lizzie, you are deplorably right on one thing at least. I don't know whether I was fit to make such a decision when I made it, but I'm *not* fit now. As far as you personally are concerned . . ." He trails off looking Tireder than ever, then picks up again suddenly: "You are again quite right. I am every bit as responsible for the other people on board as I am for you."

He climbs slowly to his feet and walks out.

* * *

The door is left open and I take this as an invitation to Freedom and shoot through it in case it was a mistake.

No because Ram is opening doors all along the corridor and ten of Russett's brightest come pouring out like Mercury finding its own level and coalesce in the middle of the floor.

The effect of release is such that after four minutes Peter's head appears at the top of a stairway and he says The row is lifting the deck plates, will we for Time's sake go along to the Conference Room which is Soundproofed.

The Conference Room is on the next deck and like our cabins shows signs of hasty construction; the soundproofing is there but the Acoustics are kind of muffled and the generator is not boxed in but has cables trailing all over, and the fastenings have a strong but Temporary look.

Otherwise, there is a big table and a lot of chairs and a small projection box in front of each with a note-taker beside.

It is maybe this very functional setup or maybe the dead flatness of our voices in the damped room, but we do not have much to talk about any more. We automatically take places at the table, all at one end, leaving seven vacant chairs near the door.

Looking round I wonder what principle we were selected on.

Of my special friends B Laydon, Eru Te Whangoa and Kirsty Lammergow are present but Lily Chen and Likofo Komom'baraze and Jeanne LeBrun are not; we have Cray Patterson who is one of my special Enemies but not the Astral Cad: the rest are P. Zapotec, Nick Howard, Addo Quartey, Dillie Dixie, Lennie diMaggio, Pavel Christianovich and Shootright Crow.

Eru is at the end of the table, opposite the door, and

maybe feels this position puts it up to him to start the discussion; he opens by remarking "So nobody took the opportunity to withdraw."

Cray Patterson lifts eyebrows ceilingwards and drawls out that the decision was supposed to be a Private one.

B says Maybe but it did not work out like that, everyone who learned Morse knows who was on the ship, anyway they are all still here so what does it matter? And M'Clare would not have picked people who were going to funk it, after all.

My chair gets a kick on the ankle which I suppose was meant for B; Eru is nearly two meters tall but even his legs do not quite reach; he is the only one of us facing the door.

M'Clare has somehow shed his weariness; he looks stern but fresh as a daisy. There are four with him; Ram and Peter looking serious, one stranger in Evercleans looking determined to enjoy the party and another in uniform looking as though Nothing would make him.

M'Clare introduces the strangers as Colonel Delano-Smith and Mr. Yardo. They all sit down at the other end of the table; then he frowns at us and begins like this:

"Miss Laydon is mistaken. You were not selected on any such ground as she suggests. I may say that I am astonished at the readiness with which you all engaged yourselves to take part in such a desperate gamble; and, seeing that for the last four years I have been trying to persuade you that it is worthwhile, before making a decision of any importance, to spend a certain amount of thought on it, I was discouraged as well."

Oh.

"The criterion upon which you were selected was a very simple one. As I told you, you were chosen not by me but by a computer; the one in the College Office which registers such information as your home addresses and present whereabouts. You are simply that section of the class which could be picked up without attracting attention, because you all happened to be on holiday by yourselves or with other members of the class, and because your nearest relatives are not on Earth at present."

Oh, well.

All of us can see M'Clare is doing a Deflation job on us for reasons of his own; but it still works.

He now seems to feel the job is complete, and relaxes a bit.

"I was interested to see that you all, without exception, hit on variations of the same idea. It is of course the obvious way to deal with the problem." He smiles at us suddenly and I get Mad at myself because I *know* he is following the Rules for inducing a desired state of mind but I am still responding as meant. "I'll read you the most succinct expression of it; you may be able to guess the author."

Business with bits of paper.

"Here it is. I quote: "Drag in some outsider looks like he is going for both sides so they will gang up on him."

Yells of laughter and shouts of "Lizzie Lee!" Even the two strangers produce sympathetic grins; I do not find it so funny as all that myself.

"Ideas as to the form the 'outsider' should take were more varied. This is a matter I propose to leave you to work out together, with the assistance of Colonel Delano-Smith and Mr. Yardo. Te Whangoa, you take the chair."

Exit M'Clare.

This leaves the two halves of the table eyeing one another. Ram and Peter have been through this kind of session in their time; now they are leaning back preparing to watch us work. It is plain we are supposed to impress the abilities of Russett near-graduates on the two strangers and for some moments we are all occupied taking them in.

Colonel Delano-Smith is a small neat guy with a face

Unwillingly to Earth

that has all the muscular machinery for producing an expression; he just doesn't use it very often. Mr. Yardo is taller than any of us except Eru and flesh is spread very thin on his bones, including his face which splits now and then in a grin like an amiable skeleton. Where the Colonel fits is guessable enough. Mr. Yardo is presumably Expert at something but no data on *what*.

Eru rests his hands on the table and says we had better start; will somebody kindly outline an idea for making the Incognitans "gang up"? The simpler the better and it does not matter whether it is workable or not; pulling it to pieces will give us a start.

We all wait to see who will rush in; then I catch Eru's eye and see I am elected Clown again. I say "Send them a letter postmarked Outer Space signed BEM saying we lost our own planet in a nova and will take theirs over two weeks from Tuesday."

Mr. Yardo utters a sharp "Ha! Ha!" but it is not seconded; the Colonel having been Expressionless all along becomes more so; Eru says "Thank you, Lizzie." He looks across at Cray who is opposite me; Cray says there are many points on which he might comment; to take only one, two weeks from Tuesday leaves little time for "ganging up" and what happens when the BEMs don't come?

We are suddenly back in the atmosphere of a Seminar; Eru's glance moves to P. Zapotec who is sitting next to Cray and he says "These BEMs who lost their planet in a nova, how many ships have they? Without a base they cannot be very dangerous unless their fleet is very large."

It goes round the table.

Pavel: "How would BEMs learn to write?"

Nick: "How are they supposed to know Incognita is inhabited? How do they address the letter?"

The Crow: "Huh. Why write letters? Invaders just invade."

Kirsty: "We don't want to inflame these people against

alien races. We might *find* one some day. It seems to me this idea might have all sorts of undesirable by-products. Suppose each side regards it as a ruse on the part of the other. We might *touch off* a war instead of preventing it. Suppose they turn over to preparations for repelling the invaders, to an extent that cripples their economy? Suppose a panic starts?"

Dixie: "Say, Mr. Chairman, is there any of this idea left at all? How about an interim summary?"

Eru coughs to get a moment for thought, then says:

"In brief, the problem is to provide a Menace against which the two groups will be forced to unite. It must have certain characteristics;

"It must be sufficiently far off in Time for the threat to last several years, long enough to force them into a real combination.

"It must obviously be a plausible danger and they must get to know of it in a plausible manner. Invasion from outside is the only threat so far suggested.

"It must be a *limited* threat. That is, it must appear to come from one well-defined group. The rest of the Universe should appear benevolent or at worst neutral."

He just stops, rather as though there is something else to come. While the rest of us are waiting, B sticks her oar in to the following effect.

"Yes but look, supposing this goes *wrong*; it's all very well to make plans but suppose we do get some of Kirsty's side-effects just the same, well what I mean is suppose it makes the mess *worse* instead of Better we want some way we can just switch it off again.

"Look, this is just an illustration but suppose the Menace was pirates, if it went wrong we could have an Earth ship making official contact and they could just happen to say By the way have you seen anything of some Pirates, the Fleet wiped them up in this sector about six months ago."

"That would mean the whole Crew conniving so it won't do, but you see what I mean."

There is a bit of silence and then Addo says, "I think we should start afresh. We have had criticisms of Lizzie's suggestion, which perhaps was not wholly serious, and as Dillie says there is little left of it except the idea of a threat of invasion. The idea of an alien intelligent race has objections and would be very difficult to fake. The invaders must be *men*, from another planet. Another unknown one. But how do the people of Incognita come to know that they exist?"

More silence, then I hear my own voice speaking although it was my intention to keep Quiet for once; it sounds kind of creaky and it says "A ship. A crashed ship from Outside."

Whereupon another voice says "Really! Am I expected to swallow this?"

We had just about forgotten the Colonel, not to mention Mr. Yardo who contributes another "Ha! Ha!", so this reminder comes as a slight Shock, nor do we see what he is Talking about but this he proceeds to explain.

"I don't know why M'Clare thought it necessary to stage this discussion. I am already acquainted with his plan and have had orders to cooperate. I have expressed my opinion on using undergraduates in a job like this and have been overruled. If he, or you, imagine that priming you to bring his ideas out like this is going to reconcile me to the whole business you are mistaken. He might have chosen a more credible mouthpiece than that child with the curly hair—"

Here everybody wishes to Reply at once. The resulting Jam produces a moment of silence and I get in first.

"As for the curly hair I am rising twenty-four and I was only saying what we all thought. If we have the same ideas as M'Clare it is because he taught us for four years. How *else* would you set about it, anyway?"

My fellow students pick up their stylers and tap solemnly three times on the table; the Russett equivalent of "Hear! Hear!" The Colonel looks surprised.

Eru says coldly, "This discussion has not been rehearsed . . . As Lizzie . . . As Miss Lee says, we have been working together and thinking together for four years and have been taught by the same people."

"Very well," says Delano-Smith testily. "Tell me this, please; Do you regard this idea as practicable?"

Cray tilts his chair back and remarks to the ceiling, "This is rather a farce. I suppose we had to go through our paces for the Colonel's benefit—and Mr. Yardo's of course—but can't we be briefed properly now?"

"What do you mean by that?" snaps the Colonel.

"It's been obvious right along," says Cray, balancing his styler on one forefinger, "so obvious none of us has bothered to mention it, that accepting the normal limits of the Mass-Time drive, the idea of interfering on Incognita was doomed before it began. No conventional ship would have much hope of arriving before War broke out; and if it did arrive it couldn't do anything effective. Therefore I assume that this is *not* a conventional ship. I might accept that the Government has sent us out in a futile attempt to do the impossible, but I wouldn't believe it of M'Clare."

Cray is the only Terrie I know that acts like an Outsider's view of one; many find this difficult to take and the Colonel is plainly one of them. Eru intervenes quickly.

"I imagine we all realized that. Anyway this ship is obviously *not* a conventional model. If you accept the usual Mass-Time relationship between the rates of transition and the fifth power of the apparent acceleration, we must have reached about four times the maximum already."

Unwillingly to Earth

"Ram!" says B suddenly. "What did you do to stop the Hotel scope registering the Hopper you picked up me and Lizzie in?"

Everybody cuts in with something they have noticed about the Capabilities of this ship or the Hoppers, and Lennie starts hammering on the table and chanting "Brief! Brief! Brief!" and the others are starting to join in when Eru bangs on the table and Glares us all down.

Having got Silence he says very quietly, "Colonel Delano-Smith, I doubt whether this discussion can usefully proceed without a good deal more information: will you take over?"

The Colonel looks round at all the eager interested Maps hastily put on for his benefit and decides to take the Plunge.

"Very well. I suppose it is . . . Very well. The decision to use students from Russett was made at a very high level and I suppose—" Instead of saying "Very well" again he shrugs his shoulders and gets Down to it.

"The report from the planet we decided to call 'Incognita' was received thirty-one days ago. The Department of ExtraSolar Affairs has certain resources which are not publicized. This ship is one of them. She works on a modified version of Mass-Time which enables her to use about a thousand channels instead of the normal limit of two hundred; for good and sufficient reasons this has not been generally released."

Pause while we are silently dared to doubt the Virtue and sufficiency of these Reasons which personally I do not.

"To travel to Incognita direct would take about fifteen days by the shortest route. We shall take eighteen days as we have to make a detour."

But presumably we shall take only fifteen days back. Hurrah we can spend a week round the planet and still be back in time for Commemoration. We shall skip maybe a million awkward questions and I shall not disappoint Dad.

It is plain the Colonel is not filled with joy; far from it, he was not Happy revealing a departmental secret however obvious, but he likes the next item even less.

"We shall detour to an uninhabited system twelve days' transit time from here and make contact with another ship, the *Gilgamesh*."

At which Lennie diMaggio who has been silent till now brings his fist down on the table and exclaimes "You *can't*!"

Lennie for some reason is much upset; Delano-Smith gives him a peculiar look and says What does he know about it? and Lennie starts to stutter.

Cray remarks that Lennie's Childhood hobby is known to have been Space Ships and he suffers from Arrested Development.

B says it is Well known that Lennie is mad about the Space Force and Why not? it seems to have its uses, Go on and tell us, Lennie.

Lennie says "*G-G-Gilgamesh* was lost three hundred years ago!"

"The flaw in that statement," says Cray after a pause, "is that this may be another ship of the same name."

"No," says the Colonel. "Explorer Class cruiser. They went out of service two hundred and eighty years back."

The Space Force, I remember, does not reuse names of lost ships; some say Very Proper Feeling others Superstitious Rot.

B says "When was she found again?"

Lennie says it was j-j-just thirty-seven revolutions of his native planet which means f-f-fifty-three Terretrial years ago, she was found by the Interstellar scout *Crusoe*.

Judging by the Colonel's expression this data is Classified. He does not know that Lennie's family come from one of the oldest settled planets and are space-goers to a

Unwillingly to Earth

man, woman and juvenile; they pick up ship gossip the way others hear about the relations of people next door.

Lennie goes on to say that the Explorer Class were the first official exploration ships sent out from Earth when the Terries decided to find out what had happened to colonies formed during the Exodus. *Gilgamesh* was the first to re-make contact with Garuda, Legba, Lister, Cor-bis and Antelope; she vanished on her third voyage.

"Where was she found?" Eru asks.

"Near the p-p-pole of an uninhabited planet—maybe I shouldn't say where because that's a secret, but the rest is History if you know where to look."

Maybe the Colonel approves his discretion, anyway his face thaws very slightly, unless I am Imagining it.

"*Gilgamesh* crashed," he says. "Near as we can make out from the log, she visited Seleucis system. That's a swarmer sun. Fifty-seven planets, three settled; any number of fragments. The navigator calculated that after a few more revolutions one of the fragments was going to crash on an inhabited planet. Might have done a lot of damage. They decided to tow it away.

"Grappling-beams hadn't been invented. They thought they could use Mass-Time on it—a kind of reverse thrust—throw it off course.

"Mass-Time wasn't so well understood then. Bit off more than they could chew. Set up a topological relation that drained all the free energy out of the ship. Drive, heating system, life-support—everything.

"She had emergency circuits. When the engines came on again those took over—landed the ship, more or less, on the nearest planet. Too late, of course. Heating system never came on—there was a safety switch that had to be thrown by hand. She was embedded in ice when she was found. Hull breached at one point—no other serious damage."

"And the . . . crew?"

Dilly ought to know better than that.

"Lost with all hands," the Colonel says shortly.

"How about weapons?"

We are all startled. Cray is looking whitish but maintains his normal manner, i.e. offensive affectation, while pointing out that *Gilgamesh* can hardly be taken for a Menace unless she has some means of aggression about her.

Lennie says The Explorer Class were all armed—

Fine, says Cray. Presumably the weapons will be thoroughly obsolete and recognizable only to a Historian—

Lennie says that the construction of no weapon devised by the Space Department has ever been released; making it plain that anyone but a Nitwit knows that already.

Eru and Kirsty have been busy for some time writing notes to each other and she now gives a small sharp cough and having collected our attention utters the following Address.

"There is a point we all seem to have missed. To recapitulate: the idea is to take this ship *Gilgamesh* to Incognita and make it appear as though she had crashed there while attempting to land. I understand that the ship has been buried in the polar cap; though she must have been melted out if the people on *Crusoe* examined the engines. Of course the cold—All the same there may have been—well—changes. Or when . . . when we thaw the ship out again—"

I find I am swallowing good and hard, and several of the others look sickish, especially Lennie. Lennie has his eyes on the Colonel; it is not Prescience but a slight sideways movement of the Colonel's eyes causes him to blurt out "What is *he* doing here?"

Meaning Mr. Yardo who seems to have been asleep for some time, with his eyes open and a grin like the spikes on a dog collar. The Colonel gives him another sideways look and says "Mr. Yardo is an expert on the rehabilitation of space-packed materials."

This is stuff transported in unpowered hulls towed by grappling-beams; the hulls are open to space hence no need for Refrigeration, and the contents are transferred to specially equipped orbital stations before being taken down to the planet. But—

Mr. Yardo comes to life at the sound of his name and his Grin widens alarmingly.

"Especially meat," he says.

It is maybe two hours afterwards, Eru having adjourned the meeting so that we can . . . er . . . take in the implications of the new data. Lennie has gone off by himself; Kirsty thinks he needs Mothering and has gone after him; Eru, I suspect, is looking for Kirsty: Pavel and Aro and Dilly and the Crow are in a cabin arguing in whispers; Nick and P. Zapotek are exploring one of the Hoppers, Cargo-carrying, Drop-shaped, and I only hope they don't Hop through the hull.

B and I having done a tour of the ship and ascertained all this have withdrawn to the Conference Room because we are tired of our cabins and this seems to be the only other place to sit.

B breaks a long silence with the remark that However often you see it M'Clare's technique is something to watch; like choosing my statement to open with, it broke the ice beautifully.

I say "Shall I tell you something?"

B says Is it interesting?

"My statement," I inform her, "ran something like this: 'The best hope of inducing a suspension of the aggressive attitude of both parties, long enough to offer a hope of ultimate reconciliation, lies in the intrusion of a new factor, such as an outside force seen as hostile to both.'"

B says "Gosh . . . Come to think of it, Lizzie, you have

not written like that for years; you have gone all pompous like everyone else; well, that makes it even *more* clever of M'Clare."

Enter Cray Patterson and drapes himself sideways on a chair, announcing that his own thoughts begin to Weary him.

I say this does not surprise me at all.

"Lizzie my love," says he, "you are twice blessed, being not only witty yourself but he cause of wit in others; was that bit of Primitive Lee with which M'Clare regaled us really hot from the hand of the mistress or was it a mere pastiche?"

I say Whoever wrote that it was not me anyway.

"It struck me as pale and lukewarm compared with the real thing," continues Cray languidly, "which brings me to a point that, to quote dear Kirsty, seems to have been missed."

I say "Like what language these people wrote their log in that we can be *certain* the Incognitans won't know?"

"More than that," says B, "we didn't decide who they are or where they were coming from or how they came to crash or anything."

"Come to think of it," I point out "the language and a good many other things must have been decided already, because of getting the right hypnotapes and translators on board."

B suddenly lights up.

"Yes but look, I bet that's what we're here for, I mean that's why they picked us instead of Space Department people—the ship's got to have a past history, it has to come from a planet somewhere only no one must ever find out *where* it's supposed to be. Someone will have to fake a log, only I don't see how—"

"The first reel with data showing the planet of origin got damaged during the crash," says Cray impatiently.

"Yes, of course—but we have to find a reason why they

Unwillingly to Earth

were in that part of Space and it has to be a *nice* one, I mean so that the Incognitans when they finally read the log won't hate them any more—"

"Maybe they were bravely defending their planet by hunting down an interplanetary raider," I suggest.

Cray says it will only take the briefest contact with other planets to convince the Incognitans that interplanetary raiders can't and don't exist, modern planetary Alarm and Defense systems put them out of the question.

That's all *he* knows, B says, interplanetary raiders raided Lizzie's father's farm once; didn't they Liz?

(Yes in a manner of speaking, but they were bums who pinched a spaceship from a planet not many parsecs away, a sparsely inhabited mining world like my own with no real call for an alarm system; so that hardly alters the argument.)

"Well," says B, "the alarm system on Incognita can't be so hot or the observation ships could not have got in and out; unless of course they have *other* gadgets we don't know about.

"On the other hand," she considers, "to mention Interplanetary raiders raises the idea of Menace in an Unfriendly Universe again, and this is what we want to cancel out.

"These people," she says at last with a visionary look in her eye, "come from a planet which went isolationist and abandoned space travel; now they have built up their Civilization to a point where they can build ships of their own again, and the ones on *Gilgamesh* have cut loose from the ideas of their ancestors that led to their going so far afield—"

"*How* far afield?" says Cray.

"No one will ever know," I tell him. "Don't interrupt."

"Anyway," says B, "they set out to rejoin the rest of the Human Race just like the people on *Gilgamesh really* did, in fact a lot of this is Truth kind of backwards—they were looking for the Cradle of the Race, that's what. Then there was some sort of disaster that threw them off course to crash on an uninhabited section of a planet that couldn't understand their signals. And when Incognita finally does take to space flight again I bet the first thing the people do is to try and follow back where *Gilgamesh* came from and make contact with *them*. It'll become a legend on Incognita—the Lost People—The Lost . . . Lost—"

"The Lost Kafoozalum," says Cray impatiently. "In other words, we switch these people off a war only to send them on a wild goose chase."

At which point a strange voice chimes in, "No, no, no, son, you've got it all *wrong*."

Mr. Yardo is with us like a well-meaning skeleton.

During the next twenty-five minutes we learn a lot about Mr. Yardo including material for a good guess at how he came to be picked for this expedition; doubtless there are many experts on Reversal Of Vacuum-Induced Changes in Organic Tissue but maybe only one of them a Romantic at heart.

Mr. Yardo thinks chasing the Wild Goose will do the Incognitans all the good in the Galaxy, it will take their minds off controversies over interhemispherical trade and put them on to the quest of the Unobtainable; they will get to know something of the Universe outside their own little Speck . . . Mr. Yardo has seen a good deal of the Universe himself in the course of advising how to recondition space-packed meat and he has found it an Uplifting Experience.

We gather he finds this desperate bit of damfoolery we are engaged on now pretty Uplifting altogether.

Cray keeps surprisingly quiet but it is as well that the rest of the party starts to trickle in about twenty minutes later, the first arrivals remarking Oh *That's* where you've got to!

Unwillingly to Earth

Presently we are all congregated at one end of the table as before, except that Mr. Yardo is now sitting between B and me; when M'Clare and the Colonel come in he firmly stays where he is evidently considering himself One of Us now.

"The proposition," says M'Clare, "is that we take *Gilgamesh* to Incognita and land there in such a way as to suggest that she crashed. In the absence of evidence to the contrary the Incognitans are bound to assume that that was her intended destination, and the presence of weapons, even disarmed, will suggest that her mission was aggressive. Firstly, can anyone suggest a better course of action? or does anyone object to this one?"

We all look at Lennie who sticks his hands in his pockets and mutters "No."

Kirsty gives her little Cough and says there is a point which has not been mentioned.

If a heavily armed ship crashes on Incognita, will not the Gov. of the hemisphere in which it crashes be presented with new ideas for Offensive weapons? And won't this make it more likely that they will start aggression? And won't the fear of this make the other hemisphere even *more* likely to try and get in first before the new weapons are complete?

Hell, I ought to have thought of that.

From the glance of unwilling respect which the Colonel bestows on M'Clare it is plain these points have been dealt with.

"The weapons on *Gilgamesh* were disarmed when she was rediscovered," he says. "Essential sections were removed. The Incognitans won't be able to reconstruct how they worked."

Another fact for which we shall have to provide an explanation. Well how about this: The early explorers sent out by these people—the people in *Gilgamesh*—oh, use

Cray's word and call them the Lost Kafoozalum—anyway their ships were armed, but they never found any enemies and the Idealists of B's story refused even to carry arms any more.

(Which is just about what happened when the Terries set out to rediscover the Colonies, after all.)

So the Lost Kafoozalum could not get rid of their weapons completely because it would have meant rebuilding the ship; so they just partially dismantled them.

Mr. Yardo suddenly chips in, "About that other point, surely there must be some neutral ground left on a half-occupied planet like that?" He beams round, pleased at being able to contribute.

B says "The thing is," and stops.

We wait.

We are about to give up Hope when she resumes, "The thing is, it will have to be neutral ground of course, only that might easily become a thingummy . . . I mean a, a *causus belli* in itself. So the *other* thing is it ought to be a place which is very hard to get at, so difficult that neither side can really get to it *first*, they'll have to reach an agreement and Cooperate."

"Yeah," says Dillie, "sounds fine, but what kind of place *is* that?"

I am sorting out in my head the relative merits of Mountains deserts gorges et cetera when I am seized with Inspiration at the same time as half the group; we say the same thing in different words and for a time there is Babel, then the idea emerges:

"Drop her into the Sea!"

The Colonel nods resignedly.

"Yes," he says, "that's what we're going to do."

He presses a button and our projection-screens light up, first with a map of one pole of Incognita, expanding in scale till finally we are looking down on one little bit of coast on one of the polar islands. A glacier descends into

Unwillingly to Earth

it from mountains inland and there is a bay between cliffs. Then we gct a stereo pic of approximately the least hospitable scenery I ever did see—(except maybe when Parvati Lal Dutt's brother made me climb what he swore was the smallest peak in the Himalayas).

It is a small bay backed by tumbled cliffs. A shelving beach can be deduced from the contours and occasional boulders big enough to stick through the snow that smothers it all. A sort of mess of rocks and mud at the back might be a glacial moraine. Over the sea the ice is split in all directions by jagged rifts and channels; the whole thing is a bit like Antarctica but nothing like high enough or white enough to Uplift the spirit, it looks not only chilly but kind of *mean*.

"This place," says the Colonel, "is the only one about which we have any topographical information, that seems to meet the requirements . . . Got to know about it from an elementary Planetography textbook. One of the Observers had the sense to see we might need something of the sort. This place"—the stereo jogs as he taps his projector—"seems it's the center of a rising movement in the crust . . . that's not to the point. Neither side has bothered to claim the land at the poles . . ."

I see why not if it's all like this—

". . . and a ship trying to land on those cliffs might very well pitch over into the sea. That is, if she were trying to land on emergency rockets."

Rockets; that brings home the ancientness of *Gilgamesh*—but I suppose the ships that colonized Incognita probably carried emergency rockets too.

This settled, the meeting turns into a briefing session and merges imperceptibly with the beginnings of the Job.

The Job of course is Faking the background of the crash: working out the past history and present aims of the Lost Kafoozalum. We have to invent a Planet and what's more difficult convey all the essential Information about it by the sort of sideways hints you gather among people's personal possessions: diaries, letters et cetera: and what is even *more* difficult we have to leave out anything that could lead to definite Identification of our unknown world with a Known one.

We never gave that world a name; it might be dangerous. Who speaks of their world by name, except to strangers? They call it "Home" or "The World" as often as not.

Some things have been decided for us. Language, for instance—one of the two thousand or so Earth tongues that went out of use late enough to be plausible as the main language of a colonized planet. The settlers on Incognita were not the sort to take along Dictionaries of the lesser-known tongues, so the computers at Russett had a fairly wide choice.

We had to take a hypnocourse in that language. Ditto the script, one of several forgotten phonetic shorthands. (Designed to enable the tongues of Aliens to be taken down. The Aliens have never been met, but it is plausible enough that some colony might have kept the script alive: after all Thasia uses something of the sort to this day.)

The final result of our work looks pretty small. Twenty-three "Personal Background Kits"—a few letters, a diary in some, an assortment of artifacts.

Whoever stocked the ship we are on supplied wood, of the half-a-dozen different species that have been taken wherever men have gone; stocks of a few plastics—known at the time of the Exodus or easily developed from those known, and not associated with any particular planet. Also books on design, a Formwriter for translating drawings into materials, and so on. Somebody put in a lot of work before this voyage began.

Most of the time it is like being back at Russett doing a group Project. What we are working on has no more and no less reality than that. The written work is all read into a computer and checked against everyone else's. At first we keep clashing. Gradually a consistent picture builds up and gets translated in the end into the Personal Background Kits. The Lost Kafoozalum start to exist like people in a History book.

Fifteen days' hard work and then we reach—call it Planet *Gilgamesh*.

I wake in my bunk to hear that there will be a brief Cessation of weight—strap down, please.

We are coming off Mass-Time to go on Planetary Drive.

Colonel Delano-Smith is in charge of operations on the planet, with Ram and Peter to assist. None of the rest of us sees the melting out of fifty years' accumulation of ice, the pumping away of the water, the fitting and testing of the mounts for the grappling-beams. We stay inside the ship, on five-eighths G which we do not have time to adapt to, and try to work, discarding the results before the computer gets a chance to. There is hardly any work left to do, anyway.

It takes nearly twelve hours to get the ship free, caulked, and ready to lift. (Her hull has to be patched because Mr. Yardo's operations use several sorts of vapors and gases.) Then there is a queer blind period with Up now one way, now another, and sudden jerks and tugs that upset everything not in gimbals or tied down; interspersed with periods of Weightlessness without any warning at all. After an hour or two of this it would be hard to say whether Mental or physical discomfort is more acute; B, consulted, however, says my Autonomic system must be quite something, after five minutes *her* thoughts were with her viscera entirely . . .

Then, suddenly, we are back on Mass-Time again.

Two days to go.

At first being on Mass-Time makes everything seem normal again. By sleep-time there is a strain, and next day it is everywhere. I know as well as any that on Mass-Time the greater the mass the faster the shift; all the same I cannot help feeling we are being slowed, dragged back by the dead ship coupled to our Live one.

When you stand by the hull *Gilgamesh* is only ten feet away.

I should have kept something to work on like Kirsty and B who have not done their Letters for Home in Case of Accidents. Mine is signed and sealed long ago. I am making a good start on a Neurosis when Delano-Smith announces a Meeting for one hour ahead.

Hurrah! now there is a time-mark fixed I think of all sorts of things I should have done before; such as taking a look at the controls of the Hoppers.

I have been in one of them half an hour and figured out most of the dials—Up Down and Sideways are controlled much as in a helicar, but here a big viewscreen has been hooked into the autopilot—when across the hold I see the airlock start to move.

Gilgamesh is on the other side.

It takes forever to open. When at last it swings wide on a dark tunnel what comes through is a storage rack, empty, floating on antigrav.

What follows is a figure in a spacesuit; modern type, but the windows of the Hopper are semipolarized and I cannot make out the face inside the bubble top.

He slings the rack up on the bulkhead, takes off the helmet and hangs that up too. Then he just stands. I am beginning to muster enough sense to wonder Why when he comes slowly across the hold.

Reaching the doorway he says "Oh, it's you, Lizzie. You'll have to help me out of this. I'm stuck."

M'Clare.

The outside of the suit is still freezing cold; maybe this is what has jammed the fastening. After a few seconds'

Unwillingly to Earth

tugging it suddenly gives way. M'Clare climbs out of the suit leaving it standing and says "Help me with these, will you?"

These are a series of transparent containers from a pouch slung at one side of the suit. I recognized them as the envelopes in which we put the Personal Background Kits.

I say "There ought to be twenty-three."

"No," says M'Clare dreamily, "twenty-two, we're saving one of them."

What in Space is the use of an extra set of faked documents and oddments—

He seems to wake up suddenly and says "What are you doing here, Lizzie?"

I explain and he wanders over to the Hopper and starts to demonstrate the controls.

There is something odd about all this. M'Clare is obviously dead tired, but kind of relaxed; seeing that the moment of Danger is only thirty-six hours off I don't understand it. Probably several of his students are going to have to risk their lives—

I am on the point of seeing something Important when the speaker announces in the Colonel's voice that Professor M'Clare and Miss Lee will report to the Conference Room at once please.

M'Clare looks at me and grins. "Come along, Lizzie. Here's where we take orders for once, you and I."

It is the Colonel's Hour. I suppose that having to work with Undergraduates is something he could never quite forget, but from the way he looks at us we might almost be Space Force personnel—low-grade, of course, but Respectable.

Everything is at last worked out and he has it on paper in front of him; he puts the paper four square on the table, gazes into the middle distance and proceeds to Recite.

"One. This ship will go off Mass-Time on 2nd August at 11:27 hours ship's time—"

Thirty-six hours from Now—

"—at a point one thousand kilometers vertically above Coordinates 1650 E, 7320 S, on Planet Incognita, approximately one hour before midnight local time."

Going on planetary drive as close as that will indicate that something is pretty badly wrong to begin with.

"Two. This ship will descend, coupled to *Gilgamesh* as at present, to a point seventy kilometers above the planetary surface. It will then uncouple, discharge one Hopper, and go back on Mass-Time. Estimated time for this stage of descent forty minutes.

"Three. The Hopper will then descend on its own engines at the maximum safe speed; estimated time thirty-seven minutes. *Gilgamesh* will complete descent in thirty-three minutes. Engines of *Gilgamesh* will not be used except for the gyro auxiliaries. The following installations have been made to allow for control of the descent: a ring of eight rockets in pentathene mounts around the tail end, and one heavy-duty antigrav unit inside the nose. Sympathizer controls hooked up with a visiscreen and a computer have also been installed in the nose.

"Four. *Gilgamesh* will carry one man only. The Hopper will carry a crew of three. The pilot of *Gilgamesh* will establish the ship on the edge of the cliff, supported on antigrav half a meter above the ground and leaning towards the sea at an angle of approximately 20° with the vertical. Except for this landing will be automatic.

"Five."

The Colonel's voice has Lulled us into passive acceptance; now we are jerked into sharper attention by the faintest possible check in it.

"The worst possible outcome of the Project would be for the Incognitans to discover that the crash has been faked. This would be inevitable if they were to capture (a) the Hopper (b) any member of the crew (c) any of the new installations in *Gilgamesh*, but especially the anti-grav.

"The function of the Hopper is to pick up the pilot of *Gilgamesh* and also to check that ground appearances are consistent. If not, a landslip will be produced on the cliff-edge, using power tools and explosives carried for the purpose. That is why the Hopper will carry three people; but the probability of such action being required is low."

So I should think; Ground appearances are supposed to show that *Gilgamesh* landed using emergency rockets and then toppled over the cliff and this will be exactly what Happened.

"The pilot will carry a one-frequency low-power transmitter activated by the change in magnetic field on leaving the ship. The Hopper will remain at one hundred and fifty meters until this signal is received. It will home on the signal and pick up the pilot, check ground appearances and rendezvous with this ship at a height of three hundred kilometers at 18:27 hours.

"The ship and the Hopper are both radar-absorbent and therefore will not register on alarm systems; by keeping to local night-time they should be safe from visual detection.

"Danger (c) will be dealt with in two stages. The rocket-mounts being in pentathene will be destroyed by half an hour's immersion in sea water. The installations in the nose will be destroyed with Andite."

Andite produces complete molecular disruption in a short range, hardly any damage outside it; the effect will be as though the nose broke off on impact. I suppose the Incognitans will waste a lot of time looking for it on the bed of the sea.

"Four ten-centimeter cartridges will be inserted within the nose installations. The fuse will have two alternative settings. The first will be timed to act at 12:50 hours, seven minutes after the estimated time of landing. It will not be possible to deactivate it before 12:45 hours. This takes care of the possibility of the pilot's becoming incapacitated during the descent.

"Having switched off the first fuse the pilot will get the ship into position and then activate a second, timed to blow after ten minutes. He will then leave the ship. When the antigrav is destroyed the ship will of course fall into the sea.

"Six. The pilot of *Gilgamesh* will be dressed in a spacesuit of the pattern used by the original crew and will carry Personal Background Kit number 23. Should he fail to escape from the ship no attempt will be made to rescue him."

The Colonel takes up the paper, folds it in half and puts it down one centimeter farther away.

"It will give the whole game away," he says, "if one of the Hopper's crew should fall into Incognitan hands, alive or dead. Therefore they don't take *any* risk of that."

He lifts his gaze ceilingwards. "I'm asking for three volunteers."

Silence. Manning the Hopper is definitely Second best. Then light bursts upon me and I lift my hand and hack B on the ankle.

I say "I volunteer."

B gives me a dubious glance and then lifts her hand too.

Cray on the other side of the table is slowly opening his mouth when there is an outburst of Waving on the far side of B.

"Me too, Colonel! I volunteer!"

Mr. Yardo proceeds to explain that his special job is Over and done, he can be more easily spared than anybody, he may be too old to take charge of *Gilgamesh* but will back himself as a Hopper pilot against anybody.

The Colonel cuts this short by accepting all three. He then unfolds his paper again.

"Piloting *Gilgamesh*," he says. "I'm not asking for volunteers now. You'll go to your cabins in four hours' time and those who want to will volunteer, secretly. To a computer hookup. Computer will select on a random basis and notify the one chosen. Give him his final instructions, too. No one need know who it was until it's all over. He can tell anyone he likes, of course."

A very slight note of Triumph creeps in. "One point. Only men need volunteer."

Instant outcry from Kirsty and Dillie; B turns to me with a look of Awe.

"Nothing to do with prejudice," says the Colonel testily. "Just facts. *Gilgamesh*'s crew was all male. Can't risk one solitary woman being found on board. Besides—spacesuits, Personal Background Kits—all designed for men."

Kirsty and Dilly turn on me looks designed to Shrivel and B whispers Lizzie you are wonderful, really you are.

The session dissolves. We three get an intensive course of Instruction on our duties and are ordered off to sleep. After breakfast next morning I run into Cray who says Before I continue about what is evidently pressing business would I care to kick him, hard?

Not right now, I reply, what for?

"Miss Lee," says Cray, dragging it out longer than ever, "although I have long realized that your brain functions in a manner much superior to Logic I had not sense enough yesterday to follow my own instinct and do what you did as soon as you did it; therefore that desiccated meat handler got in first."

I say "So you weren't picked for pilot? It was only one chance in ten."

"Oh," says Cray, "did you really think so?" He gives me a long look and goes away.

I suppose he noticed that when the Colonel came out

with his remarks about No women in *Gilgamesh* I was as surprised as any.

Presently the three of us are issued with protective clothing; we just might have to venture out onto the Planet's surface and therefore we get white one-piece suits to protect against Cold heat moisture desiccation radioactivity and Mosquitoes; quite becoming, too.

B and I drag out dressing for thirty minutes; then we just sit while Time crawls asymptotically towards the Hour.

Then the speaker calls us to go.

We are Out of the cabin before it says two words and racing for the hold; so that we are just in time to see a figure out of a Historical movie—padded, jointed, neckless metal dome for head and blank reflections where the face ought to be—stepping through the airlock.

The Colonel and Mr. Yardo are there already. The Colonel packs us into the Hopper and personally closes the door, and for once I know what he is thinking; he is wishing he were *not* the only pilot on the ship who could possible rely on bringing her on and off Mass-Time at one particular defined spot of Space.

Then he leaves us: Half an hour to go.

The light in the hold begins to alter. Instead of being softly diffused it separates into sharp-edged pools and patches with Dark between. The air is being pumped into store.

Fifteen minutes.

The hull vibrates and a hatch slides open in the floor so that starry black Space looks through; it closes again.

Mr. Yardo lifts the Hopper gently off its mount and lets it back again. Testing.

Five minutes to go.

I am hypnotized by my chrono; the numbers are moving through glue. I am still staring at them when, at the exact second, we go off Mass-Time.

Unwillingly to Earth

No weight. I hook my heels under the seat and persuade my esophagus back into place. A new period of waiting has begun. Every so often comes the impression that we are falling head-first; the Colonel using ship's drive to decelerate the whole system. Then more free fall.

The Hopper drifts very slowly out of the hold and hovers over the hatch, and the lights go. There is only the glow from the visiscreen and the instrument board.

One minute thirty seconds to go.

The hatch slides open again. I take a deep breath.

I am still holding it when the Colonel's voice comes over the speaker: "Calling *Gilgamesh*. Calling the Hopper. Goodbye and good luck. You're on your own."

The ship is gone.

Yet another stretch of time has been marked off for us; thirty-seven minutes, the least time allowable if the Hopper is not to pick up more gravitational acceleration than it can cancel. Mr. Yardo is a good pilot; he is concentrating completely on his instruments and the visiscreen. B and I are free to look around.

I did not know or have forgotten that Incognita has many small satellites; from here there are four in sight.

I am still looking at them when B seizes my arm painfully and points down.

I see nothing and say so.

B whispers It was there a moment ago, it is pretty cloudy down there—Yes Lizzie there it is *look*.

And I see it. Over to the left, very faint, a pinprick of light.

Light in the polar wastes of a sparsely inhabited planet, and since we are still ten kilometers up it is a very powerful light, too.

No doubt about it, as we descend further; about fifty

miles from our objective there are men, quite a lot of them.

I think it is just then that I *really* understand the hazard of what we are doing. This is not an Exercise. This is in dead earnest and if we have missed an essential factor or calculated something wrong the result will Not be a bad mark or a failed exam, or even our personal deaths, but incalculable harm and misery to millions of people we never even heard of.

Dead earnest. How in Space did we ever have cheek enough for this?

The lights might be the essential factor we have missed, but there is nothing we can do about them now.

Mr. Yardo suddenly chuckles and points to the screen.

"There you are! He's down!"

There, grayly dim, is the Map the Colonel showed us; and right on the faint line of the cliff-edge is a small brilliant dot.

The map is expanding rapidly, great lengths of coastline shooting out of sight at the edges of the screen. Mr. Yardo has the cross-hairs centered on the dot which is *Gilgamesh*. The dot is changing shape; turning into a short elipse; a long one . . . . The gyros are leaning her out over the sea.

I look at my chrono; 12:50 hours exactly. B looks, too, and grips my hand.

Thirty seconds later the Andite has not blown; first fuse safely turned off, Surely she is leaning far enough out by now?

We are hovering at a hundred and fifty meters. I can actually see the white edge of the sea beating at the cliff. Mr. Yardo keeps making small corrections; there is a wind out there trying to blow us away. It is cloudy here; I cannot see any of the moons, or stars.

Mr. Yardo checks the radio. Nothing yet.

I stare downwards and fancy I can see a metallic gleam.

Unwillingly to Earth

Then there is a wordless shout from Mr. Yardo; a bright dot hurtles across the screen and at the same time I see a streak of blue fire tearing diagonally downwards about twenty meters away.

The Hopper shudders to a flat concussion in the air, we are all thrown off balance, and when I claw my way back to the screen the moving dot is gone.

So is *Gilgamesh*.

B says numbly "But it wasn't a meteor. It can't have been."

"It doesn't matter what it was," I say. "It was some sort of missile, I think. They must be even nearer to war than we thought."

We wait. What for, I don't know. Another missile, perhaps. No more come.

At last Mr. Yardo stirs. His voice sounds creaky.

"I guess," he says, then clears his throat. "I guess we have to go back up."

B says "Lizzie, who was it? Do you know?"

Of course I do. "Do you think M'Clare was going to risk one of us on that job? The volunteering was a fake. He went himself."

B whispers "You're just guessing."

"Maybe," says Mr. Yardo, "But I happened to see through that faceplate of his. It was the Professor all right."

He has his hand on the controls when my brain starts working again. I utter a strangled Noise and dive for the hatch into the cargo hold. B tries to grab me but I get it open and switch on the light.

Fifty-fifty chance—I've lost.

No, this *is* the one that picked up B and me, the people who put in the new equipment did *not* clear out my fishboat, they just clamped it neatly to the wall.

I dive in and start to pass up the package. B shakes her head.

"Lizzie, we can't. Don't you remember? If we got caught it would give everything away. Besides . . . there isn't any chance—"

I tell her "Take a look at the screen."

Sharp exclamation from Mr. Yardo. B turns to look, then takes the package and helps me through the hatch.

Mr. Yardo maneuvers out over the sea till the thing is in the middle of the screen; then drops to a hundred feet. It is sticking out of the water at a fantastic angle and the waves are hardly moving it. The nose of the ship.

"The antigrav," B whispers. "The Andite hasn't blown yet."

"Ten-minute fuse," says Mr. Yardo thoughtfully. He turns to me with sudden briskness. "What's that, Lizzie girl? A fish-boat? Good. We may need it. Let's have a look."

I tell him "It's mine."

"Now look—"

"Tailored to fit," I say. "You might get into it, folded. I doubt it. You couldn't work the controls."

It takes him fifteen seconds to realize there is no way round it; he is over 1.90 meters and I am 1.53. Even B would find it hard.

His face goes grayish and he stares at me helplessly. Finally he nods.

"All right, Lizzie. I guess we—you have to try. Things certainly can't be much worse than they are. We'll go over to that beach there."

On the beach there is wind and spray and breakers but nothing unmanageable; the cliffs on either side keep off the worst of the force. It is queer to feel moving air after eighteen days in a ship.

It takes six minutes to unpack and expand the boat and

Unwillingly to Earth

by that time it is ten minutes since the missile hit and the Andite has not blown.

I crawl into the boat. In my protective suit it is a fairly tight fit. We agree that I will return to this same point and they will start looking for me in fifty minutes' time and will give up if I have not returned in two hours. I take two Andite cartridges to deal with all eventualities and snap the nose of the boat into place. At first I am very conscious of the two little white cigars in the pouch of my suit, but presently I have Other things to think about.

I use the "limbs" to crawl the last few yards of shingle into the water and on across the sea bottom till I am beyond the line of breakers; then I switch on the motor. I have already set the controls to home on *Gilgamesh* and the radar will steer me off any obstructions. This journey in the dark is as safe as my trip around the reefs before all this started—though it doesn't feel that way.

It takes twelve minutes to reach *Gilgamesh*, or rather the fragment that the antigrav is supporting; it is about four-fifths of a kilometer from the beach.

The radar stops me two meters from her and I switch it off and turn to Manual and inch closer in.

I switch on the light, using a very small beam. The missile struck her about one-third of her length behind the nose. I know, because I can see the whole of that length. It is hanging just above the water sloping at about 30° to the horizontal. The ragged edge where it was torn from the rest is just dipping into the sea.

If anyone sees this I don't know what they *will* make of it but nobody could possibly think an Ordinary spaceship suffered an Ordinary crash, and very little investigation will show up the Truth.

I reach up with the forward set of "limbs" and grapple onto the break. I now have somehow to get the hind "limbs" up without breaking that grip. I can't.

It takes several minutes to realize I can just open the nose and crawl out.

Immediately a wave hits me on the head and does its best to drag me into the sea. However the interior of the ship is relatively sheltered and presently I am inside and dragging the boat up out of reach.

I have to get to the nose, find the fuse, change the setting to twenty minutes—maximum possible—and get out before it blows—out of the water, that is. The fishboat is not constructed to take Explosions even half a mile away. But the first thing is to find that fuse and I cannot make out how *Gilgamesh* is lying and therefore cannot find the door through the bulkhead; everything is ripped and twisted. In the end I find a gap where the bulkhead itself has been torn away from the hull, and squeeze through that.

In the next compartment things are more Recognizable and I eventually find the door. Fortunately Ships are designed so that you can get through doors even when they are in the ceiling; actually here I have to climb an overhang, but the surface is provided with rungs which make it not too bad. Finally I reach the door. I shall have to use my antigrav belt to get down—(Why did I not turn it on and Jump? Because I forgot I was wearing it.)

Th door was open a little way when the missile hit; it buckled in its grooves and jammed fast. I can get an arm through. No more. I switch on antigrav and hang there directing the light round the compartment. No gaps anywhere, just buckling. This compartment is divided in halves by a partition and the door in that is open. There will be another door into the Nose on the other side.

I bring back my feet ready to kick off on a dive through that doorway.

Behind me, something moves.

* * *

Unwillingly to Earth

My muscles go into a Spasm like the one that causes a falling dream, my hold tears loose and I go tumbling through the air, rebound from a wall, twist, and manage to hook one foot in the frame of the door I was aiming for. I pull myself down and turn off the antigrav; then I just shake for a bit.

The sound was—

This is Stupid, with everything torn to pieces in this ship there is no wonder if bits shake loose and drop around—

But it was not a metallic noise, it was a kind of soft dragging, very soft, that ended in a little thump.

Like a—

Like a soft piece of plastic dislodged from its Angle of rest and slithering. Pull yourself together, Lizzie Lee.

I look through the door into the other half of this level. Shambles. Smashed machinery every which way, blocking the door, blocking everything. No way through at all.

Suddenly I remember the tools. Mr. Yardo loaded the fishboat with all it would hold. I crawl back and return with a fifteen-inch expanding beam-lever and overuse it; the jammed door does not Slide back in its grooves but flips right out of them, bent double. It flies off into the dark and Clangs its way to rest.

I am halfway through the opening when I hear the sound again. A soft slithering; a faint defeated Thump.

I freeze where I am, and then I hear the sigh; a long long weary sound, almost musical.

An airleak somewhere in the hull and wind or waves altering the Pressure around it.

All the same I do not seem able to come any farther through this door.

Light might help . . . I turn the beam up and play it cautiously around. This is the frontmost compartment, right in the nose; a sawn-off cone-shape. No breaks here, though the hull is buckled to my left and the current "floor"—the partition, vertical when the ship is in normal operating position, which holds my door—is torn up; some large heavy object was welded to a thin surface skin which has ripped away leaving jagged edges and a pattern of struts below.

There is no dust here; it has all been sucked out when the ship was open to space; nothing to show the beam except a sliding yellow ellipse where it touches the wall. It glides and turns, spiraling down, deformed every so often when it crosses a projection or a dent, till it halts suddenly on a spoked disk, more than a meter across and standing nearly half a meter out from the wall. The antigrav.

I never saw one this size, it is like the little Personal affairs as a giant is like a pigmy, not only bigger but a bit different in proportion. I can see an Andite cartridge fastened among the spokes.

The fuse is a "sympathizer" but is probably somewhere close . . . The ellipse moves again. There is no feeling that I control it; it is hunting on its own. To and fro around the giant wheel. Lower. It halts on a small flat box, also bolted to the wall, a little way below. This is it. I can see the dial.

The ellipse stays still, surrounding the fuse. There is something at the very edge of it.

When *Gilgamesh* was right way up the antigrav was bolted to one wall, about a meter above the floor. Now the lowest point is the place where that wall joins what used to be the floor. Something has fallen down to that point and is huddled there in the dark.

The beam jerks suddenly up and the breath whoops out of me; a round thing sticking out of the wall—then I realize it is an archaic space-helmet clamped to the wall for safety when the wearer took it off.

I take charge of the patch of light and move it slowly down, past the fuse, to the thing below. A little dark scalloping of the edge of the light. The tips of fingers. A hand.

Unwillingly to Earth

I widen the beam.

Gilgamesh was fitted with a special computer. Space Force job, quintuply redundant on all functions and heavily armored against God knows what. When the missile struck, it was not damaged at all, so far as I can see, but it was wrenched loose from its moorings and careened down as the floor tilted, taking with it anything that stood in its way.

M'Clare was just stooping to the fuse, I think. The computer smashed across his legs and pinned him down in the angle between the wall and the floor. His legs are hidden by it.

Because of his spacesuit he does not look crushed; the thick clumsy joints are still rounded, so far as they are visible; only his hands and head are bare and vulnerable looking.

I am halfway down, floating on ten percent gravity, before it really occurs to me that he could still be alive.

I switch to half and land beside him. His face is colorless but he is breathing all right.

First aid kit. I will never make fun of Space Force routine again. Rows and rows of small squeezable ampuls. Needles sheathed.

Pain-killer first. I read the directions twice, sweating. *Emergencies only*: this is one. One dose *only* to be given and if the patient is not in good health use—never mind that. I fit on the longest needle and jab it through the suit, at the back of the thigh, as close to the knee-joint as I can get because the suit is thinner there. Half one side, half the other.

Now to get the computer off. At a guess it weighs about two hundred kilos. The beam-lever would move it but would not stop it from falling back.

Antigrav. My belt is supposed to take up to three times the weight of an Average man. I take it off and buckle the strap round two lugs sticking out from the computer's sides—I suppose they helped attach it to the wall. I have my hands under the computer when M'Clare sighs again.

He is lying on his belly but his head is turned to one side, toward me. Slowly his eyelids open. He catches sight of my hand; his head moves a little and he says "Lizzie? Lizzie Lee?"

I say not to worry, we will soon be Out of here.

His body jumps convulsively and he cries out. His hand reaches my sleeve and feels. He says "Liz! Oh, God—I thought—"

I say Things are under control and just keep quiet a bit.

His eyes close. After a minute he whispers "Something hit the ship."

"A missile, I think."

I ought not to have said that, but it seems to make no particular impression; maybe he guessed as much.

I was wrong in wanting to shift the computer straight-away, the release of pressure might start a hemorrhage. I dig out ampuls of blood-seal and inject them into the space between the suit and the flesh, as close to the damage as I can.

M'Clare asks how the ship is lying and I explain, also how I got here. I dig out the twenty-by-five-centimeters packet of expanding Stretcher and read the directions. He is quiet for a minute or two, gathering strength; then he says sharply "Lizzie. Stop that and listen.

"The fuse of the Andite is just under the antigrav. Go and find it. Go *now*. There's a dial with twenty subdivisions. Marked in black—see it? Turn the pointer to the last division. Is that done?

"Now you see the switch under the pointer—? Is your boat ready to go? I beg your pardon, of course you left it ready. Then turn the switch and get out of here."

I come back and see by the chrono that the blood-seal

should be set. I get my hands under the computer. M'Clare bangs his hand on the floor.

"Lizzie, you little idiot, don't you realize that even if you get me out of here, which you can't, you'll be delayed all the way—and if the Incognitans find either of us the whole plan's ruined? Much worse than ruined. Once they see it's a hoax—"

I tell him I have two Andite sticks and they won't find us; and on a night like this any sort of Explosions will be put down to lightning and Sudden gusts.

He is silent for a moment while I start lifting the computer, carefully; its effective weight with the antigrav full on is only about ten kilos but it has all its Inertia. Then he says quietly "Please, Lizzie—can't you understand that the worst nightmare in the whole affair has been the fear that one of you might get injured? Even killed? When I realized that only one person was needed to pilot *Gilgamesh*—it was the greatest relief I ever experienced. *Now* you say . . ." His voice picks up suddenly. "Lizzie, you're beaten . . . I'm losing all feeling. Even pain. I can't feel anything behind my shoulders . . . it's creeping up—"

I say That means the pain-killer I shot him with is acting as advertised, and he makes a sound as much like an explosive Chuckle as anything and is quiet again.

The curvature between the wall and the floor is not Helpful; I am trying to find a place to wedge the computer so it cannot fall back when I take off the antigrav. In the end I get it pushed onto a sort of ledge formed by a dent in the floor. I ease off the antigrav and the computer stays put, but I don't like the looks of it so let's get *out* of here.

I push the packaged stretcher under his middle and pull the tab before I turn the light on his legs to see the damage. I cannot make out very much; the joints of the suit are cracked some but as far as I can see the inner lining is not broken which means it is still air and water-tight.

I put a hand under his chest to feel how the stretcher is going; it has now doubled size in both directions and I can feel it pushing out but it is *slow*, what else do I have to—oh, yes, get the helmet.

I am reaching for it when M'Clare says "What are you doing? Yes . . . well, don't put it on for a minute. There's something I would like to tell you, and with all respect for your obstinacy I doubt very much whether I shall have another chance. Keep that light off me, will you? It hurts my eyes.

"You know, Lizzie, I dislike risking the lives of any of the students for whom I am responsible, but I find the idea of you—blowing yourself to atoms particularly objectionable because . . . I happen to be in love with you. You're also one of my best students. I used to think that was why I'd been so insistent on your coming to Russett, but I rather think . . . my motives were mixed even then. I meant to tell you this after you graduated, and to ask you to marry me, not that . . . I thought you would. I know . . . you never quite forgave me, but I don't want . . . to have to remember . . . I didn't . . . have the guts . . ."

His voice trails off. I get a belated rush of Sense to the head and turn the light on his face. His head is turned sideways and his fist is clenched into the side of his neck. When I touch it his hand falls open and five discharged ampuls fall out.

Pain-killer. Maximum dose one ampoule.

All that talk was just to keep my attention while he got hold of them and—

I left the kit spread out right beside him.

While I am taking this in some small cold corner of my mind is remembering the instructions that are on the pain-killer ampul. It does not say outright that it is the last refuge for men in the extremity of pain and despair; therefore it cannot say outright that they sometimes despair too soon; but it does give the name of the Antidote.

Unwillingly to Earth

There are only three ampuls of this and they also say, Maximum dose one ampul. I try to work it out but lacking all other information the best I can do is to inject two and keep one till later. I put that one in my pocket.

The stretcher is all expanded now; a very thin but quite rigid grid, two meters by a half. I lash him on it without changing his position and fasten the helmet over his head.

I point the thing towards the open door and give it a gentle push; then I scramble up the rungs and get there just in time to guide it through. It takes a knock then and some more while I am getting it down to the next partition, but he can't feel it.

This time I find the door, because the noise behind it acts as a guide. The sea is getting higher and dashing halfway to the door as I crawl through. My boat is awash, pivoting to and fro on the grips of the front "limbs."

I grab it, release the "limbs" and pull it as far back as the door. I maneuver the strecher on top and realize there is nothing to fasten it with . . . except the antigrav. I get that undone, holding the stretcher in balance, and manage to pass it under the stretcher and thread it through the bars of the grid . . . then round the little boat, and the buckle just grips the last inch. It will hold, though.

I set the boat to face the broken end of the ship, but I don't dare put it farther back than the door. I turn the antigrav to half, fasten the limb-grips and rush back towards the nose of the ship. Silver knob under the dial. I turn it down, hear the thing begin a fast, steady ticking, and turn and run.

Twenty minutes.

One and a half to get back to the boat, four to get inside it without overturning. Nearly two to get down to the sea—balance is tricky. One and a half to lower myself in.

Thirty seconds' tossing before I sink beneath the wave

layer; then I turn the motor as high as I dare and head for the shore.

In a minute I have to turn it down again; at this speed the radar is bothered by water currents and keeps steering me away from them as though they were rocks. I finally find the maximum safe speed but it is achingly slow. What happens if you are in water when Andite blows less than a kilometer away?

A moment's panic as I find the ship being forced up, then I realize I have reached the point where the beach starts to shelve. I turn off radar and motor and start crawling. Eternal slow Reach out, grab, shove, haul, with my heart knocking my uvula; then suddenly the nose breaks water and I am hauling myself out with the last wave doing its best to Overbalance me.

I am halfway out of the boat's nose when the Andite blows behind me. There is a flat slapping sound; then an instant roar of wind as the air receives the Binding energies of several tons of matter; then a long wave comes pelting up the beach and snatches at the boat.

I huddle into the shingle and hold on. I just turned the antigrav right off, otherwise I think the boat would have been carried away. There are two or three more big waves and a brief downpour; then it is over.

The outlet valve of M'Clare's suit is still working, so he is still breathing; very deep, very slow.

I unfasten the belt of the antigrav from around the boat; then I move the stretcher sideways and rebuckle the antigrav underneath it. I switch on just long enough to get the stretcher Off the boat. Then I drag the boat down to the water, put in an Andite cartridge with the longest fuse I am carrying, set the controls to take the boat straight out to sea at maximum depth the radar control will allow, and push it off. The other Andite cartridge starts burning a hole in my pocket; I would like to have put that in too, but I must keep it in case.

I look at my chrono. Five minutes before the Hopper is due.

Five minutes.

I am halfway back to the stretcher when I hear a noise farther up the beach. Unmistakable. Shingle under a booted foot.

I stand frozen in mid-stride. After launching the boat I turned my light out, but my eyes have not recovered yet; the blackness is murky. Even my white suit is only faintly paler than my surroundings.

Silence for a couple of minutes, while I stand still. But it can't have gone away. What happens when the Hopper comes? Mr. Yardo will see whoever it is on the infrared vision screen. He won't land—

Footsteps again. Several, this time.

Then the clouds part and one of those superfluous little moons shines straight through the gap.

The bay is not like the stereo the Colonel showed because that was taken in winter; now the snow is melted, leaving bare shingle and mud and a tumble of rocks; more desolate than snow. Fifteen meters off is a man.

He is Huddled up in a mass of garments but his head is bare, rising out of a hood which he has pushed back, maybe so as to listen better. He looks young, hardly older than me. He is holding a long thin Object which I never saw before, but it must be a weapon of some sort.

This is the end of it. All the evidence of the faking is destroyed; except for M'Clare and me. Even if I use the Andite he has seen me—and that would leave M'Clare.

I am standing here on one foot like a dancer in a jammed stereo, waiting for Time to start again or the world to end—

Like the little figure in the dance instruction kit Dad got when I was seven, if you switched her off in the middle.

Like a dancer—

My weight shifts on to the forward foot. My arms swing up, forwards, back. I take one step. Another.

Swing. Turn. Kick. Sideways.

Like the silly little dancer who could not get out of the plastic block; but I am moving forward little by little, even if I have to take three steps roundabout for every one in advance.

Arms, up. Turn, round. Leg, up. Straighten out. Step.

Called the Dance of the Little Robot. For about three months Dad thought it was no end cute, till he caught on I was thinking that, too.

It is just about the only dance you *could* do on shingle, I guess.

When this started I thought I might be going crazy, but I just had not had time to work it out. In terms of Psychology it goes like this: To shoot off a weapon a man needs a certain type of Stimulus, like the sight of an Enemy over the end of it. So if I do my best not to look like an Enemy he will not get that Stimulus. Or put it another way, most men think twice before shooting a girl in the middle of a dance.

If I should happen to get away with this nobody will believe his story; he wouldn't believe it himself.

As for the chance of getting away with it, i.e. getting close enough to grab the gun or hit him with a rock or something, I know I would become a Stimulus to shooting before I did that but there are always the clouds, if one will only come back over the moon again—

I have covered half the distance.

Five meters from him, and he takes a quick step back.

Turn, kick, step. I am swinging away from him, let's hope he finds it reassuring. I dare not look up but I think the moonlight is dimming. Turn, kick, step. Boxing the compass. Coming round again.

And the cloud is coming over the moon, out of the corner of my eye I see darkness sweeping towards us—and I see his face of sheer horror as he sees it, too; he jumps back, swings up the weapon, and there is a Bang straight in my face.

And it is dark. So much for Psychology—

There is a clatter and other sounds—

Well, quite a lot for Psychology, maybe, because at five meters he seems to have missed me.

I pick myself up and touch something hot which apparently is his weapon, gun or whatever. I leave it and hare back to the stretcher, next-to fall over it but stop just in time and switch on the antigrav. Up; level it; now where to? The cliffs enclosing the bay offer the only cover; they are thirty meters off to my left.

The shingle is relatively level and I make good time till I stumble against a rock and nearly lose the stretcher. I step up on to the rock and see the cliff as a blacker mass in the general darkness, only a meter away. I edge the stretcher round the projecting end of it.

It is almost snatched out of my hand by a gust of wind. I pull it back and realize that in the bay I have been sheltered, but there is pretty near half a gale blowing here.

Voices and footsteps, far back among the rocks where the man came from. If the clouds part again they will see me, sure as shooting.

I take a hard grip on the stretcher and scramble round the point of the cliff.

After the first gust the wind is not so bad; for the most part it is trying to press me back against the cliff. The trouble is I can't *see*. I have to shuffle my foot forward, rubbing one shoulder against the cliff to feel where it is because I have no hand free,

The stretcher is tugging to get away; I step blindly upwards in the effort to keep hold of it. One foot lands on a narrow ledge, barely a toehold. I am being stretched upwards. My other foot loses the ground, then finds the top of a boulder just within reach. I bring the first foot beside it.

Now I am on top of the boulder, but I have lost touch with the cliff and the full force of the wind is pulling the stretcher upwards. I get one arm over it and fumble underneath for the control of the antigrav; I must give the stretcher weight and put it down on this boulder and wait for the wind to drop.

Suddenly I realize my own weight is going, bending over the stretcher has put me in the field of the antigrav. A moment later another gust comes, and I find I am rising into the air.

Gripping the edge of the stretcher with one hand I reach out with the other, trying to find some projection I can hang on to. All that happens is that I push the stretcher farther out from the cliff.

We are still rising.

I haul myself onto the stretcher; there is just room for me to kneel on either side of M'Clare's legs. The wind roaring in my ears makes it difficult to think.

Rods of light slash down at me from the edge of the cliff . . . For a moment all I can do is Duck; then I realize we are still well below them, but rising. The cliff face is about two meters away. The wind reflecting from it keeps us from being blown into it.

I must get the antigrav off. I let myself over the side of the stretcher, hanging by one hand, and fumble for the controls. I can just reach them. Then I realize this is no use. Antigrav controls are not meant to go off with the click of a finger; they might get switched off accidentally. To work the switch and the safety you need two hands, or one hand in the optimum position. Mine is about as bad as it could be; I can stroke the switch with one finger, no more.

I haul myself back on the stretcher and realize we are only about two meters under the beam of light. Only one thing left. I feel in my pocket for the Andite. Stupidly at the same time I am bending over the outlet valve of the suit, trying to see whether M'Clare is still breathing or not.

The little white cigar is not fused. I need one hand to hold on to the stretcher. In the end I manage to stick the Andite between the thumb and finger-roots of that hand while I use the other to find the fuse and stick it over the end of the Andite. The shortest; three minutes.

I think the valve is still moving.

Then something drops round me; I am hauled tight against the stretcher; we are pulled strongly Downwards with the wind buffeting and snatching, banged against the edge of something, and pulled through into silence and dark.

For a moment I do not understand; then I recognize the feel of Fragile Cargo, still clamping me to the stretcher, and I open my mouth and scream.

Clatter of feet. Hatch opens. Fragile Cargo goes limp.

I stagger to my feet. Faint light through the hatch; B's head. I hold out the Andite stick and she turns and shouts; the outer door slides open so that the wind comes roaring in.

I push the stick through and the wind snatches it away.

After that, for a while, nothing, I suppose, though I have no recollection of losing consciousness; only without any sense of break I find I am Flat on my back on one of the seats of the Hopper.

I sit up and say "How—"

B who is sitting on the floor beside me says that when the Homer was activated of course they came at once, only while they were waiting for the boat to reach land whole Squads of land cars arrived and started combing the area, and some came up on top of the cliffs and shone their headlights out over the sea so Mr. Yardo had to lurk against the cliff face and wait until I got into a position where he could pick me up and it was *frightfully* clever of me to think of floating up on antigrav—

I forgot about the Homer.

I forgot about the Hopper, come to that, there seemed nothing in the world except me and the stretcher and the Enemy.

Stretcher.

I say "Is M'Clare—"

At which moment Mr. Yardo turns from the controls with a wide smile of triumph and says "Eighteen twenty-seven, girls!" and the world goes weightless and swings upside down.

Then still with no sense of any time-lapse I am lying in the big lighted hold, with the sound of trampling all round; it is somehow filtered and far off and despite the lights there seems to be a globe of darkness around my head. I hear my own voice repeating "M'Clare? How's M'Clare?"

A voice says distantly, without emphasis "M'Clare? Oh, he's dead."

The next time I come round it is dark. I am vaguely aware of having been unconscious for quite a while.

There is a single thread of knowledge connecting this moment with the last: M'Clare is dead.

This is the central fact; I seem to have been debating it with myself for a very long time,

I suppose the truth is simply that the Universe never guarantees anything; life, or permanence, or that your best will be good enough.

The rule is that you pick yourself up and go on; and lying here in the dark is not doing it.

* * *

I turn on my side and see a cluster of self-luminous objects including a light switch. I reach for it.

How did I get into a Hospital?

On second thought it is a cabin in the ship, or rather two of them with the partition torn out; I can see where it was attached. There is a lot of paraphernalia around; I climb out to have a look.

Holy horrors what's happened? Someone borrowed my Legs and put them back wrong. My eyes also are not functioning well, the light is set at Minimum and I am still dazzled. I see a door and make for it to get Explanations from somebody.

Arrived, I miss my footing and stumble against the door, and on the other side someone says "Hello, Lizzie. Awake at last?"

I think my heart stops for a moment. I can't find the latch. I am vaguely aware of Beating something with my fists, and then the door gives, sticks, gives again and I stumble through and land on all fours the other side of it.

Someone is calling "Lizzie! Are you hurt? Where the devil has everyone got to? Liz!"

I sit up and say "They said you were *dead*!"

"*Who* did?"

"I . . . I . . . someone in the hold. I said How's M'Clare? and they said you were dead!"

M'Clare frowns and says gently "Come over here and sit quietly for a bit. You've been dreaming."

Have I? Maybe the whole thing was a dream—but if so how far does it go? Descending in the Hopper? The missile? The boat? Crawling through the black tunnel of the broken ship?

No, because he is sitting in an improvised wheelchair and his legs are evidently strapped in place under the blanket; he is fumbling with fastenings.

I say "Hey! Cut that out!"

He straightens up irritably.

"Don't you start, Lysistrata. I've been suffering the attentions of the damnedest collection of amateur nurses who ever handled an osteoscope, for nearly a week. I don't deny they've been very efficient, but when—"

Nearly a *week*?

He nods. "My dear Lizzie, it's six days since we left Incognita. Amateur nursing again! They have some unholy book of rules which says that for Exposure, Exhaustion and Shock the best therapy is sleep. I don't doubt it, but the thing goes on to say that in extreme cases the patient has been known to benefit by as much as two weeks of it. I didn't find out that they were trying it on *you* until yesterday, when I began inquiring why you weren't around. They kept *me* under for three days—in fact until their infernal Handbook said it was time for my leg muscles to be exercised. Miss Lammergaw was the ringleader."

No wonder my legs feel as though someone exchanged the muscles for cotton wool, just wait till I get hold of Kirsty.

If it hadn't been for her I wouldn't have spent six days remembering, even in my sleep, that—

I say "Hell's feathers, it was you!"

M'Clare makes motions as though starting to get out of his chair, looking seriously alarmed.

I say "It was *your* voice! When I asked—"

M'Clare, quite definitely, starts to blush. Not much, but some.

"Lizzie, I believe you're right. I have a sort of vague memory of somebody asking how I was—and I gave what I took to be a truthful answer. I remember it seemed quite inconceivable that I could be alive. In fact I still don't understand it. Neither Yardo nor Miss Laydon could tell me. How *did* you get me out of that ship?"

Well, I do my best to Explain, glossing over one or two

points. At the finish he closes his eyes and says nothing for a while.

Then he says "So except for this one man who saw you, you left no traces at all?"

Not that I know of, but—

"Do you know, five minutes after the Hopper left there were at least twenty men in that bay, most of them scientists? They don't seem to have found anything suspicious. Visibility was bad and you can't leave footprints in shingle—"

Hold on, how does he know all this?

M'Clare says, "Two couriers have docked with this ship while you were asleep. Yes, I know that's not ordinarily possible for a ship on Mass-Time. One of these days someone will have an interesting problem in Cultural Engineering, working out how to integrate some of these Space Force gadgets into our economic and social structure. Though courier boats make their crew so infernally sick I doubt whether the present type will ever come into common use. Anyway, we've had recordings of a good many broadcasts from Incognita, the last dated two days ago; and so far as we can tell *Gilgamesh* is being interpreted just as we meant it to be.

"The missile, by the way, was experimental, waiting to be test-fired the next day. The man in charge saw *Gilgamesh* on his screens and got trigger-happy. The newscasters were divided as to whether he should be blamed or praised; they all seem to feel that he averted a menace, at least temporarily, but some of them seem to think the "invaders" could have been captured alive.

"The first people on the scene came from a scientific expedition. You remember that area is geophysically interesting? By extraordinary good luck an international group was there studying it. They actually saw *Gilgamesh* in the sky, and she registered on some of their astronomical instruments too. They rushed straight off to the site of the landing—must be a reckless lot. What's more, they started trying to locate her on the sea bottom as soon as it was light. Found the rear and the middle pieces; they're still looking for the nose. They were all set to try raising the smaller piece when their Governments both announced in some haste that they were sending out a properly equipped expedition. Jointly.

"There's been no mention of anyone seeing fairies or sea-maidens—I expect the poor devil thinks you were an hallucination."

So we brought it off.

I am very thankful in a Distant sort of way, but right now the Incognitans are no more real to me than the Lost Kafoozalum.

M'Clare came through alive.

I could spend a good deal of time just getting used to that fact, but there is something I ought to say and I don't know how.

I inquire after his Injuries and learn they are healing nicely.

I look at him and he is frowning.

He says, "Lizzie. Just before my . . . er . . . well-meant purloining of those ampuls—"

I say quick that if he is worrying about all that nonsense he talked while he was trying to distract my attention, Forget it; I have.

Silence, then he says wearily "I talked nonsense, did I?"

I say there is no need to worry, under the circumstances anyone would have a perfect right to be raving off his Nut.

I then find I cannot bear this conversation any longer so I get up saying I expect he is Tired and I will call someone.

I get nearly to the door when—

Unwillingly to Earth

"*No*, Lizzie! You aren't going to let Kirsty loose on me just in order to change the conversation. Come back here. I appreciate your wish to spare my feelings, but it's wasted. We'll have this out here and now.

"I remember quite well what I said, and so do you; I said that I loved you. I also said that I intended to ask you to marry me as soon as you ceased to be one of my pupils. Well, the results of Finals were officially announced three days ago.

"Oh, I suppose I always knew what the answer would be, but I didn't want to spend the rest of my life wondering, because I never asked you.

"You don't dislike me as you used to do—you've forgiven me for making you come to Russett—but you still think I'm a cold-blooded manipulator of other people's lives and emotions. So I am; it's part of the job.

"You're quite right to distrust me for that, though. It is the danger of this profession, that we end up looking on everybody and everything as a subject for manipulation. Even in our personal lives. I always knew that: I didn't begin to be afraid of it until I realized I was in love with you.

"I could have made you love me, Lizzie. I could! I didn't try. Not that I didn't want your love on those terms, or any terms. But to use professional . . . tricks . . . in private life ends by destroying all reality. I always treated you exactly as I would the other students—I think. But I could have made you think you loved me—even if I am twice your age—"

This I cannot let pass. I say "Hi! According to College records you cannot be more than thirty-six; I'm twenty-three."

M'Clare says in a bemused sort of way He will be thirty-seven in a couple of months.

I say "I will be twenty-four next week and your arithmetic is still screwy; and here is another datum you got wrong: I do love you. Very much."

He says "Oh, Liz."

Then other things which I remember all right, I shall keep them to remember any time I am Tired sick cold hungry Hundred-and-ninety—but they are not for writing down.

Then I suppose at some point we agreed it is Time for me to go, because I find myself outside the cabin and there is Colonel Delano-Smith.

He makes me a small Speech about various matters ending that he hears he has to Congratulate me?

Huh?

Oh Space and Time, did one of those unmitigated soandsos, my dear classmates, leave M'Clare's communicator on?

The Colonel says he heard I did very well in my Examinations.

Sweet splitting photons I forgot all about Finals.

It is just as well my Education has come to an honorable end, because . . . well, shades of . . . well, Goodness Gracious and likewise Dear me, I am going to marry a *Professor*.

Better just stick to it that I am going to marry M'Clare, that makes Sense.

But Gosh we are going to have to do some Readjusting to a Changed Environment. Both of us.

Oh, well, M'Clare is Professor of Cultural Engineering and I just passed my Final Exams; surely if anyone can we should be able to work out how you live Happily Ever After?

THE BEST IN SCIENCE FICTION

☐	54310-6	A FOR ANYTHING	$3.95
☐	54311-4	*Damon Knight*	Canada $4.95
☐	55625-9	BRIGHTNESS FALLS FROM THE AIR	$3.50
☐	55626-7	*James Tiptree, Jr.*	Canada $3.95
☐	53815-3	CASTING FORTUNE	$3.95
☐	53816-1	*John M. Ford*	Canada $4.95
☐	50554-9	THE ENCHANTMENTS OF FLESH & SPIRIT	$3.95
☐	50555-7	*Storm Constantine*	Canada $4.95
☐	55413-2	HERITAGE OF FLIGHT	$3.95
☐	55414-0	*Susan Shwartz*	Canada $4.95
☐	54293-2	LOOK INTO THE SUN	$3.95
☐	54294-0	*James Patrick Kelly*	Canada $4.95
☐	54925-2	MIDAS WORLD	$2.95
☐	54926-0	*Frederik Pohl*	Canada $3.50
☐	53157-4	THE SECRET ASCENSION	$4.50
☐	53158-2	*Michael Bishop*	Canada $5.50
☐	55627-5	THE STARRY RIFT	$4.50
☐	55628-3	*James Tiptree, Jr.*	Canada $5.50
☐	50623-5	TERRAPLANE	$3.95
☐		*Jack Womack*	Canada $4.95
☐	50369-4	WHEEL OF THE WINDS	$3.95
☐	50370-8	*M.J. Engh*	Canada $4.95

Buy them at your local bookstore or use this handy coupon:
Clip and mail this page with your order.

Publishers Book and Audio Mailing Service
P.O. Box 120159, Staten Island, NY 10312-0004

Please send me the book(s) I have checked above. I am enclosing $ _____
(Please add $1.25 for the first book, and $.25 for each additional book to cover postage and handling.
Send check or money order only—no CODs.)

Name _____
Address _____
City _____ State/Zip _____
Please allow six weeks for delivery. Prices subject to change without notice.

SCIENCE FICTION FROM POUL ANDERSON

☐☐	50270-1	THE BOAT OF A MILLIION YEARS	$4.95 Canada $5.95
☐☐	53088-8	CONFLICT	$2.95 Canada $3.50
☐☐	53050-0	THE GODS LAUGHED	$2.95 Canada $3.50
☐☐	53091-8	THE GUARDIANS OF TIME	$3.50 Canada $4.50
☐☐	53068-3	HOKA! *with Gordon R. Dickson*	$2.95 Canada $3.50
☐☐	51396-7	THE LONG NIGHT	$3.95 Canada $4.95
☐☐	53054-3	NEW AMERICA	$2.95 Canada $3.50
☐☐	53081-0	PAST TIMES	$2.95 Canada $3.50
☐☐	53059-4	THE PSYCHOTECHNIC LEAGUE	$2.95 Canada $3.50
☐☐	53073-X	TALES OF THE FLYING MOUNTAINS	$2.95 Canada $3.50
☐☐	53048-9	TIME WARS *Created by Poul Anderson*	$3.50 Canada $4.50

Buy them at your local bookstore or use this handy coupon:
Clip and mail this page with your order.

Publishers Book and Audio Mailing Service
P.O. Box 120159, Staten Island, NY 10312-0004

Please send me the book(s) I have checked above. I am enclosing $ _____
(please add $1.25 for the first book, and $.25 for each additional book to cover postage and handling.
Send check or money order only—no CODs).

Name _____
Address _____
City _____ State/Zip _____
Please allow six weeks for delivery. Prices subject to change without notice.

SCIENCE FICTION FROM GORDON R. DICKSON

☐☐	53577-4	ALIEN ART	$2.95 Canada $3.95
☐☐	53546-4	ARCTURUS LANDING	$3.50 Canada $4.50
☐☐	53550-2	BEYOND THE DAR AL-HARB	$2.95 Canada $3.50
☐☐	53544-8	THE FAR CALL	$4.95 Canada $5.95
☐☐	53589-8	GUIDED TOUR	$3.50 Canada $4.50
☐☐	53068-3	HOKA! *with Poul Anderson*	$2.95 Canada $3.50
☐☐	53592-8	HOME FROM THE SHORE	$3.50 Canada $4.50
☐☐	53562-6	THE LAST MASTER	$2.95 Canada $3.50
☐☐	53554-5	LOVE NOT HUMAN	$2.95 Canada $3.95
☐☐	53581-2	THE MAN FROM EARTH	$2.95 Canada $3.95
☐☐	53572-3	THE MAN THE WORLDS REJECTED	$2.95 Canada $3.75

Buy them at your local bookstore or use this handy coupon:
Clip and mail this page with your order.

Publishers Book and Audio Mailing Service
P.O. Box 120159, Staten Island, NY 10312-0004

Please send me the book(s) I have checked above. I am enclosing $ _____
(please add $1.25 for the first book, and $.25 for each additional book to cover postage and handling.
Send check or money order only—no CODs).

Name _____
Address _____
City _____ State/Zip _____
Please allow six weeks for delivery. Prices subject to change without notice.

ADVENTURE
FROM FRED SABERHAGEN

☐	55327-6	BERSERKER BASE	$3.95
☐	55328-4	Anderson, Bryant, Donaldson, Niven, Willis, Zelazny	Canada $4.95
☐	55329-2	BERSERKER BLUE DEATH	$3.50
☐	55330-6		Canada $4.50
☐	50981-1	BERSERKER'S PLANET	$3.99
☐			Canada $4.99
☐	51402-5	THE BERSERKER THRONE	$3.95
☐			Canada $4.95
☐	50101-2	THE BERSERKER WARS	$3.95
☐			Canada $4.95
☐	55341-1	A CENTURY OF PROGRESS	$3.95
☐	55342-X		Canada $4.95
☐	55877-4	COILS	$3.50
☐	55878-2	Zelazny & Saberhagen	Canada $4.50
☐	55293-8	EARTH DESCENDED	$3.50
☐	55294-6		Canada $4.50
☐	51357-6	MASK OF THE SUN	$3.99
☐			Canada $4.99
☐	52579-5	SPECIMENS	$3.95
☐			Canada $4.95
☐	55324-1	THE VEILS OF AZLAROC	$2.95
☐	55325-X		Canada $3.95

Buy them at your local bookstore or use this handy coupon:
Clip and mail this page with your order.

Publishers Book and Audio Mailing Service
P.O. Box 120159, Staten Island, NY 10312-0004

Please send me the book(s) I have checked above. I am enclosing $ _____
(Please add $1.25 for the first book, and $.25 for each additional book to cover postage and handling.
Send check or money order only—no CODs.)

Name _____
Address _____
City _____ State/Zip _____
Please allow six weeks for delivery. Prices subject to change without notice.